The Death of Me

The Legacy Series: Book 1

Carolyn M. Bowen

The Death of Me
The Legacy Series: Book 1

Copyright © 2021 by Carolyn M. Bowen

This book is a work of fiction. Names, characters, places, and incidents are the product of the author's imagination or are used fictitiously. Any resemblance to actual events, locales, or persons, living or dead, is coincidental.

The scanning, uploading, and/or distribution of this book without permission is theft of the author's intellectual property. If you would like permission to use material from the book, other than for review purposes, please contact Carolyn Bowen. Thank you for your support of authors' rights.

ISBN 978-1-7336858-5-6

ALSO, BY CAROLYN M. BOWEN

FICTION

Cross-Ties
The Long Road Home
Sydney Jones Series Books
Primed for Revenge
Chance
ONE

Contents

Chapter 1 1
Chapter 2 5
Chapter 3 9
Chapter 4 11
Chapter 5 15
Chapter 6 21
Chapter 7 33
Chapter 8 37
Chapter 9 43
Chapter 10 49
Chapter 11 53
Chapter 12 57
Chapter 13 61
Chapter 14 69
Chapter 15 73
Chapter 16 79
Chapter 17 85
Chapter 18 89
Chapter 19 93
Chapter 20 97
Chapter 21 101
Chapter 22 107
Chapter 23 113
Chapter 24 119

Chapter 25	129
Chapter 26	131
Chapter 27	137
Chapter 28	141
Chapter 29	147
Chapter 30	151
Chapter 31	155
Chapter 32	159
Chapter 33	163
Chapter 34	171
Chapter 35	175
Chapter 36	181
Chapter 37	185
Chapter 38	189
Chapter 39	195
Chapter 40	199
Chapter 41	203
Chapter 42	207
Chapter 43	211
Chapter 44	215
Chapter 45	221
Chapter 46	225
Chapter 47	229
Chapter 48	233
Chapter 49	239
Chapter 50	249
Chapter 51	253
Chapter 52	257
Chapter 53	265
Chapter 54	269
Chapter 55	277
Chapter 56	283
Chapter 57	289
Chapter 58	295
Chapter 59	299
Chapter 60	303
Chapter 61	313
Chapter 62	319

Chapter 63	327
Chapter 64	331
Chapter 65	335
Chapter 66	339
Chapter 67	343
Chapter 68	349
Chapter 69	353
Chapter 70	357
Chapter 71	363
Chapter 72	369
Chapter 73	373
Chapter 74	377
Chapter 75	383
Chapter 76	387
Chapter 77	393
Chapter 78	399
Acknowledgements	405
From the Author, Carolyn Bowen	407

Chapter 1

David unfolds his muscled bulk and rubs his sore knees from his tall and athletic body being tucked into a first-class seat before waking Jason.

They'd arrived in Florence 4635 miles away from Bridgetown his former home. He'd wanted to put some distance between him and family. The Italian estate inherited from his mother was the natural choice.

He observed other travelers as Jason yawned and showed signs of life. An attractive, well-dressed young woman with erect shoulders and graceful ballet dancer steps strolled past his first-class compartment. He thought he recognized her and caught himself before calling out. Perhaps, the long flight caused his confusion.

Anxious to disembark the plane, he nudged Jason to move faster toward the exit. A car and driver from the estate would be waiting to take them to their new home. A faint memory of their departure and saying goodbye to Godwin flashed across his mind as they sheepishly moved through the corridor. Gabby was left at home sleeping for she was having a melt-down about his leaving the island. The way she acted you'd think he was leaving forever, and that wasn't the case at all.

They'd plan reunions and remain safe at the same time. He and Godwin had covered the basics of security away from Gabby's prying curiosity. His move to Tuscany was intended to lead no trail back to them should his new life's purpose of keeping the planet safe from climate change and nuclear war meet deadly repercussions.

Jason, his friend from the island, jumped at the chance to study under the estate's master vintner. He was eager to learn the craft for developing a hybrid by blending his native sea grapes with Tuscan vines. And build a distillery to take the indigenous plants and herbs and use them for making diverse flavors of liqueurs. This craftmanship would diversify the island's spirit offerings. The apprenticeship would provide directions for his becoming a successful producer.

They were met with fanfare and an ample buffet of Italian dishes cooked to perfection awaited their homecoming. The chef said, "Not knowing your culinary preferences we decided to introduce you to Italian staples. Later, you can let me know your favorites and we'll serve them at your request."

Tired, but keen on making a good impression for what would be his new home; he smiled and said, "You've outdone yourself. It all looks delicious. Thank you."

Relaxing and taking in the breath-taking beauty of their Tuscan surroundings with delicious food and drink they eased into their new work. David's focus was building a data base of global climate change initiatives now in place. The results would supply a starting point for pinpointing and funding new research ideas.

The ramifications of finding solutions would forever change the world's environment and lead to credible steps for the estate's continued production of excellent wines and olives.

His investigation into the latest dooms day predictions listed climate change and nuclear arms as obstacles to the planet's survival. He wanted to do his part in keeping the global community alive and thriving.

He couldn't shake the vision of the woman from the airplane from his mind. Using his computer skills, he hacked into the airline's passenger manifest breaching the traveler's list from their flight.

With facial recognition software he recognized her as Lilia Siciliano, and quickly learned she was a spy with the Italian Intelligence Agency, The Agenzia Informazioni e Sicurezza Esterna known as AISE/AISI.

With his family's long-term history as fighters of the underworld he wonders if he's on their watch list. Although, attracted to her, it'd be best to keep his distance, but could he?

Tracking her movement online he learns she's also monitoring nuclear production sites, particularly scientist working on projects for governments in the arms race. Information she gained would help his research and plans to stop the dooms day clock from clicking forward.

Chapter 2

Jason was settling into the routine of learning about the wine and spirits business. A chance of a lifetime his friend made possible at his family's Italian estate.

His living suite had a view he'd like to have one day on the island. The cellars were visible below within a rock-laden foundation. With the plush green orchard in the background stretching for acres across the landscape.

He and David enjoyed an easy friendship each with his own personal career goals and clear direction for the future. They had a late to him Italian dinner in the dining hall after 8 pm. On the island his family ate much earlier. But he was adjusting by eating the robust lunch with pasta or rice, fresh meat or seafood, vegetables, and sweets or fruits the kitchen staff supplied lead workers during the day.

Tonight, he was reflecting on how far he'd come since meeting David on the island during one of his summer vacations. He'd learned martial arts by sparring with him under Godwin's watchful eye. Truth be told, the two of them brought out the best in him.

He was introduced to the wine and spirit-making business during a Christmas vacation with his family and realized where his passion laid. Since David moved to the estate, he was offered a chance to be mentored by the expert vintner. Life was better than he'd dreamed possible.

The hours had passed quickly while reflecting on his new career opportunities. He gazed out the ceiling to floor triple insulated glass windows at the Tuscan moon one last time before calling it a night. Below the old-world lighting and wrought iron wall scones cast images of a heavy shadow as a man walked by the entrance to the cellars.

This was out of character, but the main door was locked unless the worker was a key holder. He'd not bother David with his insight until he checked it the next day. Perhaps, someone left belongings behind and came to reclaim them. He'd wait until sunrise and the morning light to investigate before alarming David.

An earlier riser he was at the wine cellar checking to see if anything unusual happened during the night. He gasped at the scene. Droplets of wine were still seeping from the aged oak wine barrels. Most of the contents had already spilled covering the recently refurbished ultramodern flooring designed for its mold-free and clean-up capabilities.

He was sweating profusely and agitated for not waking David and catching the culprit in the act. Now it was too late. Someone had wheeled an axe into the barrels. He quickly called David and confided the problem when the head vintner entered the building. The shocked and disappointed smirk on his face made him feel faint. What if he blamed him?

"Jason, what's going on?"

"I walked in and found where someone violently sabotaged the cellar and called David."

"Well, he'll report it to Dorian, and they'll be down in a few."

He shook his head knowing the outcome wouldn't repair the damage done. Nonetheless, a deadly message would be sent to others considering crossing the threshold to vandalize estate property.

David and Dorian arrived to examine the mutilated inventory. The person responsible was found from the cam feed as an employee who was reprimanded and put on notice for insubordination.

You could hear the sticky squeaking sound of the soles of their Bontoni Italian shoes as they stepped across the floor to figure out the extent of damage. Speaking to the master vintner Dorian turned and said, "Get your men to clean up and sanitize the area. We can tap into our reserve to keep our bottling on schedule. I'll deal with the worker responsible for this."

The master vintner said, "As you say, business as usual." Blushing, he remembered past employee problems and mentally readied for the story the estate workers would be told.

Dorian turned to David and said, "We'll talk in my office about the handling of this personnel problem." *Now, was as good a time as any to prepare David for his future role in the family business when he could no longer wield the power.*

Chapter 3

Antonia learned the estate's heir arrived and set out to entice him with her sexy poses and flirty conversation. She'd recently lost her job at a popular speakeasy in Florence. The restaurant closed for renovations with plans for reopening in eight months.

Customers would flock back for the relaxed ambiance for chatting and flirting while enjoying food and drink. She didn't plan to return for new options were available for personal advancement.

She was surprised when David brushed off her advances. A beauty all her life she wasn't accustomed to rejection. His friend Jason would be her next seduction target. Since taking a job in the villa's kitchen with her mother, she'd decided to climb the career ladder in the estate's business.

She'd be a natural at event planning to orchestrate wine-tasting and special events. Foreign tourists would book vacations to explore the colossal wine cellars and sample the culinary perfections created by their top chef. And the workers could benefit from the parties she planned to keep them motivated and excited about the estate's world-wide brands. Now, to get the idea past the snobby steward, Dorian, she'd then work her way into learning more about David and the family's secrets.

David was tracking Lilia's movements to determine if her investigations would lead to his work on tracking weapons of mass destruction. She was working on nuclear arms agreements with countries helping Italy. Since the country had none of their own, they depended on foreign governments to supply them. They'd reached an agreement with the US for planes with nuclear weapons capabilities.

He friended her on a professional social media website and hoped she'd respond. She did. They talked a couple of times, and he asked her to meet him at an open-air café in town. She agreed.

They met, and the liking was mutual. They enjoyed lunch and conversation. When preparing to leave she said, "I'll be out of the city for a few days but would love to see you on my return."

He couldn't believe his luck. He smiled and said, "Call me."

Chapter 4

Antonia, Tonia to her friends and family smiled. She had Jason wrapped around her little finger. He'd do her bidding. She wanted to be the events manager for the winery. And, although he said, he couldn't promise her anything, she knew better for he and David were best friends.

She needed entrance into the villa to develop a relationship with David when Jason wasn't around and have access to the steward's private office. The job would give her an office close enough to snoop out his business interests and learn about his secret past. There was a pay-off somewhere and even if he shrieked off her advances because of his best friend, she'd win. They didn't call her a social butterfly for nothing.

Jason was beginning to understand what his Mama told him about unscrupulous women. He recognized Tonia enjoyed their mad sex or maybe not for he was beginning to see her for whom she was - a player. She was after something, but he wasn't sure what. His guess was something threatening David. She wanted something he had, and his gut said money. But what extreme did she have in mind?

He'd invited this python into their home and he'd clean-up his mess. David was not only a friend but someone who invested in making his dream come true - a distillery in Barbados his home. Not to mention, the opportunity for tutelage under an expert vintner.

Tonia wouldn't get her dream job for he'd talk with David in the evening. His days of fanatical sexual encounters with her would end when she heard the news. There was no turning back to keep his friend out of her net and away from the opportunist.

He couldn't concentrate on his job wondering what David's reaction would be. The clock slowly ticked off the hours to quitting time. He wiped the sweat from his forehead with a towel and splashed his face with chilly water preparing for the worst.

They met in the dining hall for dinner. He said, "I've discovered something about the woman I've been sleeping with since arriving."

"From the look on your face, you need to talk. Is she pregnant? "I'll catch the wrath from your mother for taking you from the island and her oversight of your dating life."

"No, she's not pregnant or I don't think so."

"Spill it, man before our dinner gets cold."

"She wants to work in marketing, but I suspect she's got ulterior motives. She's looking for something and I am clueless about her plans. Yet, I'm certain they pertain to you."

David laughed. "Looking out for me, are you? No worries, she'll not gain access to our business center."

Jason's somber expression immediately changed, and he smiled for the first time since Tonia made her request and said, "She'll not be invited back into the villa once I tell her."

"Good idea. Your suspicions are probably correct."

Jason quit twirling the ice in his cocktail glass with his finger when the server entered again to ask if they were ready to dine. He didn't need to ask a second time, for both were ravished and ready to eat. They ate dinner together and enjoyed light conversation about their hopes for their distillery in Barbados.

Feeling the weight lifted from his shoulders. He'd make things right the next morning when Tonia came over. She wouldn't like the news and their trysts would end. This would be the last time she'd be welcomed into the villa. He'd make sure the butler was aware of her change in status.

Chapter 5

Tonia couldn't wait to see Jason and learn she'd landed the job in marketing. She strolled along the perfectly manicured walkway from her parent's cottage to the grand entrance to the villa. Thinking about the years her mother had trudged the same path to the back door to enter the kitchen to work. She was pleased with her plan to make something of herself and not become peasants like her family.

The butler allowed her entry, and she quickly went to Jason's quarters. He opened the door and the look on his face wasn't promising. But she knew how to get him in a condescending mood with her sexual prowess.

They enjoyed one another, and she sensed it would be the last time. He rolled off the bed and begins dressing for work. Then, turned and said, "Tonia, I talked with David about your joining the staff, but there are no jobs available in marketing."

Tonia figured as much from his greeting and had already made plans.

"No problem. I'm sure something will become available in the city soon."

She took the news better than he thought she would. He smiled and said, "You probably wouldn't want to build a career here since your family works on the estate."

He pulled on his pants and slipped a shirt off the rack from his closet and said, "Take your time getting dressed and let yourself out. I've got to hurry for I'm running late."

She waited until his steps were no longer heard on the terracotta floors. Then tip-toed into the estate manager's office and read the mail neatly stacked in piles on his desk. She wasn't surprised the old foggy still communicated with wax seals and handwritten letters.

She scanned the documents one-at-a-time and realized she was holding a landmine of opportunities in her hands. She smirked for she could read between the lines from the rumors she'd overheard. This illustrative family was up to their elbows in murderous intentions of anyone who crossed their paths or fortunes. She smelled a payoff of gigantic proportions.

Time was on her side for developing an extortion scheme. The milking of Jason for information and their rendezvous supplied access to the family's living quarters and private meeting rooms. Now, she had a chance to make her dreams come true.

Taking a deep breath, she patted her chest and felt the sticky sweat from the heart pounding fear of the old coot finding her in his office. Quickly returning to Jason's suite, she grabbed her Gucci shoulder bag and left as he had intended. If he knew the reason for her delay, she'd not been left unattended. She smiled at her foolery.

The estate manager had closed-circuit surveillance of his downstairs private office. He saw Tonia enter and read the fake documents on his desk. He rarely communicated in writing for it to lead back to the family and expose their mafia global stronghold.

His trusted tech guru, Godwin, had devised other methods where messages were deleted after being read. The planted documents were to catch enemies of the family who crossed the threshold of their home and to silence them. Although there was no truth in what she discovered, he'd found a rat that needed exterminating.

The steward had been a family confidant for generations and head of the estate since Donatella, David's great-grandmother died. He wouldn't let some gold diggers wreck their reputation and financial success with her demands.

He had weighty things to consider with her parents being long-time workers at the estate and vineyard. They lived on the premises and pulled their weight when things were tough. A payoff wasn't his usual strategy, but the circumstances were different this time. The question was would a payoff be enough to silence her?

He'd been careful to avoid activities that could threaten the estate or him personally. He checked the Mandarino family name and stayed clear of bank loans to business and individuals to keep off the radar for organized crime syndicates during the challenging times.

Long gone was the image of a gun-toting godfather-sequel gangster: although, more calculating in recent years, the mafia remained strong in areas such as drug trafficking and prostitution. Now, the crime syndicates were into industries such as transport and public health, extortion with a clean face.

But that wasn't this Italian family's premise. They organized to create a global market for their goods, wine, and olives. The godmother created a brand unlike any others and vowed repercussions on anyone who harmed their image. Many tried but lost for she protected her own.

Today he was the one to carry the torch, and he'd not quit his allegiance. The high stakes were set, and he'd not bend rules if the family name or finances were in jeopardy. He rubbed his head, wondering if this one was an exception to the rule.

Tonia's parents realized she was a bad seed from childhood. They dreaded the day she'd come of age to do as she pleased without a thought to how it would affect the family or their employers. She was blind to their compassion when they'd nursed them when sick and bailed them out financially when their son was caught in a gaming scheme.

The steward had turned their son, Luca's life around. He was now a vignero, cultivating the grapes they harvest, and loved his life. They owed gratitude to the steward for treating them like family.

The estate workers and locals alike whispered stories about the family's illustrative past for years. No one dared to approach the estate manager with their suspicions. His formidable image was of a mafia boss, and he ran the estate with fine precision.

From an outsider's view, the estate appeared as a commercial enterprise built on a longstanding family fortune and excellent wine making and olive production. Not a word against the family would be uttered, and Antonia needed to come to that understanding. Her life and the family's well-being depended on it.

Chapter 6

David was distressed about the family secrets he must keep. How was he ever to be honest with a partner? His family's lives depended upon his discretion for no one except those involved knew the truth. The rest of the world believed they were dead. Involvement with an Italian Intelligence Agent could potentially expose them. He couldn't chance that happening.

He'd not even had a one-night stand and didn't want one. And opportunities were numerous since his arrival in Italy. Frustration galled him especially seeing his long-time friend enjoying the company of beautiful women.

Sometimes he'd like to throw a *"Hail Mary,"* and just go for what he desired. Then he remembered how Gabby couldn't walk unaided from being car bombed after a lengthy recovery when she returned home to Barbados. Enemies of the family were real, and vigilante about ways to destroy them. He shook himself mentally, and remembered his pact with fate.

He quickly refocused and planned a trip to the US to meet with top university scientists about climate change and potentially back research with a promising record. The one believed to have the most significance was overlooked by prominent trackers of climate change research. What the scientist needed was funding to test her hypothesis and the one source onboard wasn't enough.

Travel outside of Italy was mindboggling in today's world. He had his vaccination passport and was free to travel — a godsend for his purposes. The merits for climate change predominating world-wide policy were noted from his surroundings. The healing of the country's natural resources was overwhelming. It was like looking at Italy when the first settlers arrived. The rebirth of tourism needed to be curtailed with restrictions of cruise liners docking at their ports and leaving waste in their wake.

The ocean was healing itself. Now the waters in Venice were pristine with dolphins playing where cruise ships once docked and littered. The seascape was now as his ancestors saw — a timeless snapshot of green technology for the future. He would do his part to keep it healthy. Tourism plays a significant role in the economy and needs to be done right — no unlimited number of cruise ships with thousands of passengers to stampede their land and leave debris behind.

The universities he researched had the same itinerary as Italy. Climate change was an eminent problem for the Florida coastline cities much like the coast of Italy. He'd discovered a scientist at a research university in FL was publishing papers about climate change that intrigued him. He wanted to meet Dr. Leslie Grantham and examine her work closer.

After being granted an interview, he booked his flight to coincide with the appointment. Later deciding while near the emerald coast of Florida he'd book reservations in the world renown fishing village of Destin, a vacation paradise. Who knows he might catch some fish on one of their charters?

From scrolling photos on the internet, it was likely, and reminded him of his home in Barbados and fishing with Godwin. He'd sell his catch to a local restaurant according to the charter boat captain something he and Godwin did regularly on the island.

David met with the prominent scientist and believed her research warranted a contribution to further her theories. Leaving he was excited about the future of green technology and the part he'd played in bringing it to fruition. His excitement grew when realizing the two major FL universities in the city were collaborating to address climate change. The state was much like Italy with the encroaching ocean a major concern in the future.

Fishing the aqua blue waters of Destin FL was next on his list. And he couldn't wait. It had been a long time since he'd dappled bait into the ocean to catch a fish.

Lilia didn't want to follow David. The agency thought she was the best choice to enlist him into their services. She got a buy on his upcoming trip home to Barbados, but was ordered to follow him in the US.

What if he recognized her? And did she really want to see his being with another woman, even for a night? She wanted to kick herself for that wasn't a part of her training. But he made her crazy for desire when in his proximity. Every fiber of her being tingled with sexual heat, and she had no doubt there was more to him than appearances.

David couldn't wait for his chartered deep-sea fishing trip early morning outing in Destin. That night he dined at a local restaurant, and overheard conversation from a table nearby about the gigantic fish the younger son had caught from the beach. He couldn't help himself — he interrupted.

"Sir, I'm sorry to barge into your family time, but I overheard your talking about the fish your son caught today. I'm going deep-sea fishing tomorrow and couldn't believe what I overheard. Do you mind showing me the picture from your phone?"

"Not a problem, Chayton's proud of his catch and rightly so. By the way, my name is Jerett, and this is my family."

He turned his phone around and played the video recording the boy landing a prize catch. He congratulated him and was invited to the family's table to dine.

The meal was exceptional, and he'd found a new source for fishing and pleasure boats for Godwin's business. Jerett was in boat sales and from learning about him and his family; he was in the right business. It seemed his young son was an angler, and could fish anywhere; he just had the knack.

He discretely picked up the check for the evening by making eye contact with the server and traded numbers with Jerett to keep in touch. He promised to send photos of his catch the next day if he'd send photos of Chayton's sporting adventures. They agreed.

The next morning, he boarded the charter boat, *Sea Urchin*, with anticipation of snagging a fish larger than the one Chayton caught from the shore. The captain would need to put them on his honey hole for reeling in a fish to compare. Otherwise, he'd have nothing to share with his new friend. And it would be laughable that Chayton landed a catch from the shore that a charter boat captain couldn't equal.

Luck was on their side; they filled the saltwater tank with fish. He messaged Jerett to meet him at the dock to take home the catch for his family. He was thrilled for he had a party planned at his home and was grilling fish for dinner.

This was the most fun and connected outing since leaving Barbados. He wanted this young family to become successful, and a connection with Godwin would put them on track for he bought only superior salt-water crafts for his fleet. He pinned Jerett in as close friend to his contact list to stay in touch.

When returning he strolled to his resort suite to wash off the salty fish grime from the fishing expedition and noticed his smile in the bathroom mirror. The following morning he'd hop a flight and return to the estate pleased with his trip.

Showing Jason his fishing photos, and the video of Chayton's catch would make his day. He'd not believe the size of the fish in the Gulf of Mexico. Their planned departure for Barbados would spike Jason's interest and competition for catching the largest fish.

David recognized Lilia in the restaurant. The wig was becoming, and the sun hat added pizzazz to her stunning appearance. He'd located her suite at the resort using his tech skills and planned to surprise her later in the evening.

They were worlds away from Italy and perhaps she'd let her hair down and tell him why the agency was tracking him. Plus, he'd like to learn more about her. Question number one was why she was employed in the Italian Intelligence Service? And next, didn't she realize it was a dangerous career path?

Lilia was careful in her surveillance of David. She didn't want to blow her cover. The wig she brought and summer wear including a sun hat to conceal her identity gave her confidence when following him to a local restaurant. She wanted to track who he'd meet and to discern if any of his activities warranted further investigations.

She was the first to admit that she was attracted to him, for who wouldn't be? He had the deep, dark good looks and demeanor every woman fantasized about — a manly man.

He was not meeting other women, since arriving. She'd tailed his movement and believed given the right opportunity they could be a force for good. She surmised enough to understand he wanted what's best for Italy-her homeland. But he didn't trust her. Her work with the Italian Intelligence Agency was a turn off. She'd worked hard to land a spot in the agency, and she'd not let her enamored state curtail her career plans.

The agency was bent on tracking him until they learned if he was trustworthy for a specific role important to the agency that even she didn't have clearance to be read in. There was a knock on the door, and she quickly drew her pistol before answering. A peek-hole wasn't available at the resort. She said, "Who's there?"

"It's me Lilia. Open the door and let's talk. You've come a long way for us not to meet and discuss your tracking me."

Uh-oh, her disguise didn't work. He was on to her.

"Let me dress and I'll be right there."

David quickly pictured her tanned naked body and caught himself. He needed a clear mind to talk with her.

She opened the door and defeat was riddled across her face. He quickly soothed her by saying, "Your superiors will never learn we met. I just need some answers about their interest in me and my travels."

Lilia welcomed him into to the luxurious suite and offered him a night cap. He accepted.

He watched as she elegantly strolled to the mini bar to make drinks with her cover-up flowing around her as she moved. Her sexy image would be cataloged for another time.

She made him a rum and coke, and sat across from him on a white leather sofa perfect decor for the ocean-front property. His eyes traveled to the master bedroom where a luxurious king-sized bed's sheets were folded back for the evening. His eyes clouded with desire and a natural erection interrupted his thoughts. He pressed his finger against the spot between his thumb and index finger; one of the techniques for calming himself Godwin had taught him. He needed to get an upper hand on his rampant sexual feelings about her, or he'd have to say goodnight without learning answers to his questions.

Focus was what he needed now. Lilia was beautiful, brave, and persistent, not lacking courage in her pursuit of him. He wondered if it was all business or if she had a personal interest. Dangerous as it was, he'd love to caress her body and feel her feminine warmth.

Lilia said, "Yes, I'm following you, but this isn't a personal trip. I was ordered to trail you to the US and my boss won't be happy to learn my cover was blown."

"Not to worry, he'll never hear it from me. What you tell them is your business. However, my question is why is the Italian Intelligence Agency interested in me?"

"I honestly haven't been told. All my superiors shared is you have special skills for an assignment important to our country, and they want to verify your trustworthiness to carry it out."

"Well, what have you learned?"

"You're interested in green technology, love fishing, and make friends easily."

"Well, tell that to your superiors for you'll have your facts right."

He strode to the suite door and said, "Someday maybe we can allow the chemistry between us loose and discover where it takes us."

He kissed her on the cheek, and closed the door behind him and checked the lock.

She was conscious of the chemistry too, and wondered if their sexual attraction was equally passionate.

The highlight of her trip was body surfing in the gulf while he went deep-sea fishing and was now two shades darker than when arriving. There was nothing unusual about his trip. He met with a research scientist and went deep-sea fishing. Her superiors would be disappointed. Except — his restaurant dinner with the family might've been a guise. She caught the name and would run a check to learn if it was more than coincidence.

David couldn't wait to tell Jason about his trip to the US and show him photos of the fish Chayton had caught. They'd already booked their flight home to Barbados for business and pleasure.

They planned to establish a distillery on the island. Jason had carefully stored the cuttings for the trip home. The new species developed from integrating the Tuscan vines with the island sea grape would be planted in the sandy terrain of his family's homeland. The hybrid variety was a well-researched plant for their new enterprise. Jason's anxiety showed in his face, and trying to calm him, said, "If this one doesn't take root, they'll be others. We're in this for the long haul."

Arriving in Barbados.

He was glad to be home and when Gabby welcomed him with open arms, he sensed her love. At dinner, he told

Godwin about his friend Jerett and asked him to buy his crafts and recommend him to other charter businesses.

The family deserved support to keep his son in fishing tackle and gear. Playing the video of his catch was all it took. He laughed and said, "If tourist reeled in fish like that from the shore, we wouldn't have many charters. Wow, what an angler."

Early the next morning he met Jason at their new *Island Grove Orchard & Distillery* in Bridgetown. They would plant the hybrid vines and meet with Jason's family members they'd hired to keep them healthy. He realized Jason had learned a lot from his tutelage under the expert vintner and viticulturist, head of the vineyards as he had supplied detailed instructions for care taking of the plants.

Jason's face was beaming when he spades the fertilized soil to root the first planting, one he'd never forget. His solemn hopeful expression said it all. This was his baby, and he'd care for it like a newborn.

He in turn planted their vines as numerous family members gathered to participate in the first planting of the orchard. He told Jason, "Just breathe, everything will be alright."

There was no doubt Jason wanted to stay on the island as caretaker of their new enterprise. He waited.

"I believe I need to stay and take care of our orchard and follow through on our business plans."

David laughed, and hugged him. "I expected no less my friend."

Jason's surprised expression should go down in history.

What Jason did not realize was he was ready to go ahead. But he'd just provided proof his training provided confidence for moving forward in their shared venture.

"You have contacts at the estate for discussion and updates about the latest in the industry. Stay and do your grape growing and develop your tropical liqueurs."

Before Jason turned away, he saw the tears in his eyes. This was one business venture he prayed would become successful and with the heart behind it, growth should be the norm.

When leaving the orchard, he told Jason he'd meet him at the docks for their deep-sea fishing outing. He was hoping to catch fish for both their families to dine on that night. Plus, he wanted a bigger fish to message Jerett to show to his son. Maybe they'd visit someday and the lunker king would rule — likely Chayton.

Chapter 7

The steward took his time deciding about Tonia. David and Jason were both away, and she had no access to the estate. David called to say Jason wouldn't be returning for he was remaining in Bridgetown to overseer their orchard and build the distillery. He was relieved.

The more he thought about having a blackmailer on the estate, even if it was false info, verified his intention toward her. The timing had to be right. He'd not been the head of the estate since the grand dame had died for nothing. She taught him well. Never had a non-family member been chosen for the appointment.

She allowed her son, the restaurateur in the US a buy. Her granddaughter Sydney would've been a perfect fit. But she saw greatness in her career path. Now, the great-grandson David was the heir. He wondered how he'd take the news.

David returned to the Italian estate and went about business as usual with vigor and determination. He sometimes met with the workers for a drink after hours. He'd known many of them for years from vacations there. When he became closer friends to Luca in Jason's absence, the steward became concerned. He didn't want any misunderstanding between him and David, the next leader of the family business.

He probably hadn't been told, but his great-grandmother did a trade off with his mother's father by backing his restaurant business in the US. David's grandfather changed his last name so friends of the Italian mafia wouldn't request help in laundering their drug money. The practice was common in the hospitality business. Now, the next generation male heir would run the estate and become head of the Mandarino family.

The Steward thanked God every day for Godwin, who'd shielded Gabby, the granddaughter of the godmother from learning secrets she'd fought to keep. She'd made her own battles and was lucky to be alive, and adding mafia contacts to her portfolio would make things worse.

He still couldn't believe the boldness of Tonia when she called. In a nervous high-pitched voice, she said, "I'm turning you and the estate over to the Italian Intelligence Agency for being a leader of organized crime. They're tightening the net to catch crooks for crime is rampant with mafia headpins doing as they please."

"I think you're mistaken," he said.

"No. You are if you don't pay my asking price of 3M euros to keep silent and leave the city."

He recognized her mindset so there was no use saying the info was bogus. Her contacting the spy agency would send up a red flag and bring unwanted attention to the estate. Her extortion plan caught him off guard.

He was expecting a different approach — a payoff from sensing the enormous wealth of the operation. His strategy would be changed at once for spies who broke into their sanctuary through friendships. For no one else had penetrated their security from the outside for it'd been tested.

"Tonia, what will your parents think about your blackmailing their employer?"

"They're too simple minded for understanding my reasons. And I don't think you'll tell them. Besides, I've already told them about a job offer in the fashion center of Milan. An opportunity the wealthy Mandarino family could have made available if you cared about my success."

The steward realized Antonia Marino was indeed a beauty. Yes, she had potential to become a fashion model and if she'd come to him for help, he'd made some calls. It was too late now.

He gave it a parting shot. "Tonia, I'll contact one of the fashion houses and secure you a contract and provide monies until you get settled in."

"That's not necessary. I've already made plans."

His thoughts quickly touched on her youth when she ran the grounds of the estate and did as she pleased. She was obstinate then and allowing her privileges had whetted her appetite for more.

The estate workers were treated like family being aware of their hardships. Her parents had lost control of her, but someone should have put their foot down a long time ago. Now he was in an impossible and tricky situation for families living on the estate shared their burdens. He couldn't have her disappearance come back on him.

Chapter 8

Lilia's boss was pleased with her surveillance of David. He was everything they believed, a passion for making the world a better place to live. A sure winner for the mission they wanted him to perform.

She was rewarded for her task, and her confidence hit a high note when her superior informed her of the new assignment. Any agent would be thrilled for the clandestine mission was top secret and crucial to the country's welfare in the nuclear arms race.

She hurried home to pack the basics and book her flight from Pisa to Labuan, Malaysia. From there she'd charter a speed boat to take her to Tiga Island, one of a group of small uninhabited islands in Kimanis Bay off the western coast of Sabah, Malaysia.

The flight was an easy one less than two hours flight time from Italy. She taxied to the wharf to book a boat for the short excursion to the island. Looking around, she realized the larger speed boats were out likely with tourists. This was a part of her transportation she couldn't book online in advance.

Looking around she saw a sturdy, but weather-beaten wooden boat, with a man and two young boys preparing for a fishing trip. She fingered the banknotes out of her wallet and approached him.

"I need to get to Tiga Island before sundown and back, can you ferry me across and wait for me to return?"

The man looked around at his boys and the Malaysian currency the lady was nervously squeezing between her fingers.

"Yes, let me talk to my boys, and we'll motor to the island."

Lilia watched as the man took his sons by the hands and whispered something as they boarded the craft. Before he was seated, she pressed the bills into his palms, and waited as he yanked the long-frazzled cord to crank the outboard motor. The engine caught on his last pull making a puh-puh-puh sound.

The helmsman pressed on a makeshift horn to blast four short warnings to show they were underway. A well-used motor sputtered with smoke bellowing from the undercarriage before finding a cadence worthy of their motoring away from the dock.

Floating above the surface of the water, the boat creaked and rolled while steadily moving toward their destination. Looking toward the bow, the most forward part of the boat, she saw ocean-going yachts anchored in the bay. Then suddenly, the man slipped the engine into neutral and threw out an anchor.

She froze. He said, "There's fish feeding on top of the water, I'll make a few casts then we'll be underway."

A large fish tipped his reel into the water and spun off-line. The boys were excited and jumped to their feet to help pull in the catch.

A wave from a passing speed boat hit and jerked the boat up and sideways. The boys fell overboard.

She grasped the underside of the wooden bench and felt pricks in her fingers from the splinters as she tried to help balance the boat. The man dove overboard and quickly surfaced with the older son, she helped pull him onboard.

Seeing the other son with his head low in the water and his mouth at sea level, she shouted, "Over there" and pointed in the direction. The father again dove underneath the swells. Grabbing him, he propelled him toward her voice and shoved him into the boat with an adrenaline rush.

Climbing in after him, he tapped her on the shoulder as she was giving mouth-to-mouth resuscitation and took over until his son started gurgling the sea water. He turned him on his side as he belched the saltwater from his body. Then he'd wrapped him in a blanket from under his bench and said, "We'll go to the island now."

Exasperated and thankful no lives were lost, especially the little ones, she breathed a sigh of relief. Now, if she could conclude her business and return to the mainland she'd be done.

She didn't have to tell the helmsman where to dock the boat. He lowered the engine to neutral with its slow idle spitting water and fumes then roped the frayed synthetic fiber mooring line around a cleat. When he didn't cut the engine she thought, well, we won't have to worry whether it cranks for the return trip.

She expected him and his sons to remain onboard and wait while she met with the scientist. She turned and the skipper and his sons were two steps behind her probably thinking a cool refreshing drink would be offered.

After knocking on the terrace door, she waited. The scientist was expecting her and when no one answered she pushed open the unlocked door.

The strong murky blood stench wafts through the entrance with every step smelling of death. Then her eyes caught signs of blood splattered on the walls, with brain matter caught in the popcorn ceiling above. A dead giveaway she'd stepped into a crime scene.

She quickly remembered her transport and turned and saw the skipper carrying the younger one, with the older one and him running toward the boat. The sound of the engine revved to full throttle told her they'd gotten away.

She regained her poise and with her pistol primed for a shot took cover behind the high kitchen bar. She was alone now with no way out but through.

Lilia was in a storm of blazing gun fire while popping off rounds at unknown enemies. She crawled over to the body of the lady scientist and felt for a pulse. There was none.

She inserted a fresh magazine into her pistol and waited. The silence was deafening. Then foreign sounding voices — Russians she suspected permeated the air.

Pulling herself up to full stature, she tip-toed though the villa looking for other interlopers. At first glance, it appeared all the staff was killed in the ambush. Male and female bodies were strewn throughout the retreat. Of those, only two male guards were armed. The rest was household staff.

A man lying near a side entrance in a wet suit caught her attention. She lifted the mask and quickly snapped a photo with her cell phone to send to the agency for identification.

She wondered if the assassins knew she was arriving today for a meeting with the scientist. At the sound of the high-pitched roar of an inboard motor, she ducked away from the window. Was her meeting the reason the scientist and her staff were murdered?

The scientist consulted with many countries about nuclear weapons. The ambush didn't make sense and now she'd failed her mission and needed another reputable source to verify nuclear weapon choices in the future.

Someone didn't want her to learn about the atomic scientist's projects. Or was this a premeditated attack she stumbled upon accidentally?

The scene was bloody gruesome, and her presence could jeopardize the mission further. A peek into the scientist's office revealed her computers were sabotaged as pieces were strewn about. What was taken during the ambush was unknown.

A quick escape off the island back to the mainland to catch a flight home was her goal. She'd never expect the fisherman to return to rescue her. He had family to think about.

Without hesitation, she strolled to the leeward, protected side of the island in hopes of high jacking a boat for her return trip. This would be a haven for the owner of the villa to store a craft. Finding one, she cranks the inboard and heads away from the island returning the same way she came. She'd dock at the marina and walk-away as though nothing had happened.

Motoring through the bay the wind suddenly picked up with gusts a smaller, less powerful boat would capsize from, she wanted nothing more than be in the air headed home. In the back of her mind, she knew the mission would have gone down differently, if David hadn't turned down the offer to work with the agency. She'd love to give him a piece of her mind about his gutless ambition to help her country.

Chapter 9

David checked his text messages thinking Lilia would break with protocol and meet for a drink. *Non uno* and two days had passed since there last correspondence, and he was anxious to know her whereabouts.

She was a rising star in the agency probably because of her risk-taking personality. He'd investigated the agency and knew the skill sets of each agent. His gut said Lilia was on a dangerous mission. Her comrades were probably thanking their lucky stars they weren't selected. But what was the mission?

His fingers pressed the keys on his computer to gain info about her location. If he didn't suspect she was in danger he wouldn't invade her privacy. Shaking his head at his weakness for her, he continued the pursuit.

Locating her on Tiga Island hit home with him. He was tracking atomic scientists and their work for his own initiatives, saving the planet earth. A top-notch scientist on the forefront of designing nuclear weapons was in residency on the island. But, for what purpose would Lilia be visiting her? Italy didn't store nuclear weapons. The country had made a deal with the US to buy airplanes with nuclear capabilities. The delivery was scheduled in a few years.

Booking a flight didn't make sense, she'd not asked for his help. Or did she? Was this the secret mission the Italian Intelligence Agency wanted him to fulfill?

Suddenly, her phone signal came alive, and he could see she was moving rapidly. His guess she was on a speed boat. He tailed the pings until she reached the marina. He quickly turned on his global news source to capture activity on Tiga Island.

David continued tracking Lilia to verify no one was following her. He couldn't wait to hear about her latest escapades knowing she'd leave out parts relating to national security. But she wouldn't answer his emails or phone calls. Why?

Lilia finally gave in to meeting him at an out-of-the-way less touristy bar. He was the first to arrive and gazed on her beauty when she entered. He pulled back the chair for her to be seated and noticed her nervously looking at her cell. Something happened, likely on the island that made her restless. He needed answers for it played an important role in his nuclear arms investigations.

Lilia said, "How does it feel watching the world perched from your ivory tower?"

"What?"

"You were offered a prime spot in our foreign intelligence agency for missions of your choice — a weekender so to speak."

"I can accomplish much on my own without the involvement of your government and their oversight."

"Pray tell; they just wanted you for one important mission."

"And you think it would end with that?"

"Just so you are aware — some of my comrades' think you're a Fredo."

"Let 'em; I don't care what they believe."

Thinking he was probably right, she let it go. But why wouldn't he take the job with his suitable background according to the agency?

Lilia couldn't figure him out. He held controlling interest in a foundation looking into doomsday predictions to save humankind, specifically climate change and nuclear war. But was he trustworthy to confide in? The agency would shuttle her if they found out. Her career depended on confidentiality. She'd tried to enlist him in the foreign intelligence agency for just that reason. Her higher ups were shocked and pleased she was on speaking terms with him. They saw him as a rock star for the agency to recruit. He'd hit their radar screen when entering the country. The jubilance of her higher ups about the possibilities was one-of-its kind. What skills did David offer she was missing?

Their conversation was stifled probably because of her outburst. He didn't deserve her unkind remarks. If he'd be honest with her about refusing the assignment, it would help her understand him and respect his decision to live life on his terms. They said, goodnight, early and went their own way.

Lilia left the bar and went directly home. She wanted to be alone until she had a grip on her feelings. She wanted to cry and that wasn't like her. A normally tough woman living a dangerous life, she feared little — until now.

Since returning from Tiga Island, she'd been especially cautious in her surroundings. She was being watched, but by whom? Having David on her team would supply a confidant and someone who'd understand being scrutinized. For the buzz around town hadn't died down since his arrival.

Everyone was interested in his background, for not much was public knowledge about the younger family members. The hierarchy of the founders of the estate made the family prominent in Italy with their vineyard and wine production alongside their plush olive groves.

There was a mystic aura and intrigue around the Mandarino family. She'd love to learn their uncensored history. Her gut instinct was to continue with caution for something was eerie about the family history. She felt the vibes just whispering their name.

David was making headway in collection of data to track climate change. He wanted to know who the key players were in the green industry for he wanted to financially back the best ideas through fruition.

His actions to figure out the holders of nuclear arms was risky business. The countries involved didn't want their intelligence or stockpiles to be known or challenged. He suspected Lilia's trip to Tiga Island was tied to this, and things didn't go as planned. She wasn't forthcoming with details on her return.

At their last meeting, she suggested he work directly with the Foreign Intelligence Agency to coincide with his foundation work. The idea was tempting for he could use their intelligence to further isolate threats to humanity, particularly nuclear warfare potentials. Already he'd accessed their initiatives and used them as a filter for selecting ideas to back in green technology. Italy was one of the top countries focusing on climate change in the world and was willing to share their ideas.

To learn more about their findings about climate change and exploration of nuclear weapons, he'd need to be on the inside or have a credible source. Part of him wanted to take the plunge, yet intuitively he knew it was dangerous and outweighed the positives. His parent's lives hinged on their anonymity. The counterintelligence surrounding them was on high alert. He'd not do anything to lead enemies to their door.

Lilia's eyes watered while holding back tears when he declined the offer of working with the agency. There was something she wasn't telling him that had her rattled. He believed if he'd joined the agency, she'd confided the problem. His becoming an agent wouldn't happen. She needed to trust him.

Chapter 10

Dorian, the estate manager packed his bag with thousands of euros stuffed in the hidden compartment. Not the 3M euros she requested but flash money to complete the ruse. He could easily unlatch it and show Tonia the banknotes. He'd called her, and they planned to meet at a hotel in Milan.

The trip and the outcome of her blackmailing were planned carefully. This wasn't a job to hand off to his subordinates. He trusted no one to keep the news from traveling back to the estate — and her family.

He called and asked her to meet by the pool. It was early and no one was up and about the courtyard and shared areas. In minutes, she arrived. His stomach rolled with the thoughts of his next move.

He strolled toward the pool seating area in measured steps watching as she entered the atrium. In seconds, she was standing beside him eyeballing his Prada leather messenger bag.

She smiled and said, "I'm here, let's get this done."

He motioned toward the chaise lounge and said, "Let's sit for a minute and talk between friends."

She elegantly laid back into the lounge extending her long tanned legs out in one smooth movement and said, "I'm not interested in your friendship. My only interest is what you have in that satchel."

"Soon, it will be yours. First, I want to hear you say the documents you pilfered through were bogus."

"Were they? So that's why you're paying me off?"

"What you discovered raffling through my office was a trap set to verify inside traitors to the family business."

The nuances of her body language spoke loudly before she spoke. With a pinched face she said, "Looks like you got caught in your own varmint trap."

Her high-pitched laughter was a nuisance for he wanted no observers. He'd heard enough. Leaning over her Santino chaise lounge he grabbed her throat and squeezed until her eyes rolled into the back of her head. Briefly he thought about leaving her there for their conversation didn't go as planned. They were to drive to the wharf where the rest of her extortion was stored and there, she'd meet her demise.

He decided to stage her body as a suicide for outside the family circle she was considered emotionally unpredictable. He quickly pulled her chair beside the pool and dumped her lifeless body. Then, he moved the chaise back to its original spot for no one to be wiser.

He grabbed his bag and turned to investigate the pool. Her strappy pale blue heels were floating near the top of the water. Yes, the desire for a high life got her — a perfect ending to her life's story.

He left the city and returned to the estate where workers were busy cultivating the land, and preparing olives and wine for shipping, a world-away from the blackmailing floozy who wanted to take a bite out of their empire.

It was times like this he wished David was informed about his heritage. Protection of the family's business was of paramount importance and soon he'd hold the reins. He hoped Godwin was right about David's fit for the family business and its sometimes-deadly outcomes.

On a night out with friends, David learned Tonia a consort of Jason's since their arrival at the estate was gone. He didn't know how Jason felt about the young woman, but he had an opinion by the way she pranced and danced around him for attention. He couldn't blame his friend for taking what was offered from a beautiful woman. Jason saw her and couldn't contain his lust.

He hoped her disappearance happened after his departure to not drag him into polizia investigations if that should occur. His mother would blow a fuse and blame him for allowing it to happen. His one hope for exonerating Jason was the steward. He could make it go away.

He'd learned enough on the estate to know he controlled information and that was a powerful tool. He'd talk with him tomorrow and devise a plan to forfeit investigation of his friend if her disappearance leads back to him. He couldn't wait for the meeting he'd scheduled with the steward to learn if his friend would be involved in a potential polizia investigation.

They met at the breakfast table and dismissed the staff for their personal meeting. David quickly got to the point and asked, "Do you think Jason will be involved in the investigation about Tonia's disappearance?"

"David, Jason's name will never be mentioned if there is an investigation. The polizia are looking into schemes she's played on rich tourist for connections and euros. She's still at-large and presumed alive after fleeing the city."

David felt relieved. "Keep me informed for Jason's safety is a priority for he'd my best friend."

"I think you can go to bed tonight and believe she's no longer a threat to you or your friend."

"Thank you for your candor."

The steward was aware she'd not be a problem in the future. He couldn't wait for Godwin to get David onboard to his destiny with the family. One — no parent would want to place on an unsuspecting son. His lineage made him the heir of the estate with his destiny being the next godfather of the Italian Mafia. He hoped to live long enough for David to learn the deadly secrets, and be ready to accept the family bond. If not, he was in for a rude awakening one Donatella had personally prepared for her offspring — protect the family at all costs.

Chapter 11

Luca heard the stories circulating about his sister Tonia. He didn't believe a word of it. She'd never had to steal what she wanted for men would gladly give her the moon. Their mama's concern when she hadn't called after relocating to Milan was what started the gossip. She'd asked the estate manager to investigate her whereabouts to verify she was safe. The trumped-up stories and the buzz of rumors about her thievery came afterwards.

He couldn't confirm the source of the gossip but found it hard to believe Dorian was involved. He was good to their family and especially him. His fresh start in life was a product of his interest in the wellbeing of workers on the estate.

Sooner or later, Tonia would check in with their mama. She was probably waiting to make a name for herself in the fashion industry to strut her good fortune when visiting them.

The estate had a busy and profitable season, and the year-end was approaching. Workers whispered amongst themselves about the annual bonus the manager usually paid. Luca was no different. In years past, his bonus had equaled the cost of a relatively new car.

The estate manager, Dorian was gracious in thanking employees who added to their bottom-line. The high-spirits were contagious with anticipation of what they'd buy with their dividend. That is everyone but Luca's mama and papa.

Between crying jags his mama lamented the absence of Antonia and her gut-feeling that something was wrong. She hadn't contacted the family since leaving for Milan a month ago. Even he was beginning to have his doubts about her safety. As pigheaded as his sister acted, she was still family. He had time-off coming up and a surprise visit to his sister to encourage her to call home was warranted.

David called and they planned a night out at a popular bar in the city. He wondered if he should ask for his help to find Tonia. He shook himself when thinking about the onslaught of bad publicity when his mama asked for Dorian's help. Tonia had left her address in Milan for family emergencies, and he could search from there.

He and David enjoyed their drinks and catching up since their last outing. He teased him about there being no woman in his life. David laughed so hard tears came to his eyes when he suggested he fix him up with a friend.

He said, "My life is far too complicated now to romance a woman."

"I don't anticipate anything changing soon. Are you sure you don't want to meet one of my lady friends?"

"No, but thanks for the offer I appreciate your concern."

Luca watched as the young female servers provocatively swept their hair back from their faces and smiled at David. Like he needs my help, he thought. Perhaps, he has a girlfriend in Barbados that he's secretly dating. Who knows, as his best bud he'd set him up with a gorgeous Italian woman quickly thinking about his beautiful sister Tonia.

The night ended, and they headed back to the estate each in their own thoughts. When the silence got the better of Luca he said, "I'd love to tour Jason's orchard in Barbados and perhaps offer some tips."

"Jason would enjoy your visit and be open to any advice you offered. I'm planning to return in a few weeks. Do you want to make the trip with me?"

"Sure, I'd love to check out the orchard and explore your island paradise."

"Plan to leave two weeks from today. I've already promised Jason. He'll be ecstatic when learning you're coming too."

Luca dropped David off at the front door of the estate and on impulse went around and opened his door. They said good-night and he eased the car in gear to travel down the rock laden road to his small manor provided for lead workers and their families.

The next day Luca left for Milan to find Tonia. He knocked on the door at the address she'd given their mama. When no one answered, he peeked through the window to figure out if anyone was home. It was Tonia's place for clothes were strewn everywhere reminding him of her bedroom at home.

The apartment door next to hers opened and an attractive young woman appeared. He quickly introduced himself and asked if she'd seen his sister recently.

"She hasn't been home in a couple of weeks," she said.

"Did she say where she was going?"

"No, she didn't tell me. But she was excited about meeting someone."

Luca thanked her and rubbed his jaw dreading his next stop at the morgue. Tonia was flippant but she always came home wherever that might be.

Trying to think positive for his mama would be overcome with grief if she was harmed, he drove to the coroner's office.

The protocol was antiseptic but frantic with the increase in deaths in the region. He quickly said his purpose and was taken into a viewing area. When his sister's face hit the screen all her sins from the past were erased. She was too young to die, and someone would pay.

He arranged for her body to be transported to a mortuary at home. The police station was his next stop to receive an official report of her death.

He waited for what seemed an eternity for the detective to check his files. When handed the results of their police report and her death certificate he believed she was murdered. Suicide by drowning was stamped on the official document.

Yes, right he thought. Tonia loved herself too much to take her own life. Apparently, the person she planned to meet murdered her. He'd not stop until payback was wreaked on the killer's neck.

Chapter 12

Dorian was aware of the dampened spirits of the workers since Antonia's funeral. Her mother was a sous' chef in the estate kitchen, her father a supervisor in the brewery, and their son was an overseer of the vineyards. Her death was touching many departments of their business.

He made the arrangements for her funeral as was expected of the estate owner. He consoled family members and joined in the conversation sharing fond memories of her childhood.

The fortitude of vengeance was written on Luca's face, and he made a note to cement his whereabouts on the day of her death. Trying to stay one step ahead to keep their operation running, he'd double-checked to determine if his assistant could take over. His request for vacation time was approved, and he'd have a chance to get a firsthand look at Pauli to make the decision.

Luca wasn't accustomed to flying, especially first-class. He quickly realized why his over 6'5" friend would fly no other way. The space was barely large enough for his frame. David's body was folded up like an ironing board pressured into a storage bin. And this was a long, long flight. When drinks were offered, he wasn't surprised at David's request. Alcohol could be a good thing when cramped in an undersized space.

When the tires hit the tarmac, he saw his friend smile for the first time since boarding. David said, "Godwin will meet us and drive us home."

Luca was amazed at the beautiful terrain of the island. When they arrived at David's home he was in awe, but the interior was even more appealing with the sunset over the Caribbean visible throughout the villa. They were met with love and laughter, a homecoming anyone would dream about. David's family was gracious with food and drinks as they dined on the terrace beside the pool overlooking the ocean.

He remembered Gabby and Godwin from their stays at the estate. The sparkle in Gabby's eyes when David entered was unforgettable. An unspeakable love existed between them. It made him even fonder of his friend.

They made light conversation before going to their respective bedrooms. Talk about visiting Jason's orchard and the fishing trip permeated their saying good-night. Luca noticed David's light kiss on Gabby's cheek and as she in return ruffled his hair brought back memories of his youth. His mama, Silvana, did the same thing.

Momentarily, Tonia came to mind and the wretched grief his mother was experiencing from her death. When he returned to the estate he'd dig deeper into her disappearance and the cover-up of a murder.

Chapter 13

Silvana was crippled with grief. Her daughter was murdered, and Luca was contemplating vigilante justice to bring her killer to death. She feared what measures her son would contemplate to avenge Tonia's murder.

She'd sought out Dorian to locate Antonia to find out if she was safe. He made it worst with rumors of her bribing wealthy tourist. No doubt he was the source of the gossip, but why? They had a long history together.

In her mind, Dorian overstepped boundaries targeting Tonia for arrest and ruining her reputation. He owed her for taking on the upbringing of Luca without his wedded name. When confronted he found someone to marry her and take responsibility for their son and later a daughter born from their union.

He'd kept her on in the kitchen after she gave birth and promised the son would never want for anything. They met the last time at his villa by the sea, and no personal contact existed between them until her family was in peril.

When Luca got in trouble, he was the first one she contacted, and he made it go away and took him under his protection by positioning him to learn the growing of grapevines at the estate and it turned his life around.

She tried to believe that their love wasn't forever. Especially after learning she was pregnant, and he distanced himself from her like the servant to the family she was. Later he set up a man to become her husband with a well-paid job on the estate to give Luca a name. Her choice in the matter was slim to none.

She couldn't return home to Sicily with a child in her belly. She never asked her husband about the payment he received, and did develop a fondness for him over the years especially after Antonia was born. Now, she was gone, and her son Luca was headed for trouble. No one messed with this family and lived to tell the tale.

Dorian was sensing the sorrow surrounding the death of Tonia. The entire estate was in mourning. He didn't have a good feeling about her family's acceptance of death by suicide as indicated on her death certificate.

In times like these he missed Donatella, the former grand dame of the estate. She always knew what to do and had taught him about the business from an early age. He didn't want to fail her now.

David was next in line to become the Don of the Italian Mandarino family. Problem was he probably wasn't informed for his mother was never told. His father was reluctant to mention the possibilities knowing David's true passion for world peace and a healthy environment. He needed to talk to Godwin and soften the entry for David into the underbelly of the family business.

He picked up his phone and punched in his number.

"Hello, old friend," he said.

"What's up in your part of the world?"

"Business as usual which brings me straight to the point of my call. David needs to step-up and learn more about the expectations for running the family business."

Godwin double-checked to make sure they had a secure line before commenting.

"You've been teaching him the management of the family business since his arrival in Italy. Is there a problem?"

"No, he's smart and understood the inner workings of the business quickly. The Mandarino blood line runs strong in him. He could run the business today if necessary."

"Then, what's the problem?"

"Do I need to tell you?"

"Don't you think your acting premature?"

"No, my life may be in danger."

"You've side-stepped murderous intentions before. What makes this different?"

"This one is too close to home."

"I see. I'll talk to David and get him up to speed. Be ready to show your sources when he returns."

"You think he'll take the lead?"

"No question. He's all about family."

The next day they boarded one of Godwin's charter boats and cruised to one of his favorite coordinates. The marlin was running, and David reeled in the catch of the day. Finally, a fish photo worthy of sending his friend in Florida.

Everyone received a hefty tug on their line and reeled the fish in. No question seafood was on the dinner menu for the night. Godwin phoned Gabby to plan for their guests for the evening meal.

They washed down the boat on porting and gutted the fish at the dock basin. Jason went home to change and invite his family for a seafood dinner at Godwin and Gabby's. David and Luca climbed into Godwin's jeep and held on as they took the twists and turns home at an exhilarating speed. Gabby met them at the door and shooed them to the terrace pool's showers.

Scrubbed with no fish scent they were allowed into the villa by a smiling Gabrielle. Luca smiled. This was one-of-its-kind family — happy! Something he wished for his own grieving family.

Godwin fired up the grill and hurriedly prepared side dishes with Gabby for their company. Everyone arrived at once and there were hugs and kisses welcoming their friends.

Luca was caught in the moment and enjoyed every detail of the festivities. He was glad David was his friend, and he was allowed the opportunity to visit their island. He planned to help Jason more with his vines and revisit as often as possible.

When the company left and their guest was in bed, Godwin strolled outside to the terrace where he knew David loved to stargaze. He walked up beside him knowing he was always on alert and said, "We need to talk tomorrow in private at my office."

"Yep, was expecting a new development, this proves my native heritage is sharp as ever." He laughed.

"I'm afraid so! Let's meet early before Gabby wakes up. She's too intuitive for her own good."

"Early, it is!"

The next morning, Godwin poured them each a cup of freshly brewed island coffee. They took their insulated cups to the jeep and headed for Godwin's secure office.

David was impressed with the improvements around the compound. The heightened security alerts in and around the building had not been introduced world-wide. The latest in technology designed by him were for clients worthy of his ability with deep pockets.

Being there reminded him of the years they'd banged out tech apps to help businesses to secure their trade secrets. And later a philanthropic endeavor to combat the deadly virus with a wearable app placed David on the CIA list for future recruits. He'd learned his lesson and now flew under radars for tech innovations thanks to Godwin.

He loved this place. Spending time here while in high school gave him an outlet away from home and the recovery of Gabby. He strolled over to his favorite lounge chair and waited for Godwin's important disclosure.

"David, I think Dorian is in trouble. I don't have the details, but he's afraid for his life."

"You've got to be kidding me for he's the head of the family business."

"David, you've inherited an interesting lineage cloaked in secrecy."

"Like what? He's an Italian Mafia boss?"

"You don't miss much, do you?"

"I couldn't help but notice the transports of the estate's products are dependent upon trusted sources. I suspected this was set in place decades before he took over as estate manager."

"Yes, that's true. Dating back generations before your mother was born."

"But what has that got to do with me?"

"You're next in line to become the Don, the overseer of the family business. Dorian was a place holder until an heir could take over. This was set-up by your great-grandmother, the former godmother of the Rocco Family mafia and boss of the Mandarino clan."

David strolled to the bar and wiped his now sweating brow with a kitchen towel and took a deep breath. "Does Gabby know?"

"No. Your great-grandmother thought her career path was an excellent choice."

"What happens if I don't choose to take the role?"

"The business could go to shambles from the destruction of property, loss of inventory, and takeovers bids from competitors. Chaos in every aspect imaginable would end the stability of the family business. With most of the problems started by the Italian mafias from the North and South to take down the family in a weakened state."

"Sounds like a disaster waiting to happen. Is the Don of the family public knowledge?"

"No. Estate manager or steward is the title at the villa and business. You already understand the importance of receiving and delivering products necessary for production. The Don is the one responsible to keep ownership of the organization and protect the business."

"Dorian will explain the details and provide you with his sources in case of emergencies. But there's more..."

"Lay it on me for might as well learn the ins and outs now."

"The mafia boss not only protects the business but the Rocco family as well. You'll recognize some sophisticated surveillance equipment in the business center. The technology will be right up your alley since you'd helped me develop some apps that have since been updated to heighten security."

"I picked-up on the security measures when I arrived. And thought the business was taking measures to protect itself."

"Well, you have the truth now. Between the technologies you work with and the global surveillance equipment in the business center you'll be one of the best-informed people in the country."

"Well, at least I'll be working in my wheelhouse of expertise."

"Yep, keep me informed if problems arise and I'll have your back."

"I hope that'll not be the case."

Quickly reflecting, having Godwin shielding his back was always a plus. He could move forward under the circumstances.

Chapter 14

Lilia could feel the goose bumps rise on her arms when walking home to her apartment in Florence. She wished her boss at the agency would take her concerns seriously. Someone was following her, and she suspected the culprit related to her assignment on Tiga Island.

She asked her boss about the possibilities of a stalker from the mission. He said, "Lilia, we'd noticed any conversation about your being targeted, and we haven't. We've confirmed the photo you sent was of a Russian agent and are pinpointing others who may've been working with him. They've not entered our country. Take some time off if needed to get your head straight."

She knew the worst thing a female agent could do was to appear weak. She smiled and said, "I'll be fine. I'm looking forward to my next assignment."

"We're expanding our efforts to infiltrate the Italian mafia. When you return, we want you to look deeper into their activities and find leads for making arrests."

"Yes, sir, that'll be my next mission."

Her boss was probably right. She needs to focus on the job at hand. Yet, she'd played the scenes over and over in her mind and couldn't think of a time when the assailants had a clear visual on her on Tiga Island. What was she missing?

In times like this her thoughts gravitated to David. She suspected his global intelligence could verify a possible assailant. Perhaps, she should do as he asked and trust him. A confidant would be an added benefit. Yet, without him working with the agency she'd be walking a thin line if her boss should find out. She wasn't sure she should for he had eyes everywhere.

The weekend was coming up, and she'd planned to visit her grandfather in the country. Although unworldly, his wisdom and tender care was much-needed.

David and Luca returned from their trip to Barbados. Luca enjoyed every minute away from the estate and his mourning parents, especially his mama. His work was a relief from stress, and he saw the same passion in Jason for cultivating his orchard. He looked forward to returning to the island and checking on his progress with his plantings.

He'd wake up during the night drenched with sweat from nightmares about Tonia. The thoughts of digging deeper into her death scared him for he suspected he knew the murderer. Verifying his suspicions would be dangerous and lead him somewhere he didn't want to go for his and his parents' sake.

David scheduled a meeting with Dorian on his return. He was onboard for his new mafia status. His mother's life had been saved due to detective Thomason's diligence in keeping her alive. He'd brought her to their Italian villa to recover under a new identity since she was of Mandarino descent, and the property was family owned. Although, she may not of understood her family heritage, he was there now to make things right. He accepted his fate to continue the business and protect the family name.

He had versed himself into the family business and realized they'd not move their products without mafia connections. Times were tough and even the mafia was feeling the crunch from scrutiny into their business dealings. But he didn't expect the next request.

"David, you need to guile Luca's suspicions his sister, Antonia was murdered, or prepare to silence him."

"Is this going to come back on the family?"

"Yes."

"Enough said."

He detested the thought of murdering someone he'd made intimate contact with. But he was the new leader, and whatever was needed, his family would be safe and the business intact. He needed to call Godwin an expert in conducting the perfect hit leaving no evidence to be investigated. At the same time, he was hoping Luca would let go of his plan to avenge Tonia's murder. He and his family had lived on the estate all his life — they were family too.

Lilia's visit to her grandfather's villa was refreshing. She enjoyed the walks in nature in the early morning and conversation with her papa. The springs and waterfalls on the land were just as she remembered fun to frolic in to forget the cares of the world. In recent years, her family had reduced the crops they grew and herd of cattle. He'd said, "We don't need as much as we once did."

She understood with less help in working the land, cutting back made it manageable for himself. Her mother moved to the city years before and started her own bakery where she met and fell in love with her father. He was killed in the line of duty when she was a child, and she now remembered little about him.

Her mother was terrified when learning she was following him by joining the agency. She eased her burden by telling her she did the paperwork and used her university studies to research cases and profile persons of interest away from the action of catching the criminals. They never spoke again about her career.

Chapter 15

David and Dorian met for breakfast as was their normal routine since Jason returned to Barbados. As they were enjoying their morning Caffe Latte and fresh bread with butter and jam, Dorian said, "It's time I introduced you to the group of men who we've worked with for years."

His instinct said mafia ties. The heads of the Italian mafia groups who kept their world in motion. David knew there'd be no turning back once his participation was set in motion. "Let me know when and where we are to meet. I've reviewed your files on the expertise of each family and our sources for getting things done. If there is more info I need, let me know, so I'll be prepared for the meet."

Dorian was pleased with David's eagerness for doing things right. He felt better about stepping down and giving him the reins to the family business. They didn't need his problems to cloud their vision for the future.

He reviewed his latest criminal involvement and having taken the personnel problem into his own hands rather than handing it off to David he was sure it was a done deal. Dead men don't talk.

He'd been careful knowing Luca was sifting through Tonia's last conversations and contacts. He was hoping David's friendship with him would persuade him to look elsewhere or drop investigating her death. There were no signs of his involvement, but he had an unsettling feeling Luca considered him the cause of her death.

The meeting with the leaders of the mafia was set for the following day at their office in Livorno, the nearest seaport to Florence. He called David and said, "Be ready tomorrow morning for greeting our friends at 10 am. I have an overnight trip planned and a meeting with the estate's attorney and will meet you there."

"Sure. I'll see you then."

Dorian had already informed the leaders he was making a change. It was time to retire and handover the running of the Mandarino business to fresh blood with family ties. The locals were a buzz about David's arrival, and they weren't surprised at his news.

They wanted to meet him and size up his readiness to be a boss themselves. The family ties went back generations, and it was in their best interest to work together. Could this young man step up and carry the weight of being a leader in their secret society?

David arrived a few minutes early and sat in his Ferrari waiting for Dorian. When he saw him park his Maserati in a designated parking space, he got out of his car and walked over. Together, they strolled into a cigar smoke filled conference room.

The u-shaped table was an oddity, and he waited to be shown to his seat. Dorian pulled back the chair where he was to sit for all to decide his competence for membership. And, then he strolled to the podium to call the meeting to order. He waited for directions to be sworn in, a baptism of sorts into the clan.

The prep list Dorian had provided for the meeting was absolute in his denouncing family, and friends to become a blood brother of those present until death. He'd memorized the oath and was ready for the questions Dorian would ask him.

Dorian as an elder and guarantor introduces David to his mafia associates. "Who are you and what do you want?"

David stood and said, "My name is David of the Mandarino clan, and I seek blood and honor."

Elder: "Blood for whom?"

David: "For the wicked."

Elder: "Honor for whom?"

David: "For the Honored Society."

Elder: "Are you familiar with our rules?"

David: "I am familiar with them."

Elder: "The interest and the honor of the society come before family; from this moment on, the society is your family, and if you commit infamy, you will be punished by death. Just as you will be loyal to the society, so the society will be loyal to you and will aid you in need; this oath can only be broken by death. Are you prepared for this? Do you so swear?"

David placed his left hand, palm facing down, on the tip of a sharp-pointed stiletto, dagger, held by one of the participants while the others present placed their left hand down on top of his.

David: "I swear to the Sacred Crown of this Honored Society, that from this time forward you are my family, which I will always be loyal, and that only death can take me from you. I place myself in your hands to be judged and should I commit an act or offenses detrimental to the clan, staining my honor or that of others that may cause harm to the Honored Society, I will be punished by death."

The capo-societa, responsible for the life and death of associates, places his left hand over all the others.

Elder: "You were first known as a *contrasto onorato* from now on I recognize you as a *picciotta d'onore* (honored soldier).

David gives the elder three kisses on the cheek.

At the end of the rite, the elder turns to the formed circle and recites the formula that ends the meeting of the society.

Elder: From this moment on we have a new man of honor, the Society is formed, and the circle dismissed.

The members filed out of the conference room and went their separate ways with many patting him on the back as they left. Dorian handed him a set of keys to the building and said he'd see him at the estate after his vacation. Then he'd go over the status of the contracts in motion, clean out his living suite and retire from the business.

The Mandarino enterprise would be once again become family owned and operated. This was his final salute to Donatella for taking him under her wings. Her own flesh and blood would become a mafia boss on his resignation.

David walked to his Ferrari and waited as Dorian opened his car door and positioned himself in his seat. He'd follow him out of the maze of buildings before heading home.

When Dorian cranked his motor, a loud explosion fired bellowing flames and smoke. David ran toward him, but the intense heat made him back away. He quickly called the fire department hoping they'd arrive before the surrounding buildings ignited and to pry Dorian's body out of his car.

The Vigili del Fuoco with their fire engines arrived and the flames were exhausted from Dorian's car. The nearby buildings were soaked to insure they'd not be torched too. Dorian was burned to death for it appeared his door was locked insuring his entrapment. Someone planned today's massacre but for what purpose?

He watched as the remains of Dorian's body were recovered and emergency workers lifted him into the transport to the morgue. He thanked the firefighters and police for their readiness in securing the crime scene.

After the emergency crews left the scene, he called Godwin. He gave a quick recap and asked for his help for pinpointing the murderer. They agreed the names of the members in the secret meeting wouldn't be mentioned to the authorities. Someone targeted Dorian directly and he needed to know whom. And would he be next?

Chapter 16

The estate workers were shocked to learn about Dorian's murder. They'd known him most of their lives. David contacted their lawyer, Di Maggio in the city wondering what final papers he planned to sign and to get directives for planning his funeral.

He was glad to not have to call home with the news for telling Gabby might prove to be his undoing. She'd fear for his life and want him to return home immediately.

Godwin told Gabby about his death and convinced her attending his funeral was risky since the motive behind his murder was unknown. She accepted his conviction about her safety and worried about David. "I'd sleep better if David was working from here. I don't think he's safe in Italy."

"David will be fine, and it's important that he provides continuity for the family business. I'm in touch with him daily and will help sort through the information until we find the person/people behind his murder."

Tears came to Gabby's eyes, and she wiped them with a soft tissue before speaking. "Just do what's necessary to keep David safe."

Godwin leaned over and hugged her, and placed a light kiss on her forehead. "Yes, I will."

Dorian's funeral was attended by many in the community. David spoke using the notes he'd left behind. The man was meticulous having prepared his own funeral eulogy. A feast was prepared for mourners at the estate. David was counting down the minutes until the hall emptied and, then return to his suite to reflect on what he'd learned.

Having been an eyewitness to the crime, he'd given the police his statement. They'd concluded his door jammed from the placement and force of the explosion. The remains of a bomb were recovered at the scene and the police were looking into possible suspects.

David knew the clock was ticking fast toward it being a cold case. For there were no suspects for the police to interrogate since he had a far-reaching circle of acquaintances and friends. Any of his life-time of business dealings could've back-fired given the opportunity.

He and Godwin had their own plan for solving the murder. For he wouldn't sleep soundly until he uncovered the reason he was murdered. Security was tightened around the estate and his Ferrari was checked daily for tampering.

He received calls from leaders of the Rocco Mafia giving their condolences and offer of help for finding the murderer. He thanked them for their concern and support, and promised to call if needed. They were proud of the way he was managing the situation by not bringing their presence at the port to the police's attention.

Lilia's office was buzzing with the news about a high-profile murder at the Port of Livorno (ITLIV) Tuscany connected with a prestigious wine and olive producer in the region. Her boss took charge and briefed everyone about the car bombing of Dorian, the estate manager at Mandarino's, the producers of *Old-World Wines* and *Tuscany Olives*.

Her thoughts at once went to David and the likelihood of his being next. The boss mentioned he'd be taking over as steward of the family business effective immediately and was no longer a viable candidate to join the agency.

His facial expressions of doom and gloom didn't go unnoticed by the agents in the meeting. Many were glad the hot-shot, talented young heir wouldn't be joining their force. The elbow rib punching would have given into high-fives if the commander wasn't present.

They were pleased with the outcome for climbing the ladder was difficult at best and a savvy and rich tech guy put a damper on their personal advancement. The group was relieved to learn the local police department was investigating the murder. They were to continue the investigations previously assigned to them. The male agents quickly planned a celebration at a local bar.

Taking his directive at face value Lilia did as ask. On her desk were open files with mug shots of mafia hitmen with any one of them possible suspects for murdering Dorian. She quickly caught herself from going off on a tangent in that direction. Her boss made it clear they were to stand down from agency involvement for solving the murder. But fearing David might be in danger, could she?

David met early in the morning with the department heads of the business. First, he met with the spirits and then the olive producers. It was a long morning lasting into the early afternoon filled with calming the leaders and promising the business would continue as usual. Afterwards, he would attend a meeting with their Italian lawyer, *Avvocati*, to put the settling of Dorian's estate in motion. Then later he'd read through the personal communications he left in the safe about company business.

Aware of his downstairs office, he believed Dorian stored nothing of importance there. The office was for show and designed for meeting visitors or conversation with department heads. He would go through the contents after reviewing documents in the business center.

He eased out of the plush Italian leather chair Dorian once commanded the business from and walked to his fully stocked bar. Splashing a generous amount of whiskey into a glass, he felt relieved hoping the worst was behind him.

The evening before he met with the staff servicing the villa and consoled them for, they were in constant contact with Dorian, and many had been long-time employees of the estate. Workers he'd frequently referred to as family when describing them and their duties.

The chef took the news especially hard for he enjoyed cooking for someone who understood the delicacies of preparing and serving authentic Italian dishes. His sous chef, Silvana, sat with a blank face, so much so, he considered asking if she needed time off to grieve. Fearful of her response in a fragile state, he decided to let her boss, the head chef, manage the situation. He knew her better than himself.

Noting he'd be running late for the meeting with the AVV and wanting to check under his Ferrari before leaving, he made a dash for the door. Quickly examining his car, he sped to his appointment smiling from relief. He had no idea how close to home the family enemies stood. Not wanting to be next for a hit, he parked his car where he'd have a clear view from the AVV's office window. Their Italian lawyer quickly read Dorian's Last Will and Testament. He mentioned a change was made on the day of his death and was recorded as instructed according to Italian law.

David perked up wanting to learn more about the last-minute change but waited for the AVV to continue speaking. Most of his assets would be transferred to David along with gratitude to Donatella for making it possible.

When the business was concluded he thanked Di Maggio for his efforts in probating Dorian's will as intended. He asked, "What change did Dorian make on the day of his death?"

The lawyer looked down at his feet, and then said, "He cut Luca from inheriting funds from his estate. It was originally to be halved between you and him. He did leave him his cottage on the sea, and he's been notified."

David left wondering for what purpose Dorian planned to return to the attorney's office and asked, "Did you plan to meet with him again on the day of his death?"

"No, we'd concluded his legal affairs before his meeting at the port."

He'd like to learn the history between Luca and Dorian. For in their last conversation, he'd instructed him to deal with him if he didn't back down from investigating Antonia's death. Yet, he'd left him an inheritance showing care and concern for his future. He was missing something, but what?

Chapter 17

Silvana moped around their cottage. Her crying spells since Antonia's death had diminished to occasional outbursts. Her husband and Tonia's father had grown weary of her unrelenting mourning.

She'd packed away photos and her belongings until she became stronger. As calculating as Tonia had become, she still remembered the beautiful, smart, and sunny girl of her youth. She'd never understand why Tonia didn't receive a second chance in life like Luca. Both were priceless to her, for quite distinct reasons.

Now another unsuspecting death to deal with, a murder, and her heart skipped a beat when thinking about the possibilities of who ended his life.

David poured himself a drink, called Godwin to bring him up to date with today's events. Maybe something would stand out to him that he missed inside the gaping hole in what he understood about the relationship between Dorian and Luca.

Godwin said, "Keep digging and don't say anything to Luca about your findings. If he left anything behind to solve this, it'll be in the company safe or his personal suite. He's old school and never really trusted technology although he used the resources for business."

"I'll keep sifting through his paperwork. I locked his bedroom suite after his murder not allowing the house cleaner entry. I'll start looking over papers in the company safe tonight. Tomorrow, I'll investigate his belongings. He had a cottage by the sea; do you think the answer is hidden at the coast?"

"Likely not; he liked to keep close tabs on his personal life. Although, a day trip from the estate, the location would be too far away for him to monitor closely."

"I hope you're right for Luca will be notified of his inheritance soon and I'll not have entry without suspicion."

"Keep me posted about what you find and stay safe."

David refreshed his drink glass for he was looking at a long night of filtering through the estate's files.

Reviewing the bulk of papers in the safe, he realized he knew more about Donatella than his mother had known. The legal paperwork releasing her son from his role in the family business along with an ample payout was legally administered along with naming the family successor. Yes, he was the next Don just like Dorian and Godwin had said.

The corporate business documents and seals where intact showing thirteen generations of the family business. From vendors, corporate clients, to the holders of the family assets all were included.

Now, along with the shares he'd inherited from his mother, he was the sole stakeholder in the business. The business's success or failure were in his hands to grow and meet todays and future challenges. He was glad Godwin was his confident for he'd need help.

The demands of running the empire he'd inherited was a challenge. He was feeling trapped, and unable to work on his true passion for making earth a safer place to live. His only hope was to hire a CEO to free up his time, and that was highly unlikely with the possibility of someone learning their mafia connection.

He'd have to watch his passions from a distance by investing in companies working toward the same goals. He couldn't chance anyone learning about their mafia ties. But first he had a murder to solve and to find out how deep the murderous intent ran. Was someone trying to sabotage the business also?

Chapter 18

Luca received a legal notice he'd inherited a cottage on the Ligurian Sea and was instructed to visit a law office in town to sign the paperwork and receive the keys to the property. He stopped himself short of stopping by his mama and papas to ask if they'd heard anything about it.

He'd wait until he had the details before saying anything to them. He called and made an appointment and left Pauli in charge of the orchard for three days saying he needed a short vacation. Time-off would give him a chance to check out the property and learn his benefactor's name.

His parents' families were not landholders on the sea. At least not to his knowledge for they'd inherited long ago after their deaths. All they received was a villa in Palermo Sicily that was once his mother's home. He never learned about his papa's family except they were deceased.

He cranked the slightly used Alfa Romeo Giulia he'd purchased with his last dividend bonus and wondered if workers would continue to be rewarded annually when they met or exceeded their quota. Since Dorian's death he'd not thought about who would take over as head of the business. But, in the meeting of department heads, David did say business would continue as usual.

He suspected David would be next in line for he was related to the family. Likely, the only surviving member if his memory served him about the family descendants. He was the great-grandson of Donatella the grand dame of the estate.

He'd enjoyed his company when they took an occasional break for drinks in town and when he went with him home to Barbados to check on Jason's orchard. David could probably use a friend with having the business dumped into his lap. He'd check-in with him after he sorted through the latest event.

Luca arrived at the AVV's office and quickly identified himself. He was asked to take a seat and noted the lawyer was reviewing his appearance. He was dressed appropriately rather debonair in his opinion and waited to learn more.

The lawyer, Di Maggio read from a document about the property he was to inherit. Sliding the papers toward him, he said, "Sign here and the property will belong to you."

Luca looked over the paper noting no benefactor was listed on the page he was to sign. It was a legal description of the property and list of contents within the cottage and a nondescript fishing boat.

The lawyer handed him a pen to sign and claim his inheritance. Luca looked at him and said, "This all sounds bogus especially not knowing the source of my good fortune."

Di Maggio replied, "I take that comment as an insult that you'd believe I'd participate in a scam. This is all legitimate."

"Then why isn't the benefactors name listed on this paper?"

"Read from the top of the document s-l-o-w-l-y. It's on the first page."

The lawyer shook his head wondering if Dorian could've been wrong about his paternity.

Luca blushed then apologized for his mistake. "I never imagined I'd inherit from Dorian. He helped me straighten up my life when I was young, but we've had no communication except business in recent years.

"Well, today you are fortunate indeed. Apparently, Dorian wanted you to have a choice for your future."

Luca left the office in a daze. Di Maggio probably thought he was a dummy with his response. Sliding into the car equipped with GPS he routed the vehicle to the seaside cottage. For a moment, he let out a breath knowing he had a place to relax away from the constant pressure of the business.

Yet, in the back of his mind, he wondered why he was supplied an inheritance. Did he find out he was getting closer to pinpointing his dealings with his sister Antonia? Was this to be his payoff for letting it drop?

He couldn't prove it yet, but Dorian and his sister did talk. About what, he didn't know. But, knowing his scheming sister, she'd found a blackmail opportunity and didn't realize how dangerous it was to pursue with the family. Her latest entrepreneur plans likely got her killed. What was he to do now and could he enjoy the cottage knowing he was possible blood money for his sister's murder?

He needed to call Di Maggio and find out how long his inheritance from Dorian had been in force. The enjoyment of this gift would depend on the timeline. Did he do this before or after her murder?

He rang the lawyer and caught him just as he was leaving for the day. Di Maggio was surprised to hear from again and his voice sounded agitated. "What can I do for you?"

"How long ago did Dorian prepare to leave me his cottage?"

Di Maggio saw no harm in answering his question for it was a matter of record. He said, "Thirty-one years ago."

"Thanks, appreciate your time."

Luca felt relieved for now he could enjoy the seaside cottage without guilt or shame. He quickly calculated his age at the time the inheritance was placed in his name. He was one year old. Now, he had even more questions. He accelerated to the cottage hoping answers would be waiting there.

Chapter 19

David spent the night going over the files in the corporate safe. All were based on keeping the business successful. His great-grandmother apparently loved her family yet wanted a family member to take over the reins of a business her family had built.

When her son vacated the position, more like her husband than her family, she succumbed to his wishes as penchant for his father's murder from a mob hit when she was the one targeted.

He was in the right family for the hits never stopped. If he allowed himself, he'd believe she was smiling in the knowledge her own flesh and flood was now in charge of the business.

She had chosen Dorian as a place-holder until now to ascertain the business would continue. He was smart and with ambitious characteristics of someone to lead the business in the interval.

Donatella picked him as a young man from a seaside village in Livorno near her vacation home. She'd drawn up the legal documents for rewarding him if he'd come to the estate and learn the business from her personally.

He accepted. She'd left behind legal documents to make sure he wasn't forced into his new role. According to his own statement, he believed there was more to life than that of a fisher like his father and grandfather before him.

He wondered if Dorian utterly understood the role he accepted. Or was it a personal vendetta against him that spearheaded his murder. From appearance, Dorian was all business, and he wondered if he ever relaxed and let down the barriers. If anyone had knowledge about his personal life, it'd be Godwin. He'd ask him in their next conversation.

The next morning David arose early to go through the contents of Dorian's suite. He wanted no one in the estate to have knowledge about his plans. Remembering what Godwin had said, he surveyed his living quarters looking for a hiding place to store his personal papers. A painting of he and Donatella caught his eye. For most people, they'd look past the painting thinking it was a personal capture of his time with Donatella.

He believed his secrets were hiding in plain view. Behind the painting was a safe if he guessed right. It was a personal statement of his hopes and dreams away from the prying eyes of anyone on the estate including Donatella.

He hoped his craft of cracking safes was working for he didn't want to go get tools. He flipped back the painting in its gallery style frame and saw the safe hidden behind it, and his fingerprints imprinted from years of use. Then placed his fingers on the dial, leaned his head in to listen for clicks, and moved it from left to right. The safe clicked open. He'd not lost his touch.

David opened the safe filled with stacks of euros, papers, and photos. The creepiness of touching his belonging was surreal, but he suspected the clues would answer questions about his murder. He took the papers and photos to his desk to sort through them one at a time.

Photos of him and Donatella at various stages in their life were tied together with a yellow ribbon. He opened an aged envelope and found the deed delivering the Ligurian Sea property from Donatella to Dorian.

He quickly remembered the property was to be inherited by Luca according to Di Maggio making him suspicious of their relationship. Yet, he'd put a hit on him if he didn't back down from investigating Tonia's death.

A well-worn photo of him and a beautiful Italian woman caught his attention. He took the magnifying glass from his oak desk drawer to see the photo closer. There was no doubt the young woman with him was Silvana, the sous' chef in the estate's kitchen.

He hadn't seen any interaction between them since arriving. Quite the opposite, his contact was with the head chef who he complimented numerous times for his delicious dishes.

He continued going through the photos hoping to learn more about the man who prized his privacy. A photo of a young woman and a boy caught his attention. The likeness was of Silvana and possibly her young son. He wondered where it was taken and who made the picture. The background appeared to be a seacoast property.

An envelope beneath the stack was freshly addressed to Silvana. Godwin was right Dorian feared for his life and this was likely the last personal communication to the woman in the picture. Touching the unopened letter, he wondered if he should read his last words. But then it might lead to finding his killer if he suspected someone.

Chapter 20

Luca arrived at the seaside cottage belonging to Dorian, now his. The setting was beautiful and the landscape pristine. The property was high-value even with limited real estate experience he deduced this was a one-of-a-kind seacoast villa. Not a little cottage by the sea, like he was expecting from conversation with Di Maggio the lawyer.

Taking a minute to catch his breath before entering, he wondered if the lawyer was aware of the size of his surprise inheritance. From his description he was expecting a shanty with a rough-honed fishing boat. This was not the case if the entrance was a sign.

He was feeling queasy about entering the villa that wasn't his until today. He took the key, inserted it into the lock and turned the key to open the door. The interior décor met the requirements for being featured in any Italian magazine for the wealthy.

He was in awe and slipped his shoes off at the entrance to not soil the flooring. How did he become the benefactor of Dorian's property? Yes, he'd always shown an interest in his doing well. He thought it was due from his family's long-time standing at the estate. And, to believe he was the person responsible for Tonia's murder made him angry at himself.

Luca took his time seeing the scenery from the open foyer that expanded into a large living area overlooking the sea. A mantle with figurines and a painting of the ocean and fishing boats was hanging above the shelf.

He walked closer to examine the painting after seeing the artist's initials scrawled near the bottom. He couldn't read the letters and didn't want to damage the seascape by removing the painting from the frame.

Hoping to learn something about his benefactor and the reasons he left him the property he went into the master bedroom. The bed appeared freshly made like he visited recently and expected to return soon. The walk-in closet was filled with the latest fashion in suits and leisure wear and expensive Italian footwear worn by made-men in the mafia and their counterparts of wealthy Italians.

Needing a stiff drink, he walked to the kitchen where he had no doubt stored an ample supply. Grabbing a glass from the cabinet, he uncorked the wine bottle and poured himself a healthy drink. He didn't want to be in a drunken fog during his treasure hunt for clues.

As he placed the wine bottle on the counter, he noticed a small, framed photo nearby. Observing closer, his mouth fell open from the shock of seeing a photo of his mama as a young woman. Curious, he began looking for more wondering why her photo was in the villa. Scuffling through the drawers, he found a freshly penned letter addressed to him. He opened the envelope with a kitchen knife and sat down in the dining room to read the one-page note.

The letter didn't make sense and left no clues to why he left him the property. The note simply said he wished him well in whatever endeavors he chose in life, and to use his inheritance wisely. Directions to where his safe was in the master bedroom closet, and an antique key was included in the envelope.

Feeling the urge for a stronger drink, he went to the bar and splashed some Disaronno Amaretto into a spotless glass. The low alcohol content of 28% would keep him sober as he sorted through the contents of the safe.

Following directions, he discovered the secret passage door in the bedroom closet and slid it open by touching the hidden corner cedar wood panel. Inside was an 18th century antique double-door wrought-iron safe in pristine condition. He inserted the key into the lock and opened the doors.

On the shelves were stacks of euros and a high-quality Italian leather bag. He figured millions in banknotes in the least with no note relaying the source. The money was enough to last him a lifetime, and added confusion about his receiving the enormous gift. What would he do with his newly found inheritance?

He closed and relocked the safe, and left the passageway the same as when he entered. He needed to burn the letter with details of its location in case someone should break-in once he left. With two days of vacation left before returning to the estate; the time away would help him clear his thoughts and prepare questions for his mama. Once he returned, she'd want to meet, and find out what he'd been doing. She'd never know until she explained her presence at the villa by the sea, but would she?

Chapter 21

David gave in and opened the envelope addressed to Silvana hoping it would lead to clues about his murderer. Immediately he regretted his choice after reading the first line, *"To my dearest Silvana."* But he kept reading the love letter that should've been for her eyes only.

The tightly worded message said nothing about recent events. Only that he regretted his choices, but couldn't live with himself if his work placed her in danger. He never stopped loving her and kept his distance for peace between her and her husband. The banknotes in the safe were hers to do with as she chose. The home she lived in on the estate belonged to her during her lifetime. This was his final gift to her and signed it, love always, Dorian.

David felt Dorian's pain as he read the letter and tears filled his eyes. He was caught in a similar trap. He'd never have the woman he desired for many of the same reasons.

Since Dorian death, he was visible to many dangerous people. The Italian mafia knew him now as the new head of the Mandarino family.

He slipped the letter back into the envelope he'd carefully opened and took the banknotes from the safe and along with the letter and placed them in a nearby carrying case. Then centered the leather bag on the bed, and closed the safe adjusting the picture frame to keep his hiding place secret.

Locking the door behind him, he went into the estate's kitchen to find Silvana. He'd bring her to Dorian's suite away from prying eyes to have closure about their relationship. The door would automatically lock when she left.

Lilia was at a dead-end in the investigation of the kidnapping of young women from the city streets. Luigino Di Donato, her boss wouldn't like the progress they were making for he was taking heat from the politicians worried about the effects on regional tourism.

Every few days, more girls were snatched, even tourists. No ransom demands were made for their return, leading the agency to believe it was a human trafficking operation likely mob related.

The agency had brought in known associates of the Italian Mafia. So far, they were coming up with more questions than answers. Later today, she was to interrogate one of their newer contacts fresh off the streets. She was hoping he'd provide an original take on the case and perhaps cooperate to stay clear of law enforcement in the future.

The dimly lit room had one table and two chairs. Rafael was seated and cuffed to the table. She took a seat, and asked, "Do you understand why you are here today?"

He pounded his tightly bound fists against the table, and stared at her before answering. "I have no idea why I'm here. Why don't you educate me?"

A real smart-ass from the get-go she waited a moment before speaking. "You were seen in the same area where two girls were kidnapped from the street last night."

"So, now it's illegal to walk the streets at night? *Scema, roba da matti*, crazy, I've been homeless for a while. And I'm not aware of girls being snatched."

"Explain what you were doing last night on Via de Benci Street."

"That's my la zona. I work it every night mostly outside the bars rich tourists visit and pick-pocket them as they stumble to their ride. That's the only thing you can arrest me for, but you have no proof."

He exhaled. "How much longer are you going to hold me? I need to make a call if you're arresting me."

"Give us a lead for finding and rescuing the missing girls, and we'll let you go for now."

"Sorry, donna nel servizio di intelligence, I know nothing about the kidnappers and don't want to. But, if you'll let me go, I can tell you what I heard about the car-bombing of that Mandarino fellow, Dorian."

Lilia's interest perked up, and she hoped Rafael didn't pick up on it. Her bosses might be watching and listening through the one-way mirror. The agency was told to stand down from investigating the murder. She couldn't ask him direct questions about what happened. But the info might help David stay safe. Her instinct screamed that he was running his own investigation out of self-preservation if nothing else.

"Let's get back to the girls who are missing. Would whoever you were going to speak about be involved in human trafficking?"

"That's for you to find out. I can tell you what I've overheard if you'll release me."

She was caught in a dilemma but believed the info he offered might remain within the directives the boss gave them.

"OK, you've got a deal. I just hope something comes out of it in time to save the girls."

"Word on the street is that Dorian was hit by one of the Italian Mafia families. He thought retiring was an option from something he was involved in, and they showed him differently."

"Which family orchestrated the hit, and what is their involvement in human trafficking?"

"Signora, I've done told you I've heard nothing about snatching girls from the street."

"Well, we'll follow up and your statement, if you'll identify the mafia family who orchestrated the hit on Dorian. They may be the same."

"Leave me out of it, those folks don't play. The Solocone Sciarretta family is feared and from what I've heard rightly so. I'm dead if they learn I've triggered them for anything."

Not knowing who to trust in the agency, she'd erase the tape from the meeting to be certain of his safety.

"Our conversation will never leave this room. You are free to go but if you hear anything, you are to call me directly."

She handed him her card, and said, "Remember what I said because you don't want to be caught in this human trafficking net."

She excused herself and went into the viewing room and quickly removed the recording of the interrogation, and slipped it into her lace bra before walking out. If asked, her reply would be she believed another agent was present as usual during an interrogation making notes and recording their conversation. Although, all the agents left early when possible doubtful they'd stayed for her late interrogation.

Quickly, she went to the front desk to notify the jailer of Rafael's release. In a corner of the central office with clear view of the exit door she waited for him to leave the building. When he did, she decided to go home for it was past quitting time. She'd text David and request a meeting in an out-of-the-way place. Some heavy hitters may be tracking him now.

Chapter 22

David was mentally exhausted with everything thrown in his lap. He went to the estate's business center to read the rest of the documents he's confiscated from Dorian's personal suite. He left Silvana there earlier and told her to take her time, to close the door and leave when she was ready. If bringing her to Dorian's suite was a good deed, he'd done one today.

He poured himself a shot of whiskey, and began reading the papers Dorian left behind. There was no hint to who killed him. But he did find a letter addressed to him with instructions to contact the Polizia Locale and ask for Dante Sagese. He said, Sagese is a life-long friend and knows what to do in event of my death. Once the case is closed, it'll take the pressure off those responsible and you can quietly track and kill the person/s responsible.

The letter ended with 'watch you back' and wishing him the best. Below was the private telephone number for Sagese. He punched in the numbers and waited for his answer.

"Dante Sagese, here," he said.

"Yes, this is David from the Mandarino family, and I received a note from Dorian to contact you after his death."

"I talked with Dorian earlier in the month, and he sensed he was in danger. He explained that you'd be taking over in his place. I'm sad to learn my friend was murdered, he deserved some peace before leaving this life."

"Has your department taken over the investigation?"

"Yes, I immediately stepped in when learning about the car-bombing. My department will handle it from here and within the month the file will be closed as Dorian wished."

"Thank you, for keeping The Agenzia Informazioni e Sicurezza Esterna out of it for my own good and the family business."

"Keep my number handy in case you come up on problems you can't handle alone."

"Appreciate your help and look forward to working with you in the future."

David put down his cell and pondered if Lilia's agency were tracking the case even if they had no jurisdiction. He'd like to talk with her, but lately he'd been up to his elbows in the dirty work of sorting through Dorian's life.

Thinking like-minded, he noticed a text from her. He pulled it up and quickly responded. They agreed on an out-of-the-way place to meet. Checking his Tag Heuer wristwatch he realized he'd missed lunch, and now wouldn't make it back in time for dinner. He needed to tell the chef on his way out to save it for tomorrow. He could see his blustering red face now, thinking who would eat leftovers when they could have a freshly prepared meal.

After parking his Ferrari in front of the restaurants open air all'aperto dining area to keep an eye on it, he entered. Thankful, that unlike many restaurants today they hadn't reverted to the plaque-era wine holes, windows used for wine service. They could be served a glass of wine at the table along with some freshly made Italian dishes.

He was seated when Lilia arrived and entered like a fresh breeze and sat across from him at their rustic table. Quickly explaining he'd missed meals today, he asked what she'd like to eat. They ordered the chef's special for the day, and were pleased with their choices after tasting the pasta and sauce likely prepared from an old family recipe.

He didn't want to take his eyes off her, but it was necessary to observe his car. It was a reminder of his current situation and possible lifestyle from now on. He asked, "Lilia, you mentioned you had something to tell me in person. What is it?"

"We're interrogating associates of the mob for finding missing girls who've been kidnapped off the streets. A young man today mentioned he wasn't aware of kidnappers, but learned who put the hit on Dorian."

"I didn't think your agency was investigating Dorian's murder?"

"We're not. In fact, we have been specifically instructed to stay clear of the investigation."

"Then how did you find out about the car-bombing?"

"I was walking a tight-rope and praying my boss wasn't listening. But I felt you might be in danger, and would like info about who murdered Dorian."

"Tell me what he said."

"I linked the questions to the missing girls. By asking if it was possible that Dorian was murdered by the same people who were kidnapping girls. And, he said, yes, but we'd have to track that down for he wanted nothing to do with it.

He was visibly shaken from fear of those responsible. I assured him our conversation would never leave the room and when he answered, I thanked him and went to the viewing room and slipped the recording on my person and left after seeing him out of the building."

"What was the family name of who he believed murdered Dorian?"

"One of the most feared mafia families in Italy, the Solocone Sciarretta family."

"Did he give the reason for the hit?"

"Yes, according to the young man he'd quit something they were involved in and that wasn't allowed."

"Do you think he is a credible source? Or was he trading the info to keep from being questioned about the girls?"

"He mainly wanted his freedom and was scared to mention the name of the family. He is homeless and the mob throws him a bone or two occasionally. His livelihood is made from pick-pocketing wealthy tourists."

"Lilia don't tell anyone else what you've told me. It could put your life in danger."

"Don't worry; I don't even trust my fellow agents with this type of info. The mob has likely infiltrated our ranks. The world gone mad for a fast buck."

"Are you planning to investigate the Solocone Sciarretta family relating to the missing girls?"

"Not until we have more info to link them to human trafficking. I was hoping you'd share some of your finding about the family when you investigate them."

"I will share what I find about their network and any link to finding the missing girls. But I can't share info about Dorian's murderer for your safety and mine."

"We've got a deal. I'd like to find those girls sooner rather than later. For no ransom has been posted for their return, looking like a human trafficking operation drugging, and selling them to the highest bidder."

Lilia stood to leave, and David slid out of his chair and kissed the top of her head before saying goodbye.

He watched her get into her late model sedan and drive away. Standing alone on the sidewalk he was shaking from his unquenched desire of her.

Chapter 23

Luca was enjoying his stay at the villa by the sea. He'd inspected in and around the property as much as possible and still enjoy the ocean. He was pleased to know the home was covered by an elaborate security system. The alarm was off when he arrived making him wonder if Dorian intentionally left it unsecured for his entering without triggering the alarm.

There was no surprise in finding a sleek, cabin cruiser parked in a slip designed to leverage it in and out of the water. The reels and rods were intact and all he needed was to catch bait with the small net and fish. He motored out a short distance from the shore and easily caught sea bass for dinner and used the outdoor fryer to cook them.

His vacation was ending with only one more day left before returning to the estate and the grape orchard. Pauli would have it under control, making him wonder if perhaps with his new financial freedom he should pursue something new. But he had lifelong friends in Tuscany and was enjoying David's company when they went into town. Thoughts of leaving his mother saddened him. He didn't believe leaving was in his future.

Thinking of his mother, he remembered the conversation they were destined to have. Would she be honest with him about the cottage and the reasons behind his inheritance?

When he returned to the estate, he'd check on the vines and give his mother a call asking her to meet him at his home on the estate grounds. They'd be safely distanced to have a private conversation without his papa overhearing their discussion.

Silvana cried until she hiccupped while reading the letter from Dorian. He distanced himself from her for a reason that showed how much he loved her. They were two young people in love and the family business got in the way. She remembered how he was always at Donatella's side listening and conducting her orders.

She was jealous of his constant attention to her every whim. The only time they were not interrupted was when they took a short vacation and escaped to the cottage by the sea. She'd love to visit again if for no other reason but to remember their happy times together.

A cloud of shame overtook her knowing she caused his death. She'd blamed him for her daughter, Antonia's murder. Death by suicide the death certificate read — *Dai*! No one who knew her believed that story. She was too full of life to take her own.

When she returned home, she'd call her brother and find out if he was safe from the polizia. Hopefully, her husband would be at the brewery until she made the call. She'd never want him to learn of her treachery.

She placed the letter in the leather bag filled with banknotes, closed the door, and left. The satchel would fit into the hiding place she used for storing family treasures.

Once the bag was stashed, she dialed her brother's number and waited for him to answer. She heard the clock ticking in the background fitting for the conversation they were about to have.

"Hello, Lothario Scutari here," he said.

"Lothario, it's me Silvana. Are you safe from the polizia?"

"No problem, sis, I'm in the clear someone beat me to the job."

"Oh, my, I'm glad to hear that. I let my emotions about Antonia's murder get the best of me. I should've never asked you to avenge her death."

"Well, the deed is done now, and our hands are clean. You can quit worrying about Luca and his desire for revenge. The Solocone Sciarretta family had first dibs on killing him. I'd arrived at his location when the youngest member of the family showed up. I hid behind a loading dock and watched him crawl under the car and plant the bomb. When his car left, I jumped into my pick-up and headed out, so I'd be far away when the bomb ignited, and a distance away from possible polizia inquiries."

Smiling and pleased neither she nor her family was involved in Dorian's murder, she said goodbye.

Luca turned on the security before locking the door to leave the villa. He couldn't wait to return and explore the property more. He'd gotten carried away when the fish started biting and stayed out longer than he'd intended. After hosing down the boat, he iced the fish to take home and cook. His mother would enjoy some freshly caught grouper.

He'd like to confide in someone about his recent good fortune. But it wasn't safe to tell anyone for then he'd be afraid of attempted break-ins to steal the banknotes or worst kill him for his connection to Dorian.

Checking in with Pauli to make sure everything was on schedule was his first stop. Then he'd return home and call his mama over for a talk and some fresh fish to take home to cook for dinner.

The orchard was beautiful in the late afternoon sunlight making him proud of his commitment to the vines. In his absence, the selected grapevines were pruned, and new planting had been added to evaluate a hybrid for Jason's vineyard. Pauli did fine with keeping everything running in his absence. He called his mother and invited her over.

As soon as she answered, she asked, "Where have you been? I've been worried about you."

"Come over, mama and let's talk. I brought you some fresh fish for dinner tonight."

Silvana packed some fresh rolls and jam for his pantry. Then, put on a sun hat and rushed over to find out where he'd disappeared to for the past three days. She'd thought the worst but now knew he wasn't involved in Dorian's murder.

Luca opened the door and welcomed her in. He was unsure how much he'd tell her about his inheritance for like him she'd want to share it with someone leading to potentially deadly consequences.

The freshly cleaned and filleted grouper were wrapped in paper and stored in the refrigerator until after their visit. Then, he'd hand them to her to take home to cook his papa a good meal.

Anxiety was visible on her face when she arrived. Likely thinking he was in danger when he did not tell her about his trip. When she said, "Now Luca, can you tell your mama where you've been?"

"Yes, of course if you'll answer some questions for me first."

Silvana was uncomfortable with the direction the conversation was headed. He'd discovered something, what she was unsure, but she was afraid he had to do with her secrets.

When she didn't reply, he whispered, "Mama, how well did you know Dorian?"

"As good, as anyone else working on the estate, I suppose."

Oh, this was how it was going to be, her holding out information he deserved to learn.

"I think there's more to it than what you're saying. Why can't you be honest with me? What you say will be kept between me and you."

Silvana shook her head as tears floated to her eyes. "Some things are best left unsaid, and this is one of those times."

There was no getting through to her. He'd save the questions for another day. Eventually, she'd change her mind for he was stubborn too and would refuse to share parts of his life. He kissed her on the cheek and handed her the basket with the fish, and didn't confide the location of his three-day absence from the estate.

Silvana slowly walked the beaten path home thinking about the questions Luca asked. Nothing good would come from her showing the relationship with Dorian. She made a silent oath to never labor him with facts about his paternity. He had a papa who cared for him and that was enough. She decided her rights about his life would end where his began. Now, to abide by her decision allowing both to keep their secrets, made it a challenge.

Chapter 24

David was in the business center sifting through photos of the Solocone Sciarretta family. Ten generations of family members had managed to elude the police for criminal acts according to the reports he pulled up on his computer.

Their trucking business was well-known across Italy. Shipping containers that could easily hide people or illegal products made them untouchable with their vast network and payoffs to politicians, and the like to move supplies.

They were the premier trucking supplier for the family business and had been for decades. The leader, boss of the family was at the secret meeting at the port. He was conflicted for his supposed actions went against the tenets of the secret society, anything that would cast a shadow on the Rocco Italian Mafia name.

He wanted a closer view of the younger family members to be on the look-out for when he went out for drinks or was in the city. Taking it a step further he tapped into their phones to see if he could pick up info about Dorian's murder or the missing girls Lilia told him about.

Godwin helped him map out a plan to force their hands. He had no choice but to avenge Dorian's death. Their job was to make sure someone paid for you couldn't hit a mob boss without paybacks. He suspected the Sciarretta family was on high alert with probable cause.

Dante Sagese called to inform him that the police's investigation into Dorian's death was closed. Before ending the call, he reminded him to be on the watch for they may be coming for him next believing his vulnerability.

David was aware of the ruthless nature of the family and was hoping to surprise them when the boss acted. They'd learn the case was closed and believe they'd gotten away with another hit. He was waiting for them to relax and go about business as usual.

In the interim, he was looking into the possibilities of their human trafficking. Lilia deserved information after leading him to Dorian's murderer. He just hoped she used backup when deciding to arrest them.

The chatter picked up when the Sciarretta family realized they were in the clear. Yes, they were involved with kidnapping young girls off the streets of Florence, drugging and transporting them out of the city to sell to the highest bidder. They were planning to move them within 48 hours after the buyers were lined up.

He listened intently to their conversations and caught Lilia's name. They learned she was an agent for The Agenzia Informazioni e Sicurezza Esterna and planned to stop their investigation. A young thug on the streets was seen leaving their office. They followed him knowing he'd been involved in some of their recent petty action. Uncooperative at first, he later confessed to being interrogated by her but swore he didn't give up information about them. He said, "She's searching for those responsible for kidnapping young women. And I told her I didn't know anything."

Knowing his statement was true because they didn't allow thieves to become associates and know their business, they let him live. He was so scared he'd already pissed his pants adding belief to his fear of the family.

David closed his satellite listening portal and quickly called Lilia to warn her she might be in danger. His call went directly to her voice mail leaving no choice but to leave an urgent message.

Lilia didn't know who to trust in the agency. She wanted to check out the leads she'd gotten about the Sciarretta family before going to her boss, Di Donato. He expected concrete evidence before deciding how the agency would handle it.

The trucking facility was located outside of the city, and she wanted to get eyes on what was happening there and take photos if she saw any young girls. Using her personal vehicle to not attract attention, she parked her Fiat close enough to survey the property. She checked her phone and realized she'd missed a call from David. After listening to his urgent sounding message, she returned his call.

He answered promptly. "Lilia where are you?"

"I'm gathering intelligence at the trucking facility."

"Get out of there now. They know you're investigating them."

"How?"

"The young thug you interrogated told them you were looking into the kidnapping of the girls and asked about their involvement."

"They must have forced it out of him. I didn't take him as someone who'd share otherwise."

The next sound before the call ended, was Lilia screaming.

In an adrenaline rush, he immediately stood prepared for action. They would murder her to protect their enterprise. He wanted to rush to her aid, but they would recognize him being a member of their secret society. His hands were tied. Why, did she have to put herself in danger?

He quickly called her boss for she'd indicated there wasn't anyone else in the agency she trusted.

Without identifying himself, he told him where she was and to bring backup to immediately extract her from their hands. Her boss was rattled for a minute, until he exclaimed loudly, "This is a life-or-death situation you need to move now."

"Yes, yes, you're right. We'll take care of it."

David stopped for a minute to whisper a silent prayer for her safety. He begrudged the fact he couldn't save her without showing his hand. Out of nowhere, his thoughts went to how committed the Italian Mafia was to their own rules stating to not harm women or children of mafia heads. He'd never know for she was an intelligence agent that'd probably forfeit the claim, and she'd probably never accept a marriage proposal knowing he was boss in the Italian Mafia.

His not being present to save her knowing what was happening gave Lilia another reason to not speak to him. She'd expect him to take charge. All he could do was hope for the best.

Lilia felt the roughness against her face of a burlap sack as it was thrown over her head as she was pulled from her Fiat. She reaches for her cell and touches it with her fingers when someone pried it from her hand. She heard shattered glass as someone stomped on it.

Lifted, and thrown across a burly man's shoulder she was being carried somewhere no one could rescue her. She thought about her mama and the grief she'd feel if she was murdered today. There'd be no doubt she was lied to about her line of work. *Please God save me from these evil men.*

Luigino Di Donato quickly pressed the intercom button to summons the agents he trusted on the mission. When they came to his door, he said suit up, we have a hostage situation on our hands with one of our own Lilia Siciliano.

She was following up on a lead and was kidnapped by members of the Sciarretta family. This feared mafia family is armed and dangerous. We'll proceed with caution with the end goal of rescuing Lilia and arresting those present.

They tipped the scale in the wrong direction with their latest actions.

The agents noted the address and rushed to their vehicles and with sirens blaring drove to the trucking facility. As they turned the corner they saw Lilia's blue Fiat, and found from where she was taken. Sizing up the building nearby, they made plans for entering with Di Donato leading the team of agents.

Lilia was taken inside the building and shoved into a metal chair with its metal prongs bruising her hind side. The eerie sound of footsteps on the concrete floor vibrated through her mind as she waited for the burlap bag to be removed from her head.

A man wearing expensive woody-aromatic Italian cologne removed the covering. She blinked for the room was dimly lit with the shutters drawn.

"Who do we have here," he asked.

"Lilia Sicilliano an agent of the Agenzia Informazioni e Sicurezza Esterna. And, you have just kidnapped an official member of the domestic security and foreign intelligence team. Do you have any idea the prison term you're looking at?"

"Not if they never find your body. A lack of evidence I believe is what you call it."

"Don't be so sure of yourselves."

Off to her side, she sensed someone else in the room. Turning to get a better look, the man opens and readies a cigar. He places the cigar in his mouth and bites down and cuts the tip with his eye teeth and spits it out. He lights up the stogie and puffs until it gives off a red glow while looking at her. The boss says, "Donna nel servizio di intelligence, you've just landed yourself in a heap of trouble by trespassing on our property. What exactly are you hoping to find?"

"Why don't you tell me since I wasn't on your property until you kidnapped me," she said.

"That'd take all the fun out of our cat and mouse game."

"Do tell. Is there something or someone here you want kept a secret?"

A feisty fanciulla they'd captured scooping out their facility. He laughed for he had another plan in mind to calm her sassiness. He nodded his head toward his son standing near her, and he left the room.

As he was leaving, the sound of gunshots firing echoed from outside. In minutes, Di Donato and his team of agents entered the room with weapons drawn.

"Are you alright Lilia?"

"Yes, sir, I'm fine."

"You are under arrest Solocone Sciarretta for kidnapping an Italian Intelligence Agent."

"That won't stick."

"Don't bet on it for we have your crew and sons outside in handcuffs."

Di Donato unfastened Lilia's hands from the cords holding them down and said, "Why don't you search the premises for those girls. We just received a search warrant based on your kidnapping."

Lilia eased out the metal chair and waited to see if any agent would follow her lead. Marco said, "Let's get this done."

She and Marco listened to determine what direction they should go before deciding on their course of action.

She shouted out, "Intelligence agents call out if you're in here."

A sing-song of voices penetrated the air. She said, "Marco you take the left side and I'll take the right as they walked down the galley filled with container boxes."

They combed the circumference of the building for the girls. When they had released the captives, they totaled twenty young girls frightened to death. Knowing they were scared, she spoke in a soothing voice, "You'll be all right now. We have arrested the people responsible for your kidnappings. We'll take your statements about what happened then take you back to the city and let you freshen up and contact your family."

Some girls started crying. They were dirty, malnourished, and scared. She said, "Follow me" and lead them outside of the building to freedom.

Her boss, Luigino Di Donato was smiling when she and the rough-housed young women made contact. "Good work," he said. "You're a real chip off the old block."

Knowing he was talking about her papa, she smiled.

Two large vans were summonsed to take the women back to town. Lilia suddenly remembered the camera in her car, and wanting this experience to be over for the girls, made photos of each one for their records and proof of the crime. She walked back into the building and made shots of the containers they were freed from.

The women were divided into four groups of five for agents to take their statements. When they finished the girls were weary, and hungry anxious to be reunited with their families.

Marco videotaped the girls from out of the country with his camera. For he was certain, they'd never return for further questioning or a court date. The interviews were all much the same; they never expected to be snatched from a popular street in the city.

Luigino Di Donato radioed his agents transporting the Sciarretta family and crew and said, "Add human trafficking to the charges. We're bringing the young women back to the city and will see they are reunited with their families or provided an airline ticket home."

Lilia was up most of the night with the girls. They were afraid for the agents to leave their side. The agency provided food and drink to nourish them back to health and hotel rooms to house them with armed guards posted outside.

David couldn't go to sleep fearful Lilia remained captive. He tapped into her boss's cell and listened to his conversations. The news would make the morning paper. High ranking members in the Italian Mafia, including the mob boss was arrested for human trafficking and abducting a government agent.

He hoped when it was over Lilia would call him. He did his best for her without blowing his identity in the Italian Mafia.

Chapter 25

Luca had never been one to use his vacation time from work. He didn't have anywhere to go or an abundance of money to travel. His life was different now, and he'd decided to take his full three weeks built up over the years. He'd love a snapshot of his mama's face when learning he was on vacation. Not a word, would he say about his life until she came clean about her past.

He'd talked to Pauli; his assistant about when he wanted to take his two weeks off so one of them would be at the orchard. He planned to hire a newbie interested in learning the craft of growing vines. Since receiving an inheritance, he was motivated to move on to something new, and when the orchard was well cared for, he'd be free to choose.

He and David met for drinks in town, and it was a welcome relief to have a friend. They enjoyed themselves and talked about making another trip to Barbados to check on Jason and his grove and distillery.

David hoped Luca would talk about inheriting the villa formerly belonging to Dorian. He didn't. The idea intrigued him since Dorian wasn't acting cordial toward him in their last conversation and made last minute changes to the inheritance of his estate. At least he was off the hook, for avenging his death on him for the guilty party was found. He was relieved Luca wasn't the one responsible.

He still had family business to take care of but was waiting for the court cases against the Sciarretta family to be over. Security measures were set up to keep tabs on their conversation to keep Lilia safe. It was no secret the family-maintained power whether from prison or their Italian country home.

Now, that he had some time between running the business, and courting disaster, he'd check on the green technology concepts he'd invested into before learning his new role in life.

The foundation investments were on track with research underway as he envisioned. He wished for more time to court projects to have influence in climate change. Already, he noted a commercial push back from the tourism industry in Italy. It was to be expected. Change usually comes in steps, and he hoped the leaders of the country would stay the course for a healthy environment for its residents.

Chapter 26

Silvana stomped her petite feet, at the thought of her son Luca taking off without a word about where he was going. She'd learned he'd left after reading the notice posted on his cottage door. A cardboard sign with a fish jumping out of the water read "Gone fishing will be back in three weeks."

There was no doubt about his reasons behind it. He'd not share until she confided her past. They were at a stalemate and since when did he have the euros to go fishing for three weeks. Charter boat fishing wasn't cheap that much she'd learned.

She'd made a pact not to monitor his personal life, but a three-week fishing trip was over the top. She wondered if he said anything to his papa. After he returned from work at the brewery, they'd talk.

Wanting him to be in a good mood, she prepared his favorite Italian meal of Lasagna with extra cheese. The oversized portion would be enough for his lunch tomorrow. They were each moving on with their lives one day at the time since Tonia's death. Never speaking about it, she sensed he missed her quirky remarks and rantings as much as she did. The sadness in his face still lingered.

A tired man entered their home and his face lit up when smelling the aroma of the freshly baked Lasagna. He'd had a difficult day at the brewery when the trucks didn't show up for deliveries.

They'd been in dire straits if not for over-ordering in the past to build up their inventory. He called the company to find out the reasons for a delay in the shipment and was told not to expect deliveries until they were notified sometime in the future. He called David, the new steward to tell him about the problem. His new boss would handle it and get back with him.

Armo kissed Silvana on the cheek, and thanked her for cooking his favorite dish. She sat opposite him at the table, and they enjoyed their meal together with a glass of the estate's wine.

Waiting for him to shower, and relax, she picked a book from their bookshelves, *The Long Road Home* to read. The title hit her feelings of being far away from where she needed to be. She thought about the last time she was in Sicily at her family's villa. Perhaps, it was time to revisit her birthplace for she'd inherited the property when her parents died. She'd double check the rental status then visit between the bookings of tourist vacations. She'd call her real estate agent tomorrow.

The property had been a godsend when Antonia was growing up. The extra euros provided her with a few of the finer things she demanded to own. But it was never enough. Tonia's taste out distanced their ability to provide as she desired leaving her cranky and belligerent at times.

Seeing her husband fresh from showering, she thought about how difficult his life had been. His only family had been she and the children. Now, it seemed it was just them with Luca taking off on his own.

She said, "Sit down and relax and I'll make you an after-dinner drink."

His eyebrows lifted at her cordial state of mind. Not knowing what to expect next, he said, "That'll be nice. Make mine light for tomorrow will probably be another day in hell."

"Have you thought about retiring? We'll still have the manor house close to the friends we've known for years."

"No, I'm needed now for the new kid in charge has a lot on his plate. But I am training younger ones to take over when the day comes when I can't cut the business any longer."

"Sounds like a plan. I've been thinking about traveling to my home place in Sicily. Would you like to go?"

"No, I have business here to keep to our shipping schedule. But you go and have a good time."

"I'll tell you when I'm leaving. By the way, have you heard anything from Luca?"

"No, why do you ask? I thought you talked daily."

"He's gone for a three-week fishing trip. Did he tell you where?"

"Nope, it's news to me. He probably took off with one of his rich friends from the city."

"*Dai*, that didn't sound like Luca. He trusted few people let alone leaving for three weeks with a rich friend."

David saw a blow-up coming for he needed the delivery trucks to run on schedule. They brought in supplies and shipped their products by trucks throughout Italy. The problem needed a solution fast, but making the call to their transport company wasn't an easy task. The Solocone Sciarretta family was awaiting their trials for criminal intent.

He was locked into using their services. This action was a long-standing agreement between the mafia families. He'd look for other sources for trucking their products and investigate upping their air and postal shipments. But, for large bulk orders, they needed truck deliveries within the country and deliveries to their container shippers at the harbor.

He punched in the number for the mafia boss and waited. At first, he thought he wouldn't answer. When he did, he went directly to the point of his call. "Just learned you're not delivering or shipping supplies for a while, is that true? And are our bulk shipments still on schedule?"

"Don't you watch the news? My trucks have been confiscated putting me out of business. What do you want me to do, tote them across Italy on my back?"

"Sorry to hear that and I wished you'd called. I have no choice but to negotiate with another trucking company for our products must ship, or we're out of business."

"You do what you need to do. This will blow over soon enough, and we'll be back strong and looking to continue our agreement."

David ended the call and wondered what made him believe he'd be back soon. The whole family was facing lengthy sentences if found guilty. At least there'd be no repercussions from dealing with a non-mafia related trucking company.

He hoped the family's criminal actions took them off the streets for life. For when they returned, he'd avenge Dorian's murder. It was expected by the insiders familiar with the rules of the Italian mafia. And, he still had the upper hand by Sciarretta being unaware he'd be targeted to avenge Dorian's murder.

He started going through possible trucking companies who could deal with the volume they produced for shipping in Italy. He'd talk to the vendors they used for products shipped in to verify if they could deliver on schedule. A call to the main vendor on his list was met with excitement to be of service. A reasonable delivery fee would be added, and they'd send their trucks regularly. David grinned. Getting out of the mafia trucking deal may be for the best in the future.

His next call was to a trucking company who could ship their products in Italy and to the harbor cargo docks. His request was met with enthusiasm and a promise to deliver their products on schedule. He thanked them and wrote down the contact number to supply the shipping department the next morning. The day had slipped away from him, and he was ready to call it a night. Thoughts of Lilia flooded his mind, and he longed to be with her.

Carolyn M. Bowen

Chapter 27

Luigino Di Donato feared retaliation from the head of the Italian Mafia the Sciarretta family pledged to, a secret society even his agency couldn't identify. Now, with their being freed until their trials he was anxious. He had no doubt they had politicians in their pockets, along with some of his own agents whom he'd not yet identified. The only agent he was certain about was Lilia Sicilliano. Just like her father before her, she sought the truth wherever it took her. For him, it meant a brutal murder.

He didn't want the same fate for his daughter, but being prepared with an education in the field of highly sought agents, his guilty conscious won out. Her father's murder was linked to a case investigated by the agency. He believed she'd be good, especially if she'd train more in weapons and defense necessary for all agents and a performance goal, he'd instilled in her from day one.

She couldn't be a sheepish agent thinking her high IQ would provide the solution in deadly situations. She'd been saved once, by an unknown source to her, she either needed to prepare herself and become combat ready or be fired. Her emotions were driving her investigations, and she'd not live long on that route.

Stalking the kidnappers of the girls saved their lives, but he wasn't ready to give her a high-five until she realized she'd be dead if not for a phone call. Dammit, he recognized the voice, the young man he wanted to recruit for his agency — David Jones. With plenty of guts, smarts, and brawn, he and Lilia would've made a super-agent team. In the least his call proved someone was behind the scenes tracking the scumbags who threatened a peaceful Italy. A tech entrepreneur from an early age and now steward of one of Italy's leading wine and olive producers, he wanted to be friends for he had eyes on the world — their world. How did he get him to trust him?

David fell asleep thinking about Lilia. He was frustrated and concerned with her lack of preparation for taking on a mafia connection. It was like she'd read the latest magazine spread about the luxury life of the financial greats in Italy, mostly mobsters. She was clueless. Solocone Sciarretta was in the news constantly with his beautiful daughters parading around town flaunting the latest in Italian fashion while dining at the upscale restaurants and clubs.

They were known by him, and now he needed to count on the Italian Mafia's tenets and eject the Sciarretta family from their fold. What they were into was considered filthy business by the group. No dealings in drugs or prostitution were allowed in their enterprises. The bylaws called for zero tolerance for not abiding by the rules to protect the families and not draw attention to their way of life.

Their criminal behavior was already bringing down hell fire for all the families. Leading journalists had begun digging into their mafia affiliation linking them to a mafia group in the North known for similar escapades. They in turn may refute the mafia connection and turn eyes toward their secret society.

Action was needed before this happened. His blood brothers were aware of the family's tyranny from the news reports reaching everywhere. Their peaceful existence was being shaken to its core making it no surprise when an elder summonsed members excluding the Sciarretta family for a secret meeting.

Chapter 28

Luca was enjoying his newfound freedom on the coast of Livorno where he fished and relaxed in the villa Dorian bequeathed him. This was the vacation of a lifetime, and his only wish was to meet someone and enjoy the scenic view together. Although, he still wasn't comfortable confiding his inheritance to anyone, not even his mama. He was left wondering how to continue with care.

A night out at local seaside bar suited his purpose for meeting local women. In listening to the chatter, he might also learn something about Dorian; for he likely visited the clubs for entertainment when he vacationed.

Thinking about his mama, he wondered how she was faring. He suspected she was spewing insults by now after reading the sign on his door. He'd never taken off without letting her know his destination and return date. Hopefully, his plan worked to learn answers to his questions about her and Dorian.

Tomorrow he would explore the villa and search for secret crannies or hidden compartments notably used by the Italian Mafia. The hidden vintage safe was a dead giveaway that there's more to the villa than first meets the eyes. He wished for more details about the hiding places for he'd never found the passage leading to the safe without Dorian's letter with clear directions.

The ability to find his hiding places would require x-ray vision like the military to discover his secrets. He remembered the talk around the table about the mafia's secret bunkers at one of the workers weekend cookouts.

The news about the capture and arrest of a North mafia boss included details about his hiding place. He was found in a space not much bigger than the inside of a car behind a chicken coop. There he hid as the family took in billions from their drug trafficking business. They'd laughed at the stench the big guy breathed in while his family and associates lived the high life.

Dorian didn't fit that persona. He was meticulous in his surroundings and dress. Wherever his hiding place was it was clean and well-stocked with food, and his favorite beverages. He'd take one room at the time to discover his inner sanctuary and search outside for an escape route.

Tonight, he was going to a nearby seaside restaurant to enjoy drinks and music. Meeting a good-looking woman to befriend would add much-needed spice to his life.

He dressed after sorting through Dorian's closet for suitable attire. Finding casual wear that fit and suitable shoes, he gazed into the floor length mirror and smiled. Life was great!

He strolled into the bar and focused on his surroundings. With a clear view of the Ligurian Sea there were no bad seats in the bar and grill. Claiming a stool at the bar would take the focus off him while he looked around for a suitable companion. He quickly ordered a draft beer from the bartender who he suspected was the owner from the graying around his temples. He asked, "Have you been working here long?"

"Yes, since day one."

He pointed toward a photo hanging behind the bar of him and a smartly dressed man. Luca observed the yellowing picture, and asked, "Who's the man beside you?"

"My cousin, Dorian," he said. "He financed the start-up of the Ristorante Del Sole twenty years ago."

"Well, from here it looks like he made an excellent investment."

"I'd say so; we've done well since opening as a local bar and grill. We've expanded our menu and beverage selection over the years tapping into the tourist traveling to Livorno."

Luca cleared his throat and wondered what he'd stepped into by accepting the villa by the sea. Obviously, Dorian had family here and eventually they'd learn he owned his property. Would he be in danger once they realized it?

He knew nothing about Dorian except that he was steward of the estate and ran the business up until his murder. The man behind the bar probably had the answers, but would he share them?

Luca glanced at the menu, and then said, "I'd like the stuffed mussels in spicy tomato sauce dish. I haven't had mussels in a while."

"That's an excellent seafood choice and one of our crowd favorites."

Luca observed him typing the order into the POS System thinking they'd stayed in step with the times. The restaurant was filling up with customers as servers bounced from table to table taking orders for drinks and food.

He saw her first a beautiful woman with brown hair and green eyes, characteristic of someone from Northern Italy. She sat two bar stools away from him and quickly began talking to the bartender who appeared to be a friend.

He was intrigued and waited to introduce himself. When they had finished bantering back and forth, he leaned over and said, "Good evening, my name is Luca. What's yours?"

Her deep green eyes surveyed him and then said, "My name is Renata Cantu. I haven't seen you here before. Are you from around here?"

"This is my first visit. I'm from near Florence. But will be vacationing here often in the future."

They made idle chit chat about the things to do and see in Leghorn, its Genoese name as their dinner was being prepared. By the time their order was served they were seated side-by-side at the bar, enjoying their delicious meal. He was feeling hopeful about the possibilities of seeing her again.

He noted a chalkboard sign after he excused himself and went to the men's rest room. On the weekend a local band, Jolly Cinema, was featured during the evening. He'd ask her to meet him here for dinner and dancing. Then, wondered if that was the way to set up a date.

She eagerly accepted his invitation and said, "The weekends are meant to be enjoyed and this is the hottest place for entertainment on the coast. I'll see you around 8 pm."

Luca smiled. His living at the villa may be the best thing ever happened to him. After trading cell numbers and picking up the check for her meal, he said, "I'm looking forward to it."

He took the last sip of his drink and watched her swaying hips as she left the restaurant. She was not only beautiful, but fun to be with. His mama would be pleased he'd met a nice Italian woman.

Driving home, he reflected about the evening, and his recent luck meeting Renata. Tomorrow he'd return to his treasure hunt for secret hideouts in the villa, hoping for a successful adventure. Tonight, he would sleep like a baby knowing a girlfriend was possible, blocking out the fears of his mama's secrets and what they'd mean in his future.

Chapter 29

David prepared for the secret meeting of his blood brothers. With the high security alert, he wasn't taking any chances. Underneath his suit jacket was a Beretta 92fs 9mm pistol in case it was needed.

He was instructed by Mariano Tarantino who oversaw coordination of getting the members to the ristorante for the meeting to drive to Buontalenti, Livorno, and park. His cell phone was to be turned off and left in the car. They'd be shuttled from the crowded Livorno Central Market by cars to Bello Italiano Ristorante reducing the chances of a hit from the Sciarretta family or their associates.

Loaded into a car with his mafia brothers, he sensed the tension in their hurried conversation and manic hand motions of his fellow riders. He felt like he was sitting on a powder keg waiting for it to explode.

When they arrived, the driver, Taviano "Tight Lips" Rogolino opened the doors and rushed into the ristorante ahead of the members. From outside, he could see the blinds being drawn and in their place were food posters shielding the window frames.

When they entered, they were shown to a darkened room in the rear of the building near the kitchen where a horseshoe crafted table along with chairs was prepared for their meeting. A buffet table filled with meat and cheese appetizers was set-up in the corner of the room. An assortment of wine, beer and hard liquor were on a bar along with ice buckets and assorted glasses. Not knowing where to sit, he waited for the elders to enter and take their places. When everyone was seated, he took the empty chair noting it was within the inner circle.

The heavy wooden swinging doors to the nearby kitchen were closed for their privacy. The meeting was called to order by Mariano "Molotov" Stefania who quickly said the reason for the meeting. Solocone Sciarretta had broken rules of the society bringing unwanted attention to the group by his filthy dealings.

The oath Sciarretta had taken years ago was now breached. He said, "The interest and honor of the society comes first. He vowed to be loyal and has broken his oath by staining his honor and that of others, which caused harm to this Honored Society. This he knows is punishable by death."

David watched the faces of those present as they nodded in agreement having made the same oath to the society to do no harm. Stefania administered a roll-call vote with each member present speaking for their families. When all were heard, he said, "The Solocone Sciarretta family is dead to us."

Stefania turned to the capo-societa, Angelo Simone, responsible for the life and death of its members, and said, "The Honored Society has spoken death to the Sciarretta family. We adjourn by placing this in your capable hands."

The members filed out to the waiting transport cars with heavily armed guards securing the outside of the building. As David stood to leave with the others, Angelo Simone, said, "I need a word with you. Your car and driver will wait."

David stepped over to the bar and asked Simone, "Padrino, what would you like to drink?"

He said, "Sangiovese," and David poured some into a wine glass and returned to his chair and said, "You have my full attention."

Simone said, "I need your help to locate Solocone Sciarretta, his male family members, and the soldiers who make up his clan. I understand you're a tech guy and thought you could lend a hand."

"I can run surveillance on your targets and get back with you after identifying the places they visit often or return to occasionally."

"Catch Solocone coming out of his barber shop for him to be prepared to be photo'd for his funeral. Our soldiers will pop him and his family when you provide details about their routine."

David stood when Simone said, "Send me the details, and this will be done and over." He quickly jotted down an email address he was certain was on Dorian's server and said, "I'll be waiting to hear from you."

David nodded, kissed his cheek, and walked with him to the door and their waiting transport.

On the drive home he thought about how differently his life was than what he imagined. A crime boss wasn't on his career map and further complicated a relationship with Lilia.

He'd do what Simone asked for it served two purposes. A payback to Sciarretta for his hit on Dorian and bringing attention to the group potentially exposing him as an Italian mobster. When in fact they were an entrepreneurial group banding together to get their products to the global market. Tempting as it was to see if there were other possibilities, he remembered the blood oath he made and would abide by.

However, the business was opening for non-mafia contacts thanks to Sciarretta's present legal problems. His heart palpitated at the irony of serving an outdated business model set in motion by the family of Donatella, his great-grandmother.

Chapter 30

Luca couldn't wait to see Renata again. They'd dined and danced until the restaurant closed the night before. She was a beauty, and he was sexually attracted to her. The problem was he couldn't invite her to the villa for she might recognize the home as Dorian's and start asking questions that he couldn't answer.

She was friends with the owner of the bar and likely met Dorian on one of his stays. Who knows, she may've gone out on the cabin cruiser with him and his cousin. Sensing more problems than solutions, he decided the planning was complicated, but worthwhile.

She appeared to be interested in taking their relationship to the next level as was he. He went online to book a hotel nearby for the following weekend and their date night. He wasn't going to let this opportunity slip through his fingers.

He found a vacancy next door to the ristorante where they'd met and made reservations.

Then he remembered the fish stew slowly simmering in a large cooking pot on the stove, and went to taste the thick broth. The stew was ready to be served. He toasted the bread and spread gremolata butter over the top for dipping into the sauce then ladled the stew into a low bowl. Pouring a glass of Chablis, he sat in the dining room and enjoyed his meal. He wished his papa could taste the savory dish.

When he finished, he cleaned and stored the fish stew in the refrigerator for the next day. Remembering his earlier plans, he quickly recapped his earlier attempts of finding hiding places in the villa. He'd banged on the walls looking for an opening, looked behind furniture, pulled up rugs, looked in the fireplace for a secret opening, and found nothing. Yet, his gut said he was missing something.

He went back to the master bedroom closet and opened the passageway to the safe. The wrought-iron unit stood tall and was elaborately decorated with hobnails all-around and burin décor of a family seal on the bottom. Using his key, he opened the vintage lock to examine the contents closer. The euros were stacked as he'd left them. He looked on the shelves hoping to find something new.

On the bottom metal shelf, he found a floor plan rolled up, then went to examine the house plans in better light. He spread the paper sheets out on the nearby king-sized bed and looked for the difference in his measurement of the square metres of the villa and those on the blueprint. The numbers on the prints were inconsistent with his findings. A hidden room was attached to the villa. But how was it entered?

He took one last look at the floor plan and rolled up the papers to secure in the safe. Sometimes he got insights, afterward. He walked to the passageway and slid the plans back into their place. Frustrated, he shoved the heavy wrought-iron door shut and kicked the bottom of the safe.

His angry blow to the unit directly onto the family seal hit a mechanism that unlocked and swung open an invisible panel. Not wanting to get locked in, he noted every step he made. He walked along a corridor that opened into a large living suite with a view of the canal where the boat was docked. The hiding place was as he envisioned, furnished with food, drink, and all the comforts of home including bookshelves filled with books.

He examined the suite and noticed the filtration system complete with heat and air, electricity, WIFI modem, security system, and water. He found a console attached to the wall, and pulled the switch. Outside he heard the pulley engage for leveraging the boat into the water. He at once resets the switch to keep the cabin cruiser dry docked.

There had to be a backdoor if Dorian had planned to use the boat as a getaway if security was compromised. He felt he was in a maze with no way out. They were at sea level so the outside exit couldn't be underground unless he planned to swim to the boat.

Not believing Dorian was one for high tech gadgets, he started looking for old school clues with finesse. He searched the kitchen drawers for clues hoping to find directions as before. Nothing was in them except cooking utensils and cutlery. Next, he searched the bedroom off to the side, and his nightstands.

On the night stand he found a photo framed. Again, his mama at a younger age with a flower in her hair. She had a lot of explaining to do when they met. He picked up the photo and observed the frame closely noting its unusual characteristics.

On the bottom of the ornate frame the appearance was thicker, and he found a tiny metal latch. He pushed the lever to the side with his finger and gasped when realizing the frame cradled a high-tech remote-control device.

He touched the red button and an exit nearest the canal and the yacht appeared. The hiding place opened into a courtyard, and he watched as the yacht was being lowered into the canal for a quick getaway.

Looking back over his shoulder at his entrance, the hiding place was no longer visible. A stone wall was now covering the exit. Furthermore, the canal view he saw from the inside was gone. The mechanics of the device left no tale-tell signs from outside to show a room with a view.

He couldn't reenter the way he'd exited, so he went around to the front entrance. He was glad he'd left the front door open, or he'd been locked out. But he'd bet Dorian had a side entrance for returning to the villa, and he wanted to find its location. Inheriting the villa, called for self-preservation, since bad people could be after him.

Chapter 31

Silvana kissed her husband goodbye and hurried to the 6am train departure to Sicily 654 km away. She'd be away for the two weeks and hopefully when she returned Luca would have put their past behind them. He was asking too many questions, which could only lead to heartbreak for him. Her heart was broken many years ago and never completely mended.

Going back in time and to the villa where she was raised was painful. The purpose of her visit was to take control of the future by reclaiming the past. She'd hoped the years of a family void had erased the stigma of a mafia connection for the rental income had been a life-saver while raising Antonia.

Her brother vacated the area after realizing a hit was on him as the next male heir in the family. He went to work with the Zarrella's in the North having been introduced by a third party during a time when the Sicilian and Zarrella mafias were allies. Having been known for his hits, a requirement of becoming their soldier, he was immediately initiated into their clan.

He'd helped her find employment on an estate in Tuscany for a fresh start. Their mama was left behind for the mob rarely hit the wife or mother. Although, the now repentant boss, Livio Pirrello, broke the rules when he ordered a hit on the mother of his enemy to rise to the head of the clan.

Her mama lived at the villa with money sent home by her son Lothario, and remnants of her husband's mafia allegiance secretly supplying care and monies for the rest of her life. As a rule, the Sicilian mafias were blood thirsty and cutthroat in their dealings and still were. She was afraid of reentering their world although years had distanced her from the bloodbath of her father and the hysterics of her mother.

After the long, and tiring train ride to Palermo Sicily, she walked the streets of her youth to the red tiled roof and stucco house she once called home. The real estate manager hid a key to use during her stay. She slid the cactus planter over and removed the door key from its hiding place. Conscious of someone watching her, she eased it back in place with her foot after unlocking the door, then quickly entered.

She at once bolted the door and tip-toed through the home to make sure it was secure. Laying her handbag on a table, and out of habit taking her suitcase to her childhood bedroom, she wondered who knew she was coming.

There were only three possibilities, the real estate manager, her brother, and husband. Marabella the long-time manager of the property in her absence was the source. For her husband or brother would never expose her to violence. But why would Marabella confide her vacation plans to someone? Ah, she had a buyer from the US; the former renters had shown interest in owning it. She wondered who Marabella contracted with to scare her away.

In the back of her mind, knowing the family history, she may have contracted the Sicilian mafia family who murdered her father. With her sultry sexy looks and flirty demeanor, perhaps she was the *comare*, mistress, of one of the bosses.

Caught in an unexpected and potentially deadly dilemma was daunting. All she wanted was peace and quiet to explore her feelings about the past, so she could move forward. She gazed into the large ornate mirror in the living room and her sad eyes stared back speaking volumes about her torment. She was on her own.

Her brother, Lothario couldn't come to her aid without being exposed in the city he'd left out of fear of retribution when he whacked the soldier responsible for the murder of their father. Dorian was dead. Her husband had no idea of the family's history, and she'd not put her son, Luca in danger. But this time she'd not run like the scared young woman from her past. She picked up her handbag, and locked the door and walked toward the Ballaro street market to buy fresh meats, fruits, and produce to prepare for dinner and her vacation.

Chapter 32

Luca's vacation had turned into a treasure hunt that spiked his blood pressure just thinking about what he'd discovered. He'd still not found Dorian reentry into the hidden bunker; but believed one was available for him to ease back into hiding when the coast was clear. He was surprised when finding the high-tech gadgetry hidden in the photo frame with his mama's photo.

His thoughts immediately went to Godwin. While in Barbados he and David had left early one morning. Waking up, and finding David gone, he asked Gabrielle where they went, and she said, "To his tech office, their man cave."

Godwin probably installed the security system and was fluent in the operation. He'd call and ask him for help after talking to David when he returned to the estate. He hoped David would continue being his friend when he discovered he'd inherited Dorian's property for he couldn't explain it.

The stress of unanswered questions was getting to him. His mama needed to come clean and confess what she knows.

The day had slipped by him while he was busy looking for hidden entry points. He quickly showered and changed clothes for meeting Renata and their rendezvous at the hotel afterward. He packed a change of clothes in one of Dorian's Italian leather overnight bags and threw it into the trunk of his car.

He arrived at the Ristorante Del Sole before Renata and sat at the bar to wait and ordered a draft beer from the barkeep and made polite conversation. Renata entered swinging her hips with all male eyes staring at her beauty. She kissed him on the cheek and ordered a glass of chardonnay after greeting the bartender.

The bar became crowded quickly for word had gotten around about the popular local band playing the venue. The Jolly Cinema had a load in an hour earlier to set-up for the gig. With their soundcheck completed, they were sipping drinks before kicking off the night's entertainment.

They ordered fresh seafood and pasta as they waited for the band to gear up and play so everyone could dance and enjoy the music. Renata excused herself and went to the lady's room. The bartender caught his attention and said, "I need to talk to you for you need to be careful around Renata."

Luca's stomach turned and was dizzy-headed. "What do you mean? I've asked her out on a date."

"Trust me, she's not for you. Stop by early tomorrow morning and I'll explain it to you."

"OK, what time should I stop by?"

"Make it around 9 am and don't do anything foolish tonight."

Luca wondered when he'd ever get a break and find someone to share his life with or in the least a night. He peered at himself in the mirror behind the bar; she'd recognize something was wrong when returning. He smiled in the mirror and prepared for more small talk.

The band started playing, and he asked her for a dance. She followed him to the dance floor, and they swayed to the music. He had to remind himself to look happy for he was with the best-looking woman there.

They took a break from dancing and ate their dinner. He noticed the barkeep was never far away when they talked. His nervous watchful eyes made him decide to ditch his plans for later in the evening. His curiosity was piqued about the secrets surrounding her. For tonight, he'd say goodnight and go their separate ways.

His senses picked up on the barkeep's eyes piercing his backside as he walked out the door with her. Irritated his plans were blown, he was tempted to wave goodbye. For with his forewarning, he'd never be able to make love to her. He'd return to the bar after she left to assure the proprietor he'd listened to his warning.

Chapter 33

Silvana walked to the Ballaro street market feeling like she did as a kid, free and excited about buying the freshest produce, meats, and seafood. Returning to her roots had a purpose for rejuvenating her soul and being able to respond to Luca's questions. She was not a whore, but her secrets make it appear so. Dorian was the love of her life. She never knew why he betrayed her until reading the letter he left behind that the new steward allowed her to read.

She wished he was alive today and could circumvent the danger she was exposed to by a greedy real estate woman. Having no choice, she'd step up and call Marabella and explain in no uncertain terms the villa was not for sale now or ever.

Marabella didn't expect a call from her and apologized for holding out for a sale of the property to the previous renters.

She'd let them know the villa was unavailable. Silvana wondered if the watchdogs would be called off. She'd soon find out.

Tonight, she'd view the Sicilian sunset from one of the local seaside bars in Mondello, a small borough in the city of Palermo, the capital of Sicily where she'd lived her childhood. Now, overrun with tourist, for its beach lies between two cliffs called Mount Gallo and Mount Pellegrino she'd not stand out in the crowd. Yet, know if she was followed.

Her mama's antique car was in the garage and hadn't been driven in years unless her brother Lothario or his friends sneaked in and drove it to keep it operational. A flashback of her daughter Tonia came to mind. She'd love to own this sporty Italian car. Few had this model of Ferrari's for only the bosses in the mafia or the wealthy could afford them.

She slid behind the wheel and felt the luxurious leather seat and cranked the motor. It revved up on first try. Happy, she motored to the quaint seaside bar excited to see a Sicilian sunset once again.

She parked. Veered into the rear-view mirror and pleased with her hair and makeup, opened the door to go into the bar. Being home again to enjoy the local hangouts was a treat. One high-heel was touching the parking lot pavement when a strong arm lifted and tossed her over his shoulder. She screamed.

People were walking by but ignored her pleas for help. What had their city turned into when no one aided those in need? Did the mafia still have a stronghold on the average resident where they were afraid to get involved?

Relaxing against the torso carrying her to make him believe there was no fight left in her, he became gentler when placing her in a dark-windowed sedan and climbed in after her. The driver cranked the car and in minutes, she figured, they arrived at their destination, a Palermo coastal villa. The luxury car stopped at a security gate, and then went ahead to the main villa's entrance. Snipers were visible on the rooftop, and heavy armed soldiers were hiding in the lush landscape, and the entrance was heavily armed with guards.

The car halted at the front door and the car emptied of made-men. Her captor whispered, "Remain silent and listen to their demands". She wanted to put her arm in his and walk in like they were expected for a social visit. The madness of the evening had raddled her nerves, and she'd like to give her kidnapper a surprise.

With acute awareness, she realized this was the seaside home of her father's boss, Amabile Ghio. The Ghio Mafia was the leader of the Sicilian mafia clans. Quickly thinking back to Marabella, she wondered if she was his lover. What other reason would she be there?

Her captor led her into a stately room with overstated décor and seated her on a plush ruby red velvet sofa. She'd been here before with her father when she was a kid trailing behind him when he allowed it. Her father, Gherardo Scutari, was boss of a region and had constant contact with the godfather of the clan. His overreaching into another clan's territory was what brought his demise. He didn't realize the godfather had become an ally for it was hush-hush. Now, she was seated in the seaside villa of the man who ordered her father's murder. She'd like to disappear into a fine mist away from her captors.

Amabile Ghio, Ghio to his associates, entered the room. He said, "Silvana, it's been a long time since your last visit to Sicily. Your mother's funeral if I remember right. What brings you here now?"

"I wanted to reclaim my past, make peace, and move forward with my life. It was pastime."

Ghio nodded his head as if to understand the meaning of what she said. "And when was the last time you saw your brother, Lothario?"

"I haven't seen him since our father's murder. With each passing day, I've come to believe his body will never be recovered. By now, the fish have feasted on his remains. He'd dead to me."

"You're right. His body never washed up on our shores for we were watching."

"Now, down to business, I want to buy the villa you now own to make a statement to my soldiers. I own them and should they betray me and/or try to expand their business without my blessings they will remember what happened to your father, a traitor to the clan."

Knowing he was capo of the Sicilian Mafia; she measured her words with eloquence fearful of his response. "Amabile Ghio you're asking me to dissolve my inheritance the only connection I have to my youth. Over thirty years ago I left and haven't returned until now, and I have no plans for returning soon. I beg you to allow me the freedom to come and go as I please in the remaining years of my life."

"Silvana, I remember you when you were just a child with your dark eyes, and long flowing hair. I want to grant your request, but what does that say to my army of soldiers?"

"It says that their boss is honest in his dealings, and compassionate to those who can't help themselves from a stigma that was placed on them without their knowledge or consent."

Ghio paced the floor deliberating her remarks. He'd promised Marabella a commission on the sale when he purchased the property. Yet, he understood wanting to reclaim your youth. For he, too, wanted the ownership of his family home which the government had seized from his father before being sent to prison. He owned it now from years of backing politicians until he had them in his pocket. Then, he pounced with demands of ownership of what the government had taken. He won. His father was released from prison and their properties were returned.

Ghio admired fortitude and knowing Marabella had her eyes on a diamond that only he could afford, he gave in. "Silvana, you've made an excellent argument for keeping your family's villa. Perhaps, you're right; my soldiers should know I'm a fair and honorable man. You can go in peace and visit home as often as you wish."

"Thank you; I'll always treasure our talks."

"You'll be driven home by one of my captains with my condolences for the loss of your brother."

The hunky Italian who threw her over his shoulder tapped her on the shoulder to leave the interview. She followed him to his car and when he opened the door she slid into the seat. Neither spoke a word until they arrived at her villa. Sensing he had something to say, and his conduct throughout the harrowing kidnapping had been honest for a mafia associate, she invited him in for a drink and conversation.

She motioned for him to have a seat in the living room and asked what he'd like to drink. She hurried to the bar and mixed the cocktail and poured herself a glass of chardonnay.

He said, "You don't remember me, but Lothario and I were best friends growing up. I remember you and the cookies you baked for us."

"I must've blocked out some of my childhood, for I don't remember you."

Not knowing whether to trust him, or not for he may be acting on Ghio's instructions, she'd proceed carefully.

He said, "You can rest assured that your brother is alive and planning to avenge your father's murder. Learning the ways of the Zarrella clan has taken time. Soon, he'll rise-up and lead the attack on the Southern Italian mafia with Amabile Ghio being the prime target."

"Aren't you a captain in Ghio's clan?"

"Yes, but I understand the merits of establishing a fresh, innovative clan prepared for today's world. Ghio is living in the past and Italy is rapidly changing as should our services. He's clueless about how new technologies have changed the landscape and how to stay ahead of neighboring clans."

"So, you want to be a boss in the new regime?"

"Yes, and I will be for I leak information to your brother about our plans."

"You have a career path much like I when rising from dishwasher to sous chef."

They laughed. He said, "Tell your brother I was gentle with you, and your response to Ghio was tactful and fit his mission."

She smiled. Not knowing whether she should acknowledge she knew Lothario was alive or not, she remained silent. He said goodnight, and left.

Silvana felt relieved and hoped the remainder of her vacation would be peaceful as Ghio promised. When she returned to the estate, she'd contact Lothario and verify the captain's story. Until then, she had time to soak up the sun and enjoy the coast of Palermo while deciding on her answers to Luca's questions.

Chapter 34

Luca rose early to meet the barkeep/owner of the Ristorante Del Sole. There was no doubt in his mind; he was spooked about his dating Renata. What other secrets about his inheritance did he not understand?

After drinking an espresso, he was ready for whatever the day brought. He met Celso Mezzeo at the appointed time. Mezzeo welcome him into the now empty ristorante and asked what he'd like to drink. After last night's liberations, he said, "Espressio Corretto, please!"

His order wasn't lost on Celso who was accustomed to serving the drink laced with alcohol to hungover tourist visiting their island. Perhaps, Luca was in the right state of mind to learn family secrets, and served him his drink.

He said, "Dorian and I were cousins, and remained close during the years."

"Yes, you mentioned that on my first visit here."

"Well, Renata is related also to your father's family."

"Wait, a minute for I'm sure my father has no relatives in this part of Italy."

"That's where you are wrong. Your father is Dorian. Why else would you inherit his villa?"

Luca wanted to scream at the madness his life was taking. Everyone knew the family secrets except him. "I had no idea. Mama never told me. I assumed the father who raised me, was my real papa."

"Dorian picked him for your father. He wanted to distance those he loved from a possible mafia hit from the family he pledged allegiance to until his death."

"So, that's why his villa is equipped for a rapid escape?"

"Yes, it originally belonged to Donatella who gifted it to Dorian. It has been updated in recent years. But there's more family secrets."

Luca wasn't sure he was prepared for cloak and dagger mysteries. Yet, Celso was the only one with the details and willing to share. His mama surely wouldn't disclose her relationship with Dorian. Whether she was afraid, or feeling guilty was unclear.

He said, "I want to learn everything about my ancestry. Leave nothing out, for it might be a life saver in the future."

"I was anxious about your friendship with Renata for reasons other than she's your cousin. She has made a pact with the Rizzo family to kill a close relative to initiate herself into their clan. You were the chosen one."

"Oh, my god you're saying she was going to whack me for equal rights in an opposing Italian mafia to my biological father?"

"Yes, she's ambitious and picked one easier to take over with her smarts, political influence, and weapon expertise."

"I owe you for saving my life. I'd planned to take her to the hotel next door when you warned me."

"Stay clear of her, for she'll not let go of her plans to infiltrate and take over the clan and become godmother herself. Her jealousy of your father's life has no boundaries, she wants it all."

"Am I safe staying at the villa he owned?"

"Yes, as long as you're apprised of the escape route."

"I'm working on it but still haven't devised a way to reenter when the coast is clear."

"Can't help you with that, but Dorian's tech guru mapped out coordinates for his safety on and off the island. You need to talk to him."

"Celso, I can't thank you enough for your honesty. I plan to return to the estate tomorrow to decipher what I've learned."

"Keep your mama in the dark about the mafia connection. Dorian wanted to protect her at all costs for she was the love of his life."

Thinking back to the ultimatum he'd given his mama; he would be especially cordial on his return and let the past be forgotten. Now, sneaking away from the coast without Renata following was his goal. From the estate he'd plan his future after talking with Godwin about the villa's security.

Chapter 35

Silvana enjoyed the rest of her vacation. No one followed in her daily outings to the market and seashore excursions in Palermo. The Sicilian godfather, Ghio was keeping his promises of a peaceful coexistence during her vacation. She wished to bring Luca to her family home, but wondered if he'd be safe as the grandson of the man Ghio believed betrayed him.

She couldn't wait to talk to Lothario, her brother to find out if his captain, Alessio Volta was being honest, or if it was a trap to ensnare her to revealing he was alive.

Reeling back in time from visiting her family's home, she was ready to be honest with Luca. She hoped the discovery of his paternity didn't void his respect for his papa. No matter the monetary payoff, he'd been affectionate and fatherly to Luca. She hoped the secret would remain between them.

She braced herself for revealing blood lines destructive to her relationship with her son.

The red gravel driveway leading to the estate was breath-taking with the lush vineyard in plain view. Here he'd spent his life; it was home where his parents lived, and he learned the craft of grapevine growing. It had been a great life and gotten better with David taking over as the estate and business owner.

He liked him on their first meeting as someone with unlimited financial resources yet down to earth. He wondered how he did it. He'd just inherited a seaside villa and was ecstatic. David owned it all and probably more if his take on the Mandarino family was correct.

He wanted to feel jealous but wasn't because he liked him and enjoyed the time they spent together. David had the answers he was looking for, but should he rat out his mama to get the information. He sighed. For if what Celso said was true, David was aware of everything about him and his family. He'd soon learn the truth.

Silvana kissed her husband on the cheek when returning from Palermo. She was tired from the train ride but quickly prepared dinner knowing he'd be hungry after his long day at the brewery. She tried to be a good wife and often wondered if he'd chosen to marry her if Dorian hadn't offered a payoff. Stuck with consequences of her own making, she'd honor the vows of till death do we part.

Did she ever forget Dorian? Not in a minute. Her emotional state went from angry at his rejection, to acceptance of a man to marry to become Luca's father. Now, Luca would learn the secrets of a woman of shame. She'd rather die than be honest but, it was necessary for her son to speak to her again.

Luca called David on arrival and asked him to meet. David was busy with estate matters and asked him to come to the villa.

David was tracking Lilia's travels knowing she was ill-prepared for her assignments. Her boss said he'd bench her if she didn't learn tactical surveillance and weaponry. From his oversight, it wasn't stopping her emotional outburst to contain crime; in an arena she lacked training and experience to enter, the Italian Mafia. He wanted to shake her; then train her to be the best in the force. She was filled with ambition to be better than her dad, an excellent standard requiring demanding work. Getting her attention was a fallacy, for she didn't trust him.

Luca came to mind for he should be arriving soon. He asked the chef to prepare an authentic Italian dinner for their meeting. Missing Dorian's praise, the chef made every effort to impress to make the evening memorable.

His friend entered and David gave him a hug. He didn't have many on the estate, and he'd missed him. Luca hugged him back. And, said, "I just learned something that makes no sense. But I suspect you're aware of my problems."

"My main question is will I be safe at the seaside villa Dorian, my father left for me?"

Calmly, likened to his great-grandmother Donatella, he said, "The villa is your home and I'll put you in touch with Godwin who designed the secret in-and-outs of the villa. You are not to tell anyone of this place. This was Dorian's last resort hideaway, and may save your life if they learn you're his son."

Luca was flabbergasted and didn't know what to say. "You've known this all along?

"Only since you inherited the villa and I read the love letter to your mama by accident for I was looking for his killer."

"Have you identified his murderer?"

"Yes, it was a mafia hit and a good reason for you to be careful sharing your family secrets."

"I won't tell a soul about the villa, not even my mama. I plan to talk with her tomorrow for I need answers. My papa will never learn our secret. He's always been good to me."

David nodded understanding and said, "Let's eat our delicious looking dinner and later I'll message Godwin's number for you to call about the security features at the villa."

Silvana had made peace about telling Luca the truth about his father. He'd returned from his deep-sea fishing trip and hopefully being rested the news wouldn't be as shocking to him. She'd called her brother, Lothario, to make him aware of what transpired when she returned to their family home in Palermo. He wasn't surprised at Ghio's tactics and was relieved she'd remembered their story about his being dead. She said, "tell me about his captain, Alessio Volta. He said you were life-long friends, but I didn't trust him and said nothing."

"We're working together to overthrow Ghio's clan with the added benefit of avenging our father's murder by popping Amabile, the godfather who ordered his killing."

"Be careful, Lothario, for Ghio is diabolical in leveraging his enemies to confide their secrets. Call me when our father's murderer is dead."

"I'll contact you when it's done. I'll be unreachable for a while for I've got to go dark to put things in motion."

"I understand and will wait for your call."

Silvana glanced at her cell and realized Luca had called and left a message. Surprised, she immediately called him back.

Chapter 36

David called Godwin to tell him he'd given Luca his number. He wondered if Dorian had confided his plans for the villa if he died. He punched in his number and waited. Godwin answered, "Hello, how are you?"

"Nothing major happening here, at least for the moment. How's island life?"

"I'm enjoying another day in paradise."

After chatting about fishing, he said, "Luca will call you soon. He's inherited Dorian's villa in Livorno and is interested in learning about your security features. Did you know he was Dorian's son?"

"Yes, but Dorian swore me to secrecy and asked me to provide the getaway instructions to him when he called."

"Well, now's the time. For if the mafia learns he's Dorian's son he could be in danger from more than one family."

"Don't worry. I'll get him up to speed with a clean escape plan. I just hate that Dorian didn't get a chance to use it. He was close when they whacked him."

"He sensed it was coming for his final papers were in order. I hope Luca has better luck in owning the villa."

After sending Gabby his love, he ended the call. His thoughts at once went to Lilia. He'd try her cell again, hoping she'd answer.

Lilia picked up his call, and he went straight to the point and said, "Lilia, are you free tonight for dinner at Lo Scoglio Ristorante, or the Rock in local talk? I'd love to catch up on your latest news."

Hurriedly, she answered for she was on the way out the door to her mandatory weapons training class. "Yes, I can meet you there at 8 pm."

When the call ended, he wondered why she was quick to end the conversation. He'd find out when they met if it wasn't secret agency business.

Luca knew his mama was on estate for she'd never missed a day of work except Antonia's birth or when she was rarely sick. He waited for her to return his call. This time he wanted the truth for it could mean life or death to him.

He answered immediately when she called. He was ready to learn the full details surrounding his birth. And put this behind him and lock the secrets away in his mind to never be mentioned again.

His mama arrived with snacks of homemade Bruschetta with tomatoes and basil. He quickly asked her to sit at his dining table and scooted a plate over to her side. When both were sitting and sipping their wine and sampling her classic dish, he said, "Mama tell me your story about my birth and afterwards."

"Luca it pains me for you to learn I wasn't wed when you were born. I was in love with Dorian and a part of me still is. He couldn't marry me because of the dangers involved with his being next in line to run the business.

I was angry at first, especially when he insisted, I marry to give you a name. He hand-picked your papa and I wasn't involved in their negotiations and never asked. I've learned to love your papa since then, and he was Antonia's father."

"You've carried a big secret over the years. I never questioned if papa was my biological father, for he treated me like his son. I'll never tell him for I think it would be painful for him."

"You're probably right. He's especially fond of you and proud of the man you've become. Can we leave our secrets in the past for all our sakes?"

"Yes, mama, your secrets end with me."

Silvana sighed and said, "Thank you. I was afraid our relationship would be destroyed."

"No, we can move forward from here and make a pact to keep family secrets between us."

Silvana smiled and then thought about her father's mafia dealings. A secret best kept from Luca for Lothario planned to end Ghio's clan forever. Now, if he'd call to inform her the deal was done, she'd put it out of her mind.

Chapter 37

David sped to the Lo Scoglio Ristorante to meet Lilia for he'd lost track of time verifying locations for hits on the Sciarretta family. Angelo Simone, the boss of bosses laughed when he said, "You've got your wish. Solocone regularly goes to the barbershop on Wednesday's at 2 pm. He'll be there next week if my calculations are correct. He'll have two bodyguards with him or that's his usual number of armed comrades."

"Well done. He'll be our first hit and my soldiers will infiltrate his country home at precisely the same time. He'll never be tried for his criminal acts for we've sentenced him to death to protect all our blood brothers."

"Let me know when the deed is done for, I won't breathe easy until he's dead and our secret society is safe."

"We'll be cautious when we make the hit in case there's an outlier of his family we miss."

"I'll be on standby and have his clan's pictures waiting to identify them from the photo's your soldiers take at the scenes."

David was hoping to learn news about the Italian mafias at dinner with Lilia. And, if the agency had any leads on the mystery clan of the Sciarretta family. He hoped she'd relax and talk about herself and her plans for advancement in the agency. He arrived just in time to see her pull her blue Fiat into a parking space. After locking his car doors, he hurried to the entrance to greet her.

She smiled when seeing him, and he brushed a light kiss on her cheek. The host waved them in, and they followed him to their reserved table. After ordering drinks, he asked, "How have you been doing? I've missed you."

"Ditto," she said. "I've been exceptionally busy taking the courses my boss required of me to stay in the field."

David smiled. "How's that going?"

"I'm more proficient with weapons now but, my hand-to-hand combat needs work."

"Your petite size makes it difficult to master your opponent. You need to learn martial arts for that'll level the playing field."

"That's not an option offered by the agency."

"No worries. I can teach you mixed martial arts and your boss will be surprised at your abilities."

"You'd do that for me?"

Oh, yes, he thought and more. He said, "Set aside an hour every week for training and meet me at the estate. I have a gym there with flooring that works well for training."

"OK, when can we start?"

Remembering his earlier conversation with Simone, he said, "Why don't we begin classes the first of the month. We can track your progress monthly from there."

"Sounds like a plan. Thank you."

Their dinner arrived, and they began eating. At a break between the courses, he asked, "What have you been working on lately, anything like the kidnappers you single-handedly brought down?"

"I wish. I'm still assigned to the Italian mafia investigations, but my boss has benched me until I complete my training. I'm profiling the mafia heads in the region and later will look at the Sicilian mafias in case they come into our area."

"So, what have you learned about our regional clans?"

"Quite frankly, we believe a mafia war is pending as fallout from Solocone Sciarretta's upcoming trial. Apparently, he went rogue and is putting all the clans in danger of investigations, and they fiercely protect their secret societies."

David rubbed his chin wondering how she deduced that argument. Hoping he'd learn more, he asked, "Have you heard anything about the northern clan since they publicly decried his actions and stated he wasn't one of them?"

"No, they went silent, another reason we believe they are planning a war against Sciarretta's mafia allegiance. They were targeted by our agency because money laundering, kidnapping, and human trafficking are a few of their specialties.

We'd learned more if Sciarretta hadn't been released from jail. But he has politicians in his pocket, and unfortunately police, and agents on his payroll. He'd probably exposed his clan if the Northern mafia put a hit on his family."

"I'm glad you're doing the profiling especially not knowing what agents you can trust when the bullets start flying."

"Right now, I agree, but after my training I want to be in the mix to take down the bad guys."

Her ambitious statements reminded him of someone else who almost didn't make it out alive.

They finished their dinner and agreed to stay in touch before leaving. He kissed her goodnight and left to think about the things she'd said earlier. Was a mafia war on their landscape? He'd need to get Godwin involved to help track chatter for all the clans. Simone needed to be told after they discovered if it was an imminent danger to their society.

He couldn't lead with an Italian agent tipped him about their findings. Now, he was anxious about Lilia coming to the estate to take martial arts lessons. He'd double check the security and hire a younger man trained in protection strategies to take over the duties of the aging butler. It was time he retired to his manor and enjoyed the rest of his life.

Chapter 38

Silvana was busy cleaning their home although it was spotless when she started. She was nervous since she'd heard nothing from Lothario in weeks. She wondered if his plans were in motion to take down the Ghio clan. The leader, Amabile, lived wide-open believing his formidable ruthless reputation would make his enemies think twice before attacking him or his Sicilian clan.

She hoped Lothario's steps to destroy him were well-hidden for she'd not put it past him to attack his family, her. Blood thirsty mobsters like Ghio were not beyond revenge even if women were involved. She and her mother lucked out when her father was murdered for, they could've been killed too. Her papa was shot down as he opened his car door when he arrived home. If they'd been in the car, they'd all be dead for his luxury sedan was plastered with rounds of high-powered bullets.

Being never certain of their safety, her mother forced her and Lothario to leave the city. She remained behind for Sicily had always been her home. Now she too was afraid, miles away from Palermo. If Ghio finds out Lothario is alive and behind an attack against him, she was uncertain of what he might do.

Her spirits lifted when noticing new construction at the front entrance to the estate. The young heir was building a more secure entrance to their compound. She didn't understand why for the family had lived in peace for generations on the massive property. For no one was brave enough to attack them on their own soil.

In the city was a different story. Donatella's husband was murdered as they were leaving a ristorante one evening. The locals whispered about it being a mafia hit for years. Employees kept their thoughts to themselves and continued working as usual for their boss was gracious in commending their arduous work with excellent pay.

The high-topped dry-stone wall with a solid metal entry-gate gave her confidence in her safety on the estate. Taking a deep breath, she walked over to the villa to prepare dinner for the owner. The chef was taking time off, a luxury he seldom enjoyed. Cooking for just one wasn't what he was accustomed to at the estate. She wondered if he was considering leaving for a job in the city. Hopefully, not for they still had employee meals to prepare daily, and it was more than she could plan and cook on her own.

David was in his business center tracking the chatter of the Northern mafia clans. He and Godwin talked and decided to split up the region including members of his own secret society. When he saw Godwin was calling, he knew something was up for he was usually home with Gabby by now. He answered and waited for him to spill the news.

"You've got trouble coming your way. The Zarrella clan is planning a hit on Solocone Sciarretta with the intentions of torturing him until he gives up his associates."

"When does this supposed to happen?"

"They're tracking him now and plan to kidnap him when leaving home in the next few days. I'm listening to find out the exact time and date."

"We have a narrow window to attack him first, and there's no way we can hit him sooner than his regular barber's appointment. Call me when they've scheduled his kidnapping."

"Will do, for you'll be exposed if Sciarretta talks."

After saying goodbye, he leaned back into the plush office chair and thought about the extra security measures he'd created. In the back of his mind, he knew it was primarily for Lilia's safety for the days she trained with him.

He'd hired a top-notch security guard, Elpidio Venturi, to replace the aging butler. He'd run a deep security check on him before hiring to be sure he wasn't affiliated with a mafia group or had entanglements that could jeopardize his loyalty to him.

Pleased with his efforts for the day, he went to the dining room where the staff would serve his dinner. Then he'd call it and night and rest to prepare for another excruciating day of tracking the Italian mafia clans.

Early the next morning, Godwin called. He wondered if he went to bed the night before. Gabby was probably in a tether believing he was in danger.

Godwin said, "The Zarrella clan has finalized their hit on Sciarretta. They're snatching him on the way to a meeting with his attorney on Thursday at 11 am. I'll keep listening in case they make last minute changes to their plan."

"That's good news, for we can hit him first. I'll let Simone know this is our only chance to hit him before they grab him."

After sending Gabby his love, he hung up and called Angelo with the update. It was still early morning, but the news couldn't wait.

The boss of bosses was appreciative of his efforts for tracking Zarrella's revenge on Sciarretta for exposing their clan. He said, "They'll have to dredge the bottom of the ocean to find his body. Our soldiers have their orders and will remove his body from the scene. The others will be left on site to send a message to less honorable men in our ranks and our enemies."

"I'll be waiting to hear the hit was successful."

David rubbed his forehead for becoming the heir was more than he'd imagined. Gone were the days when he could put all his efforts into creating a better world. Now he had it compartmentalized by backing organizations with similar values and with the urgency he felt for making a difference. Running the business single-handed and dealing with the mafia was tiring. He wondered how Dorian did it for so many years. Luckily, they had a good team of loyal employees who were outstanding performers. He'd continue Dorian's plan for rewarding them at the end of the year with a generous bonus.

Lilia would arrive soon and be eager to practice martial arts. He'd given in to her request to start training earlier than planned. He'd insisted she use his equipment for strength training and warm up with stretches before they began. She'd wanted to jump right into the basics; a personality trait he'd seen her exhibit before. He slowed her down and now she enjoyed the workout prior to their sparring.

The butler announced her arrival on the intercom, and he went downstairs to greet her. "Wow," she said. "You've really taken your security up a notch. I had to show my driver's license and wait for clearance prior to entering. And your hunky butler looks as if he could take on a freight train. What gives?"

"Just bringing the estate up to my security standards for nothing has changed here in years and crime is rampant. Better to be prepared."

"I see," she said. "So, I can feel relatively safe while on your estate then?"

He smiled knowing she was the reason for the added security measures.

"Yes, you can. Are you ready to learn a new technique today?"

"I'll be ready, right after my warm-up exercises."

Lilia's athletic body was transforming into a woman of steel. He'd known there was potential, but she'd exceeded his expectations. In a few weeks, he's set up a match between her and Venturi, his new bodyguard/butler. The match should be interesting with her executing the moves she'd been taught.

When they completed the workout, he offered use of the gym's shower for a quick refresher. She said, "No, but thanks, I'm headed straight home and can shower there."

He walked her to the front door and waved as she got into her car to leave. Her boss would be pleased with the progress she'd made for becoming a top agent. She would become a leader in the force with her quick wit, and highly skilled defense mechanisms. He was proud of the work they'd done but was hoping for a date night with her. Waiting for the hit on Sciarretta and the fallout from the Zarrella clan was encroaching on his plans with Lilia.

Chapter 39

David was focused while setting up the program for verifying the hits on the Sciarretta family. Godwin was eavesdropping on the conversations of the clans. Today was the day to protect their secret society. For Solocone would eventually talk when tortured to learn the name of their clan and its members.

He went to the wet bar and splashed some whiskey into a shot glass. Downing it, he wondered if this was the way his life would be in the future, always on alert from neighboring clans. His lifestyle was making it impossible to develop a romantic relationship with Lilia. But when the latest threat was contained, he'd share his feelings. The estate goes years between clashes with other clans.

Godwin was closely guarded when it came to protection of his and Gabby's anonymity. He knew his romantic interest in Lilia was likely misguided because of his family history. He'd ask when the wait was over prior to inviting her to his home for a candlelit dinner and declaration of his feelings for her.

The antique clock on the wall slowly ticked the minutes away until the hit on Sciarretta. He waited for a call from Simone to verify he and his armed soldiers were popped as planned. And, his country estate had been swarmed by their soldiers, leaving no one alive to tell of their fate.

Silvana rushed around the manor getting ready for work. She was running late because her brother Lothario had called and said, "The plans were rapidly moving forward and soon the heads of the Sicilian mafia would be dead."

She caught herself holding her breath. Just breathe, she reminded herself. But what if Lothario was killed, and they came after her? Should she tell David, the estate steward that enemies may try crashing through their gate?

She was on pins and needles when she locked the manor door and hurried to the backdoor of the kitchen. Every step on the pristine rock-laden walkway she debated the decision. Learning her mafia background could get her fired, or he could view her honesty as being trustworthy.

The kitchen staff was already prepping the lead employees' lunches when she arrived. She decided to make David a special island dish to remind him of home to soften the blow if forced to confide her family secrets. Her phone was in her sous chef jacket handy for a call from Lothario. She waited.

David's phone lit up with a call from Simone. He quickly answered hoping Sciarretta was quashed finally. Angelo said, "You'll be receiving photos of the dead from my captain. Quickly verify we've hit them all for we can't allow any of his soldiers to escape and connect with a neighboring clan."

"Tell your captain to send them now and I'll run them through my data base of his associates."

"Done, let me know immediately if we've hit them all."

In minutes, David was receiving photos from the captain's cell of the murdered clan members. He identified the culprits all except one, a new soldier in Sciarretta's clan, a female recruit."

He quickly called Simone and verified the hit except for the outlier. "We need more information about Sciarretta's latest female recruit. Did anyone see her and perhaps believe she was a family member until she returned fire?"

"No, but we have a photo of her for you to run surveillance on."

"Send it, now before she goes into hiding."

"Will do and be quick, so we can end this before she's gone for good."

David pressed his fingers against his temples and wondered when did females become mafia criminals? Maybe it was a good thing that Lilia was training to become the best in the secret intelligence agency for most men would be unsuspecting of female killers. When the time was right, he'd share this info with her.

Silvana made fish cakes and Bajan Macaroni Pie for David's lunch. Since his arrival, the head chef ordered Bajan seasonings and fresh fish to awe his new boss. He'd even ordered the premier coffee of the island from Wyndham's Bajan Crafted Roaster to make David feel at home.

David was taking lunch in his business center. She prepared the tray to take to his office and wished Lothario would call her with an update before she spilled the family secrets. With the lunch hour approaching she hurried up the stairs to the elaborate decorated entrance to the business center with authentic Italian sculptors on the wall. She pressed the button on the solid steel entrance and waited for an answer. Little did she know that inside the massive room was a cam feed showing the person behind the buzzer?

The door automatically opened. She'd been never here before and was shocked when she entered. When did the estate become high-tech? The brochures presented a timeless capsule of Italy and its love for wine and olives on the estate. Yet, their operations center was technologically advanced. Why, she wondered. Was this the new wave in the way multigenerational businesses operated?

Chapter 40

Luca talked with Dorian's cousin Celso and found out his relative Renata didn't make the cut for the mafia clan since she didn't pop him as next-to-kin, a requirement of the clan. She'd joined a family that was already under legal scrutiny hoping to make her mark. When he confided the name of the family, instantly David came to mind, for the family was the head of the Italian trucking company for the estate.

This was something he didn't want to do but since learning Dorian was his father, he had no choice. He called David and asked if they could meet for, he didn't want to confide using his cell. David was rushed in his answer, but said, "Come on over and Venturi will alert me to your arrival."

Luca did as was requested and the new butler guided him up to David's office and pressed the button for entry and left. The door opened, and he saw David at a high-tech console working. He said, "Thank you for agreeing to meet me on short notice."

"No problem, what's on your mind?"

David got up and went to the bar and poured them a glass of the estate's wine.

"Well, I just received news from Dorian's cousin that since Renata couldn't pop me as next-to-kin to join a mafia family; she signed on with the Sciarretta family. I recognized the name from years of their trucking company servicing the vineyard. I thought you should be informed."

"Luca, thank you for your prompt update for she is dangerous. Are you taking precautions for she may try to pop you to prove her worth to the clan?"

"I'm doing all I can which is limited on what Celso tells me."

"Would you like for me to put your enemies under surveillance because of your paternity?"

"Can you do that?"

"Yes, of course. And I'll call you if there's a threat."

Luca left David's office in higher spirits with the knowledge he was protected and confident no enemy would destroy him.

David quickly phoned Simone. He said, "I've identified the female soldier. Her name is Renata Cantu and I'll have eyes on her movement in the city. Just have your soldiers ready to strike a female operative."

Before his evening meal, David had pinpointed her location before she fled the city. He called Simone with the location and said, "Get her now."

In minutes, he called back and said, "It's done, we found her exactly where you said she was hiding."

Of course, David already had cameras beamed into the location of the hit. He didn't trust anyone but Godwin and wanted nothing to lead back to him.

Thinking how fortunate he was in identifying her, he called Luca to thank him. "Luca, you can vacation in Livorno without a threat from Renata for I've verified she's dead."

"Thank you. You have no idea how much that means to me."

David went up even more in brotherly love in his eyes. He was guarding his back for he was clueless about the pit his paternity cast him into. He now understood why his biological father distanced himself from his mama and him. He was in a deadly game.

Silvana greeted her husband after work as usual with dinner of the table. Over the years they'd developed a routine that worked for both. She did her best to hide her anxiety about Lothario and realized she'd succeeded when he went to bed as usual in his bedroom.

Romance had never been an important part of their relationship which made her feel like a bought women. The few times they'd had sex were when Antonia was conceived. He tried to be more romantic perhaps to woo her; she didn't realize it was to impregnate her.

She was trying to move on as Dorian had wanted when he paid him to be her husband. Yet, he was a mystery to her, but she'd bet Dorian had the family history. Things she'd like to know.

Her phone rang; she answered hoping to hear news about the coup on the Sicilian mafia. She answered and it was Alessio Volta, the captain in the Ghio clan and friends with her brother.

He said, "Your brother, Lothario was murdered in the ambush on the Ghio clan. Amabile is dead, the murderer of your father. We've taken over and his entire family have been murdered. You can return to Palermo in peace from this day forward."

Silvana wanted to say thank you, but her brother was dead never to realize the victory for paybacks on her father's killer. All she could do was cry and her wailing was the last thing he heard before he hung up.

She wasn't aware her boss was tracking the Sicilian mafia war and had visuals of her brother, Lothario being popped from his friend, Alessio, taking over the mob and their holdings.

David never left anything to interpretation. He quickly did background checks on the winners and losers of the war to take over the Sicilian mafia. His findings sent up shock-waves for the people under his protection for their links with the Sicilian family.

Chapter 41

Hopelessness is something Silvana is accustomed to for her grief for her daughter and brother sent trembles through her body. She did her best to move forward with flashbacks of their childhood invading her mind at inopportune moments. Lothario was his papa's son and close as they were he failed to recognize the pitfalls of joining a mafia family.

He wanted to learn their methods to prepare himself for taking over the Sicilian commission to avenge his father's murder. Now, he was dead. She hoped that was the end of her family's involvement with the Italian families. She suspected it wasn't over yet for her son was alive, and they'd go after him.

David was busy looking over the fallout from the Sicilian commission bloodshed. He wondered who'd pop-up as the newly vetted boss of bosses. When the name Alessio Volta came up as head, he became afraid for his friend Luca and his mother. He zeroed in on the hit and saw that Volta popped Lothario in what they called cross-fire. Being tech savvy had its rewards especially with his deep infiltration. Alessio popped him on purpose.

Volta used him to take control of the Sicilian commission. Someone with a revenge motive and a person to blame made him free at last to take the helm. He wondered if Silvana was told her brother was dead. He thought not for her distance from news in Palermo.

Crises were all around him for fear Lilia would do something stupid, single-handed; he needed a drink to calm his nerves and get the right perspective for moving forward. The woman he lusted after and felt romantic toward and long-time employees, Dorian's next to kin were in danger. This was something he'd handle on his own for they'd messed with the wrong entity.

He'd out wizard they're dated surveillance in a heartbeat. Now to call in select soldier from the 5,000 his great-grandmother vetted into the family, to squash them and lead nothing back to the family name. He trusted only Godwin to verify his friends were in danger and stand along beside him for the fight. He wouldn't make a move on the south until it was apparent Silvana, and her son were marked for death for he had the northern clan, the Zarrella family to worry about.

Immediately calling the boss of bosses, Simone to gather information about them, he waited for an answer. By now the Zarrella clan was aware they'd hit the Sciarretta family, ahead of their planned attack. Did they identify their secret society as the professionals behind it?

Simone said, "The leader of the Zarrella clan as put out a hefty bounty on the streets to identify us."

"So, they're fishing for info. That's not good for I was hoping they'd see we had the same goal with the hit on Sciarretta and back down."

"They've wanted to come into our region for a while. This sparked their interest and fired them up for a war."

"I'm tracking them as we speak. I'll let you know what I find out. It goes to say we need to prepare for them. I have no plans to take an acid bath at their hands."

"Yes, they are especially brutal and cruel in their killings. Being drug smugglers, they use a special technique for keeping their soldiers and enemies in line and their shipments moving throughout the country and abroad."

David sighed after saying goodbye to the man in charge of the life and death of their sworn enemies in the north. He called it a night after setting up his phone to receive notices about them as he tried to sleep.

Lilia was never far from his mind, and he said a prayer for her safety since she'd been appointed to a special task force to take down the Italian mafias. In the back of his mind, he wondered what would happen if she found out about his associations?

Chapter 42

Lilia was proud of her new status in the agency. Her boss, Di Donata announced her new role and the faces of her male counterparts fell when hearing the news. She expected as much and would be close-mouthed about her investigations never being certain about who was on the take.

She'd learned the Zarrella clan was itching for a war against a yet unidentified local mafia family. Her office didn't have the Intel or resources to identify the phantom clan. From what she'd learned from her boss, David likely did, and he wanted to meet him and ask for his help.

Torn between loyalty for her boss and strong sexual feelings for David, she didn't know what to do. She was caught in a catch-22 knowing her decision might put her in the crosshairs. She picked up her cell and called David. He quickly answered and her heart skipped a beat when he said, "Ciao Bella! How are you today?"

His deep baritone voice rolling the words, "hello beautiful" off his tongue went straight to her lips. Closing her eyes, she pictured a breath-taking kiss. Then realizing her lapse in conversation, giggled like a schoolchild, and said, "I've got a special favor to ask of you. My boss wants to meet you. We need your help for finding a secret society that we fear may be headed to war."

"Oh, that's all. He laughed. "Am I a wizard who can pull the answers out of a hat?"

"He knows you're a tech genius and we don't have the resources or manpower to do what you can."

David didn't have to think about the answer for he'd not put his own head on the chopping block or his associates. "Tell your boss I'm swamped with the business right now, and have barely gotten my feet wet in running the operations. I'm learning something new every day. It's just bad timing with everything going on here. I hope he'll understand."

"I'll give him your response although I wish you'd listen and help avoid a bloody turf war."

"Maybe your Intel is wrong and there's no reason to assume a clash will take place in our region."

"Yes, you may be right. We'll double-check with our sources before continuing our investigation."

Whew, that was too close for comfort, and he needed to do something right away to back off the task force. He turned to his large screen computer console to continue tracking the leaders of the Zarrella clan. He hoped Simone would agree to take the war to them for too much attention was being focused on their region.

Luca came to mind as someone newly equipped for surveillance of the port in Livorno where he now owned a villa with an ultramodern security system. He didn't want to recruit him into the secret society for it was a heavy burden to carry. He'd ask as his friend for the Zarrella's would be putting out feelers, and his uncle Celso Mezzeo would probably have the scoop on their activities.

From his cabin cruiser, observation at the port where the clan smuggled in their narcotics would be easy. They may be marking their time at the harbor to attack them since the port was an easy commute to Tuscany territory.

A build-up of soldiers would be easily detected from the sea using binoculars. And, he had no doubt Dorian's cabin-cruiser was well stocked with cameras and other needed items. He'd invite Luca for dinner and ask for his help.

Chapter 43

Di Donato called Lilia into his office when she arrived at work. He'd received news that one of the magistrates involved with the task force and his wife were popped on the way home from a restaurant.

The investigators believed the hit fit the description of similar ones by the Zarrella clan. He was concerned for her safety and said, "Pull back your investigation, until we know who is behind this latest bloodshed."

"Yes, sir, but isn't that what they want us to do?"

"It's no matter for if you're dead, you can't catch them later. Do as I ask, and when the time comes to move forward, I'll inform you at once."

"As you say, sir, I'm on stand-by until you give me the green light."

Di Donato nodded, and she quickly exited his office. She wanted to throw something for every time she got close to unraveling the secrets, she's shut down.

Immediately her thoughts went to David and wondered what he was doing. He'd congratulated her on learning basic martial arts and postponed teaching her the next level until after the holidays. She missed seeing him and wished he'd call.

David phoned Luca and invited him to dinner. The chef would be pleased to prepare for more than one diner. When he felt safe again, he'd explore more social interactions so his talents would be put to better use. Thoughts of a candlelit dinner with Lilia came to mind.

Luca arrived and was shown into the dining room where David waited. As had become a custom for them, they hugged on greeting. David made their cocktails and invited Luca to sit and talk before dinner was served.

He said, "Luca, how would you like to take a week off with pay and go to your villa in Livorno for I need some eyes on the waterfront?"

Luca didn't need the background info for he already knew his biological father was in deep with a mafia clan. He wondered if it related to the hit on him or was a new threat to the business, David personally, or both. "Sure," he said. "I can leave tomorrow, and Pauli can run the orchard in my absence."

"Before you sign-on, you need to know this could be dangerous if you are identified. I'm gathering info about the Zarrella clan. They've smuggled drugs in and out of the port for years untouched by rival clans or the Guardia di Finanza, the agency responsible for investigating illegal trade and smuggling. My interest is on a build-up of soldiers in the area for I've heard they're planning a payback to a rival family. This could cause a disruption to our business on land and sea."

"I'm ready to do whatever I can to help. The villa is one of the safest places on the planet. Godwin filled me in on the elaborate security system. I can go in and out by land or sea without detection, or hideout in the heavily stocked luxury bunker until the coast is clear."

"OK, then. Let's get down to specifics of the plan. You can take the cabin-cruiser out to sea and watch their activities. You'll find everything you need onboard for detecting their movement. I'll send photos of the main operatives in their organization for you to track. First, check-in with your uncle Mezzeo to find out what he knows about the Zarrella clan. His Ristorante Del Sole is a popular spot for meet-ups and relaxing after hours. Listen carefully, but don't divulge any particular interest in what you learn."

"I understand and will let you know my findings. Hopefully, I can catch some fresh fish to eat for when I return."

"A perfect ending to our plan," said David.

Now that their business was concluded, David said, "Our secondi course should be arriving soon. The snack-sized bites paired with Aperitivo, a pre-dinner drink hit the mark, but I'm ready for the main feature."

On cue, a server presented the Bistecca Alla Fiorentina with its perfectly charred crust with roasted vegetables and a zesty red pepper Romesco Sauce. Their Tuscan-style dinner was paired with Chianti, a favorite red wine in the region.

After dessert, Luca thanked David for the evening and said, "I'll check in with you tomorrow after talking to my uncle."

"I'll be waiting. Buon viaggio!

Luca left David's villa thinking about the story he planned to tell his mama tomorrow before he left. She'd become especially anxious when he left the estate and went into town to meet friends or relax on his own. He had to tell her something believable for being away a week.

Then he remembered confiding about working on a new hybrid plant for Jason's orchard in Barbados. She knew he traveled there before with David, and it would be a plausible lie for he was doing something for David this week.

The next morning, he arose early and called his mama before she left for work and planted his alibi. "Mama," he said. "I'll be away this week helping Jason with his orchard in Barbados. David asked me to go and take the cuttings we've developed for he can't leave right now for he's still learning the business."

"I understand. The *Island Grove* is important to David and his friend Jason. You've helped them a lot and I would anticipate you'd continue. Stay safe, and call me when you return."

Luca felt better for she believed every word. He quickly texted David his story, in case, she mentioned the trip in passing. Then he swung his overnight bag into his car for the short road trip to Livorno. He hoped to arrive at the Ristorante Del Sole before it became crowded so he could talk to Mezzeo alone.

Chapter 44

David followed up on the Sicilian clan to figure out what was happening since the takeover by Alessio Volta, the boss of bosses, former captain. He'd not picked up on anything that made him believe he'd changed the core values from the proceeding leader or made technological advances.

Volta was likely pleased with his increase in profits since taking over as godfather. The mafia's income was from contracts with the state for construction and road building, territory protection, sometimes from both sides, and racketeering of products, and illegal drugs. This was the mainstay of their operation. As under earlier bosses, prostitution, and human trafficking were off limits for the family enterprises.

Eavesdropping on his and Lothario's earlier calls, he believed it was only a matter of time before they'd take over the drug trade from neighboring families. For he'd provided

Alessio with the methods of importing the base cocaine narcotics from South America to mafia owned refineries to be repackaged and exported to the US and Europe. A lucrative trade agreement for the Zarrella clan without external scrutiny for they'd lined politicians and enforcement officials' pockets.

It would be almost impossible to trail the financial windfalls from their illegal operations. With money wired through Switzerland or Bahama banks, the debits and credits were untraceable, and they'd do nothing to trigger interest from the state.

The Sicilian clan kept a low profile unlike their counterparts in the US who were slowly embracing the old ways out of necessity. A made-man in the Italian mafia wouldn't consider flashing money or showing off his mistresses in front of others. The standard was to do nothing that would provoke an interest in their affairs. The spouse was to be protected at all costs for the family unit was important and the wife had leverage to report his activity to the la polizia.

David was pleased Silvana and her son; Luca were not being discussed. Hopefully, Alessio would leave it in the past with the takeover of the Sicilian commission and move forward with his plans. He'd keep tabs just in case.

Luca arrived at the Ristorante Del Sole to meet Mezzeo after his road trip from the estate. He was ready for a refreshing Peroni and conversation with the owner. Mezzeo was behind the bar swiping the counter with a damp kitchen towel. He said, "Didn't figure you'd be back so soon but then again the Ligurian Sea has a way of lolling you back to her coast."

"You're right. I have a few days off and decided to recuperate on the sea and try to catch a few fish. Do you want to join me?"

Mezzeo shook his head and said, "This place takes all of me from sunrise until late at night. Maybe when I retire, I can relax and enjoy the ocean."

"My brother is a fisher who supplies the ristorante with fresh seafood. We talk about the days when we can enjoy the sea again like when we were young men."

"The off season would be a suitable time to take a break. You can turn over your business to your staff for a couple of days and enjoy a short reprieve."

"I've been thinking about that a lot lately. And, with the offers coming in for my ristorante, I may retire for time has changed and we're living in a different world now than when we began."

"Going from local to a tourist hot spot probably had its moments. I best order before the crowd files in for their dinner."

Looking over to the black chalkboard announcing today's specials, he said, "I'll take the catch of the day grilled with almond sauce, lemon, and shallots. The panna cotta with butter and orange blossom sounds good, and add Pistachio ice cream to finish it off."

Mezzeo tapped in his order and returned with a fresh brew. Luca said, "Have you seen any of Renata's mafia associates in the area since she left?"

The worried scowl on Luca's face made Mezzeo relax and tell him the latest news. "The Zarrella's sent her packing when she didn't come up to their standards, a hit on a close family member to show her allegiance. Renata found a Tuscany clan who offered equal rights and was murdered when they were attacked.

The Zarrella's are in the region now mostly at the port. I'm hearing they're planning an attack on a northern mafia group but don't have the specifics. I'm hoping the hit isn't on the clan Dorian was involved with for the overflow may reach you."

"Keep your ears open and if you hear anything let me know."

"Sure, your blood kin and I owe Dorian for my livelihood."

Luca finished his meal and was glad the ristorante was near the villa he now called home. He said, good night for all he wanted to do was lie down on a soft bed and sleep. But he needed to call David and report the conversation between him and Mezzeo. He punched in his number and waited. David answered.

"Glad you had a safe trip. Did you learn anything from your uncle?"

"Yes, this place is swarming with soldiers from the Zarrella's clan, but mostly at the port. I'll take the cabin cruiser out tomorrow and spy from the ocean about their activities. Mezzeo said he'd heard plans about their hitting a clan in the northern region, is that us?"

"Not directly, but the war may jeopardize our shipping products to the market if we're blockaded."

David thanked him and told him to rest easy and call when he was out on the water tomorrow. The photos of the leaders were at his disposal if he needed anything else to let him know.

When they hung-up David wondered how much of their activity was known by his boss of bosses, Angelo Simone. He'd not confided his suspicions to him and although a new head of the family, he had an impressive following of soldiers built-up over the previous generations of the Mandarino family.

Simone should have said something for now it was appearing as if he was on the outs with his own clan and they had products to protect and get to the market. He didn't need an internal clan battle to contend with. They were supposed to protect their own and other brothers' properties and businesses and not go to war.

The next morning when reading the newspaper, he saw Angelo's daughter engagement photo. It was a slight to not be invited to weddings of their blood brothers or godfathers. For at these spectacular events was where much of the mafia business was conducted.

This was an accepted method of transference of power and expansion of territories. As a gift to the wedding couple monies and propriety rights were transferred to the godfather for their benefit.

Marriage in the mafia was a holy sacrament with many arranged for benefits to the family and clan. The women who grew up in mafia families recognized the expectations of the wife of a made-man and many embraced the possibilities of continuing the family tradition.

Marriages between families were sacred vows with sisters and young women being prime candidates for matrimony.

He wondered why he was banished from this inner sanctum. Not that he was looking for a mafia wife, but he'd chosen the mafia life and expected inclusion.

He wondered if the color of his skin with his father's Caribbean patrimony showing proof of his ancestry was the reason. He expected the stigma in the US where he learned in his early childhood that the color of your skin made a difference in society.

He felt like he'd been cast down into a dark pit. The only person he'd confide in was Godwin. He'd call to learn why he was being exiled from the clan he recently pledged allegiance until death. For his ousting might mean eviction from the clan and a certain death.

Chapter 45

Luca boarded the *Buona Vita* and set the coordinates to the location David provided in his text. Motoring away from the launch he wondered if Dorian felt he was living the good life while at sea and aptly named his vessel accordingly. He'd never know but with the fresh salty sea breeze gently brushing his face, he understood the feeling.

He'd double-checked the items on board to complete his mission, and packed a lunch and snacks for a day on the sea. He was surprised at the high-tech items and built-in equipment for a fast get-away. Dorian wasn't as old school as many believed when it came to clandestine activities.

He was alert to the passing boats in the harbor as he motored to his point of observation. Would anyone recognize his craft as one once belonging to Dorian?

He hoped not for he needed anonymity to conduct the mission David assigned him. He lowered the anchors by touching a button on the console when reaching his destination. Then he grabbed the long-distance binoculars and an ultramodern camera and started scanning the ocean and port for activity.

The container ship, *Costantino* David mentioned was anchored in the harbor unloading its cargo. He quickly snapped a picture to send to David via the link onboard. A closer view was needed of the berth where the ship was moored. He quickly texted David and asked for coordinates for a closer shot. In seconds, David texted the numbers to enter the navigation system adding stay safe, and get out of there if they suspect you. No problem was his reply.

Luca upped the anchors and moved closer in before releasing them in the new spot. From here he had a front row seat to watch the activity around the ship. He cast out a fishing line to appear to be fishing and then cradled his reel in the holder and waited.

When recognizing no one was watching him, he snapped pictures of the men on the wharf. Some he recognized from the photos David sent to ID the mafia clan. Taking a closer look, he saw a man in a suit approach a Zarrella leader and was handed a briefcase. He caught their transaction and lowered his camera and started to reel in his line playing the part of an avid fisherman. He'd cast in another spot and continue watching to determine the number of soldiers guarding the ship. He messaged David the photos he'd taken and waited for his response.

David texted back, thanks Luca. You can go fishing now. We have what we need. He was glad Dorian left meticulous details in his personal effects about the cabin cruiser. He texted, look into the left compartment by the wheel and you'll find the fishing coordinates Dorian used to catch fish.

Luca smiled as he pulled away from the harbor and motored to a coordinate on the list. He still had the afternoon to enjoy an outing on the sea. He bit into his Muffuletta and watched as the waves lapped against the port side of the cabin cruiser. The air and sea were mesmerizing and there was no doubt seafarer was in his ancestry line.

After catching a grouper, enough for his dinner, he reeled in his lines and headed to the villa. He could grow accustomed to this lifestyle easily. Now, if he had someone to enjoy it with and could share the news with his mama, he'd be happy.

David was stunned when he received the photos Luca sent. The man receiving the briefcase was from Lilia's Intelligence Agency. Marco was with her and helped release the kidnapped girls. He wondered if her agency was trying to catch the Zarrella's in a smuggling sting, or if he was on the take and the briefcase was full of euros for protection from the agency.

He couldn't ask Lilia for she'd know he was tracking the mafia clan something she and her boss wanted him to do for them. He could bug Marco's phone to see if he answered to anyone in the agency and his contacts. He quickly set up detection of his movement and planned Luca's next mission in Livorno.

Chapter 46

Luca thought about his mama as he was preparing the grouper for his dinner. She'd enjoy sitting at his table and enjoying the view of the rocky coastline while dining on fresh seafood. He suspected she'd been at the villa before with the photos of her scattered throughout. When the Zarrella's' where no longer feared, he'd ask David if it was safe for her to visit.

He was glad a trip to Barbados was his alibi for when returning he'd have a deep tan. She'd notice. Then he would say he and Jason went fishing in the Caribbean when not tending the orchard and discussing new stock and growing the vines.

David talked to Godwin about his fear of being ousted from the clan and a possible hit by the Zarrella family. He said, "Simone is concerned about your high-profile in the region. Fearful that your presence at his daughter's wedding will bring closer scrutiny by someone not on his payroll. He's partially correct in his assumptions for the wedding will be feasted on by reporters and all of Tuscany. And you're not a long-time family friend."

"You haven't heard anything about his ordering a hit on me?"

"No, but that doesn't mean he hasn't for I can't monitor all his activities from here. I'd suggest calling and congratulating him on his daughter's wedding. He'll get the hint that you're aware of a snub and respond to protect his interest. Whether it's the truth or not, only you can determine."

"I need a genie in the bottle to monitor the threats against me. I'll let you know what I find out."

"Good, for he's your strongest opponent right now for the Zarrella's have the Sicilian commission on their backs. That's where they'll be a war, a bloody one. For they own the northern drug trade, and politicians for moving their products and will fight to death to keep their stake.

Alessio needs to remain in Palermo and protect the Sicilian territory to continue their operation and forget about taking down the Zarrella clan to gain their drug smuggling business or there will be blood on the streets."

"Well, that's one off my list for the present. I've amped up protection for our trees, fruit, and shipments along with strengthening the security around the estate. At times, I feel like a prisoner in my own home."

"Take a deep breath and relax, the hurdles you're experiencing will pan out. They always do after war between clans. You're being tested for you're the new kid on the block, and they're checking for your vulnerability. By not showing your hand, you've got leverage should they plan an attack."

"Appreciate the advice and I'll let you know what I learn from my sources here."

David hung up and wished Lilia would call. He was tracking Marco to decide if his presence at the harbor was a sting by the agency or for his own profits. The guesswork would be reduced if he had insider information.

He'd recently promoted Elpidio to his personal assistant. The longstanding position of butler wasn't much-needed since he took over the estate. The number of people on one hand would be the tally of who'd entered the villa since his inheriting the title of steward or boss.

The new responsibilities he added to Venturi's job description were to enhance internal communications between the units in the business. He'd decide later the ones that didn't need his approval after he reviewed his tact with department heads and his business acumen. He needed someone to take care of non-crucial aspects of the day-to-day operations to free up his time to pinpoint their enemies' moves.

Elpidio appeared excited to advance to a higher-level position in the estate's business. The skills he showed would factor his rise in the organization for he had another job in mind after he proved his trustworthiness.

He picked up his phone to call Angelo to congratulate him on his daughter's wedding. His response would be a revelation for their future dealings.

Simone answered and said, "Pronto?"

"Just read the news about your daughter, Guilietta's wedding in the paper. Congratulations!"

Angelo cleared his throat, and said, "Thank you, we're excited about the union between our family and hers."

David waited as the silence became deafening before saying, "I wish them a long, and happy life together."

His reply got Simone's attention for he was accustomed to the mafia's method of veiled threats. David wasn't as unschooled in mafia courtesies as he believed. He said, "An invitation wasn't sent for your protection and mine. Too many questions will be asked if you're a guest for few outside the clan knows our paths have crossed. You'll thank me later for this forethought."

"As you say, it's a family tradition to honor the bride and groom with those in your inner circle. May their day bring nothing but happiness on this special occasion for the wedding couple."

When the call ended, David felt a strange hope for a future with Lilia. If he was shielded from mafia contacts in the outer world, perhaps they'd have a life together. His secrets would be safe. Now, if the war mongers would retreat, he'd ask her out again. But would she respond after months of silence since her last visit to practice martial arts?

Chapter 47

Luca was an early riser and dressed for a meeting with Mezzeo at the ristorante. He'd promised to listen for info about the Zarrella clan. Mezzeo was waiting for him when he arrived. The look on his face wasn't promising for good news. He pulled out a bar stool and sat down. Mezzeo eyed the entrance before going over to lock the front door.

He said, "I heard Zarrella's soldiers talking about a hit in the north last night. The hit is big for retaliation against a clan that brought unwanted attention and potentially legal problems to them. They're out for blood and to make a statement about their power in the region."

"Did you hear the hit's name?"

"No, but a godfather will be popped for no one less would make the statement they want to send."

"I see. Did they say where he'd be whacked?"

"No, but they're giddy with excitement about their coup."

"Do you think it has anything with Dorian's former group?"

"Like I said, no names were mentioned."

"Thanks for sharing. I'll be returning to the estate tomorrow and will keep my eyes and ears open. I'm unaware of his mafia business and hope the same is true about me."

Mezzeo recognized Luca was in unfamiliar territory after learning Dorian was his biological father. He didn't have the tell-tale odor of a mafia consort as did Dorian. He was out of his element of lovingly tending grapevines for the estate.

"Stay safe, and return when you get a chance. The fishing will be wonderful in the coming months."

Luca thanked him and left to clean-up and ready the home for his next visit. Tomorrow he'd return to the estate and talk to David about his findings.

David was tracking Simone's family activities as they prepared for the big wedding. The security was tight for Angelo was taking precautions for his daughter's nuptials. This once-in-a-life time event would be the perfect stage for a hit on the family. Angelo had been in the business long enough to be aware for targeting.

Luca called on his return, and he invited him over for dinner. He dropped off his fresh catch from his fishing trip for the chef to prepare for dinner. Entering through the backdoor before his mama's shift, for David had already told the chef he'd ordered a fresh grouper for dinner. His secret was safe from his mama.

David's surveillance of Angelo's clan made him shake his head. They were still living in the 90s for the security measures they'd put in place wouldn't stop the new tech-savvy mafia clans. He was glad he wasn't invited for no guest would be safe if the event was the target.

When the doorbell rang at 8 pm, his new assistant and butler was still in his office, and answered the door. Seeing Luca's smiling face though the peek hole, he at once invited him in. Knowing he was a close friend of his boss, he treated him with upmost respect. He wanted to make friends on the estate himself and for his boss to be pleased with his work.

David and Luca hugged on meeting and went to the bar to pour cocktails. They had time to discuss Luca's clandestine assignment prior to dinner. They sat in the cozy luxurious chairs in the main hall and began talking while sipping their drinks. Luca said, "Thanks for the vacation, the fishing was extraordinary. I can't wait to return during the height of the fishing season."

David motioned for Luca to follow him, and they went upstairs to the estate's business center. Behind the closed secure doors with newly installed high-tech sensors, David and Luca relaxed in the steel reinforced office and talked.

David said, "What did you find out from Mezzeo?"

"The Zarrella clan plans to hit a godfather in this region. The soldiers are excited about their planned coup for paybacks for being fingered in criminal investigation earlier this year."

"It appears the Sicilian family is second on their list if they don't back away from the drug trade in Livorno."

David at once knew the paybacks they were after. When the Sciarretta family kidnapping charges were made, the

Zarrella clan was fingered for probable cause. Although they denied it, the foreign and domestic intelligence agencies started investigating them. They murdered their opponents until they backed away from their investigations.

The Zarrellas' may not have family names of the make-up of the clan families, but they'd learned Simone was the boss of bosses of the secret clan. He was the hit and his daughter's wedding might be the venue where his inner circle was targeted.

David quickly reviewed his brief history with Luca and the potential hit on him by Dorian came to mind. Luca had no knowledge about the mafia, but he'd scared his biological father. This was the close to home murderous intent he'd confided to Godwin. Dorian had receded his inheriting of his estate which included shares in the Mandarino family business. Should he trust him now with a potential death squad posed to breakthrough their gates?

Chapter 48

David never one to make quick decisions unless his life was in imminent danger said, "Let's go see if our dinner is ready, and enjoy your catch of the day."

The fresh grouper reminded David of home on the island seeming a life-time ago. He thanked Luca for remembering his favorite seafood and said goodnight. Tomorrow he'd talk with Godwin and get his insights about how to move forward and protect the estate if it was next on Zarrella's hit list.

Early the next morning, he called Godwin. He was at a loss for the mafia clan that he personally swore allegiance could be under attack. Normally that didn't happen or hadn't in years. And everyone in the clan was oblivious to the potential hits. Their outdated methods would soon become the death of them if someone with new techniques for protection didn't take charge.

He wondered what his great-grandmother would have done. Then, he remembered she was the godmother, and kept everyone safe from mafia infringements and prosecution under her umbrella. But he didn't become godfather with his inheritance. He became boss of the Mandarino family that owned the estate. He was initiated by the boss of bosses into the overall Rocco family, named for his great-great grandfather with Angelo Simone now leader. A clan built on the framework of the Freemason's secret society. And for generations were unknown to the intelligence agencies, he'd like to keep it that way.

The Simone family was made head of the Rocco clan since Donatella's death for only blood kin in the families could serve in this lofty and respected role. Otherwise, Dorian would've been the next godfather.

He wondered if it was time to step up to keep all the families safe and free to produce and sell products or services, they provided the public. The idea of becoming boss of bosses went against everything he'd planned for his future. Yet already he'd been promoted to captain in the Rocco clan. He didn't want to live his life looking over his shoulder. But what could he do? He'd inherited the allegiance to the society along with the estate.

David knew Godwin's surveillance was deep throat. He had a personal stake in protecting the family. And he was waiting for his call to tell him how to equip himself to save the estate and the family name. Some he'd love and others he'd hate without a doubt. He was aware the conversation wouldn't be stingy on results driven performance.

Godwin always seemed to know the answers when he was dumbstruck. He called. After exchanging pleasantries, he said, "You're too close to see what's in front of you. Forget about enlisting Luca into the clan his father swore allegiance to. Give him a choice to stay on at the estate tending his vines or go to his villa. I'd suggest his villa, so he won't sidetrack you with his conspiracy theories, and learn more about your family connections.

Luca's not a fighter for a commercial cause, only vengeance against who hurt his family. Anyone who would murder someone who made their life possible doesn't need to be you're confident. Distance yourself now and let the mama's boy have his ocean paradise thanks to the promises of obedience and the bloodletting of his father.

Other words, he's weak and was emotionally driven to kill for revenge of his pathetic sister's actions. She was on the take for deep pockets, and when she found that close to home it got her murdered. Brush it off and move on. I'm certain Dorian did everything in his power to persuade her otherwise. No sense in having unnecessary mental and emotional clutter impeding your progress for preparing the clan to be ready to defend the estate."

David swallowed the lump in his throat before replying for he considered Luca a friend. "Your argument for setting him free makes sense for I like you have determined he'd be worthless when bullets start flying. Yet, I considered him a friend, and he does excellent work in the orchard. However, I get your point. I need to give him freedom to make a choice and step up for what's to come next."

"You're right. Changes are coming and the estate will continue as it has for generations or be squashed and torn apart by the militant and blood thirsty Zarrella clan. You need to bring your A-game for planning strategies to overcome this war on the Rocco family. A predetermined fate when Sciarretta broke the sacred rules of honor to himself and the brotherhood. The effects of his actions will rain down hell and brimstone on the clan. They are barbaric in torture methods and will target the families who make up the clan when they are finished. They will come for you. You need to be prepared in advance to stop them before reaching you."

"Thanks for your feedback. I'll start mapping out a plan to slow them down before reaching Simone's daughter's wedding. Maybe we can soften the blow and take down some of their soldiers. Then attack again as they are leaving his country estate on the side roads they'd likely take for the next hit, the next in line to be family boss. Before, they reach our estate the numbers should be something we can manage. I'll be prepared with our men ready and armed for battle with the latest weaponry available."

They ended the call promising to stay in touch and use their education and training to oust the Zarrella clan from their territory and out of Italy. Yet, in the back of his mind he was aware another clan would step up to take over the drug smuggling business, likely the Sicilian commission with its new leader Volta.

David sat back in his leather console chair, and felt the smooth fiber against his body. Godwin was right in his predictions of disaster, and he needed to plan for war. Making matters worse was the unlimited resources available to the Zarrella clan streaming from their lucrative narcotics trade. They had the financial reserves to payoff politicians and key recruits of the Guardia Di Finanza for legal protection.

He was thankful for his foresight for ordering advance weaponry to be delivered incognito on his arrival in the estate. His upbringing never left him. He would be prepared for a fight to death with the latest arms available.

Chapter 49

Luca awoke early and prepared his caffe latte and nibbled on the bread and jam his mother brought over yesterday. He could tell she was still anxious but about what he didn't know, and she'd not tell. He thought after his forced conversation about his father, they'd have no more secrets. But she was holding back something, and it alarmed him.

He was trying to decide about whether to stay or take an early retirement to the villa on the Ligurian Sea, and she wasn't helping. He predicted she'd die on the estate where she'd lived most of her life. But he had a choice now that he didn't have earlier.

He didn't want to die on the estate, another man's property. But, if he left her, he'd need to explain his inheritance. This wouldn't be easy, and of course she'd want to check it out. But should she for her home was with his papa and their easing into their retirement years?

He was afraid that once she visited the villa, she'd want to live with him and reclaim her youth and live with memories of Dorian. He'd never find the woman of his dreams at this rate.

David had breakfast as usual in the main hall mainly to pacify the chef who was stringent in proprieties of the main house. The chef would probably live his dreams in the coming weeks when the estate became overrun with soldiers for the fight against the Zarrella's.

He couldn't wait to see if their iron chef could deliver the goods. He thought so for he'd been checking him out and his knife skills were to be envied. He'd put a plus by his name for their homeland security.

He called the chef into his downstairs office. Naturally so polite it was sickening, but something behind his facade was relatable. He said, "I want you to retire Silvana and hire a bad ass sous chef with culinary skills that can be dangerous when provoked. Don't worry about Silvana; she has a home on the estate as long as she lives."

"Were back in the trenches again, much like the stories from when your great-grandmother Donatella was alive, aren't we? We'll make you proud, sir."

"Yes, we'll be involved in a clan war. Be planned for feeding a brigade of soldiers within the week. If you need help for deliveries tell me, and we'll hire additional coaches to truck food and supplies in."

"Yes, sir, but I doubt we need anything for our pantries are overflowing and can feed the soldiers for up to a month from our reserve. We also have the livestock we can resort to if beef and poultry run low."

"Well, hopefully your reserve will hold us until the fighting is over, and we're the victor. If we should get overrun, use your repertoire of skills to defeat the enemy."

Just when he was up to his eyeballs in preparing the staff, Luca called. He prayed he didn't want a face-to-face for he wasn't into it. He said, "Hello Luca, how are things with you?"

"Well, I've decided about my future. I need to claim my inheritance and live on the Ligurian Sea and Pauli can shepherd in a newbie for tending the vines."

"Well-done, friend, I'd done the same. Are you leaving soon?"

"Yes, tomorrow matter of fact."

"Best wishes in your new domicile."

One problem solved with Luca out of the way. Next, he needed to pinpoint a location to hit the Zarrella mafia before they arrived at Simone's country estate. And, have soldiers placed at strategic points to ambush them before hitting the next boss in line. Then, block the entries into his estate for he believed the Mandarino family was third in line. He didn't want them on the property for innocents lived on the grounds. Furthermore, there had never been blood shed on their soil, and he planned to continue the tradition.

He and Godwin talked and decided the prime spots to attack were from the country back roads the route to their potential hit sites. Now, it was time to bring in Elpidio his new assistant and ask if he was willing to become a soldier in their clan. He'd already decided to immediately promote him to lieutenant for he'd researched his background before hiring him as bodyguard/butler.

Gavino DeFillippis his captain in the Mandarino clan agreed he'd be an asset to the family. If Elpidio was agreeable, they'd fast track his initiation into the clan with just a few of the blood brothers present. They needed to keep their head in this business instead of celebrating right now. They'd party when the Żarrella clan was disbanded with the few survivors likely retreating to the US to further their drug trade from South America.

He called Elpidio and asked him to come to his office. In minutes, he arrived and was pressing the button for entry. He welcomed him and offered a drink. He accepted. David pointed to a sofa and said, "Please, have a seat. I have an important matter to discuss with you."

Elpidio had no idea what was going on. He feared firing was why his boss called. And he'd done nothing to warrant it for he was diligent in his assignments always going the extra mile. He waited.

David said, "Are you familiar with the Freemason society?"

"Yes, ironic as it is, I've heard the mafia's secret society is based on their rules and formalities."

"The Mandarino estate embodies such a society, and it appears we'll soon be at war from an opposing clan to take over our properties and business. Would you be willing to place the Mandarino clan above your own family and embrace your blood brothers until death?"

"Yes. I've heard tales about the family, but no one was certain it existed."

"We want to keep it that way, a secret society for all our sakes."

"I will provide you a rule book to study and then quickly plan your initiation ceremony for 'time is of the essence'."

He handed Elpidio the instruction book along with the prompts for the initiation. He'd use the short version to hurriedly get him installed into the clan. He said, "The entire clan won't be available for your ceremony, and I believe you can understand the reasons as we prepare for war."

"I understand what I pledge makes me a blood brother until death no matter of the number in attendance."

"I believe you get the point. I'll call you with the date and time for the ceremony. It will be soon."

Realizing he was being dismissed, Elpidio set his half empty wine glass down on the bar and left. He'd been hoping for such an entrance into the family and today his wish came true. He'd make a stellar combat ready recruit for he believed in the right to free trade that the mafia provided its members. From his understanding it was a necessity to move your products to the market since the 1800s Italy. The families decided to protect their own when no outside help from the polizia or legal system was available.

David quickly called Gavino, his captain to plan the initiation of Elpidio. They agreed on the three members of the clan to be in attendance. They'd know when he stepped out of line and would deal with it. He'd not need to worry about his allegiance for it would be monitored.

He called Elpidio to tell him the time and place for his ceremony and quickly realized the excitement in his voice.

If he proved to be true to the clan, he had a lofty position for him to undertake to rid himself of the daily operations of the clan. He wanted him to become his underboss. In a few days, he'd learn his capabilities and suitability for the job.

The day before the ceremony he asked the chef to prepare appetizers and toasting beverages for the event. He'd decided on a spot within the compound for the occasion. In hindsight, likely one of the meeting places Donatella used to conduct business. The chef knew it at once when told to plan for the meeting. As a remnant from the old guard, he likely embraced the new activity and code of conduct.

The three top captains in the Mandarino clan and David entered the enclosed courtyard for the initiation of Elpidio Venturi into their family. When Venturi arrived, he was taken to a round table which had a pistol, a dagger, and a small image of a saint placed in the middle prepared for reciting his pledge to the clan. By answering the questions asked, with the first one agreeing to punishment for traitors, until he'd promised to abide by all rules of the society.

One man of honor then took his finger and pricked it with a pin; then Venturi smeared the saint's image with blood while another set fire to the image. Then David spoke the words, "If you betray the Mandarino family, your flesh will burn like this saint", cupping his own hand over the flame as he did so, to prevent the initiate from dropping it.

The ceremony ended with congratulations and a toast to their new blood brother. The appetizers were sampled then the captains left the courtyard to plan for war. David and Venturi walked back to the estate in silence.

The Death of Me

David thought about calling Godwin with the update, but it was unnecessary for he'd followed through on plans to strengthen the guard. Now, he was prepared to give Venturi his assignment. Knowing his strength was hand-to-hand combat he'd be the keeper of the villa not unlike what his assignment had been all along. He'd up his arsenal with a Beretta ARX 160 assault rifle, Spectrum M4 submachine gun, 9 mm pistols, and a choice of knives for short range. The home front would be protected with the weapons and Venturi's basal sense and refined martial arts skills.

Their strategic plan was in place and the wedding day of Simone's daughter, Giulietta was the next day. Angelo was correct when he said, he'd thank him for his forethought of not being invited later. If their plan failed a blood bath for all attendees could be expected. Tomorrow's news would pinpoint Simone as a mobster with unflattering terms. Yet hopefully the Rocco family could come out unscratched.

His cell rang and seeing Lilia's number he answered. In rapid speech, she quickly went to the reason for her call. She feared her boss Di Donato was in bed with the mob. Since her task force with him as head, had been instructed to back off investigation of the Zarrella mafia, she started investigating the unit.

Her saintly boss who feared for her safety was the lead kingpin in law enforcement for the clan. Marco next in line who reluctantly aided with the kidnapping case was next in line. He'd probably gotten the OK from the Zarrella clan to prosecute the Sciarretta family for human trafficking for that was their domain until recently. Without pausing for a breath, she continued.

David listened and every fiber in his being wanted to protect her, but he couldn't with a war coming to his own providence. He said, "Lilia you're in over your head, and they are probably aware you've been profiling them. Go to your grandpa's and lie low for you'll be their next hit."

"You won't help me?"

"No for you'll have no legal recourse when dealing with that family. They have judges and politicians in their pocket. It's a tricky situation."

She was not happy when the conversation ended for, she believed he was her knight in shining armor. Anti-mafia groups had been murdered including special units with magistrates on board to disband the blood-thirsty unit. Lilia had no idea how deep they'd infiltrated the legal system. He hoped she'd take his advice but doubted it. Her naivety could get her murdered, and he'd not be available to protect her.

The clock was ticking down the hours to the nuptials between Giulietta and Adalfieri Ricci. David was at his command console where he had eyes and ears on the strategic attacks against the family's enemies.

A repurposed Italian Trombomcino M-28 grenade launcher welcomed the Zarrella clan on their passage to the big event. A league of their soldiers was left dead, and others disembodied. The next strike would drop the advance team from their mission. This was one down and more to go before the bloody war was over.

The squad attacking from the rear of Simone's property got a surprise counterattack from his militant leaders. They were all dead with no one alive to message the leader of the Zarrella clan about their defeat.

Simone could thank him later by making him capo di tutti capi of the Rocco family for he knew how to protect his own. He'd provide video playbacks of the attacks to convince him if his puffed-up ego couldn't see the merits.

The next attacks by the Zarrella's were taking place. Stupid on their part, for the families were at the wedding they did not crash. Now, they were no smarter than they began. The Mandarino estate and Rocco family was safe for they'd not learned their allegiance to the clan.

He sought out Venturi to tell him the news. His body was conditioned for a fight, and he slowly saw the adrenaline rush recede as they talked. He thanked him for his preparation and told him he may need him for a more personal business assignment.

Now, to curtail Lilia's rash belief that good overcomes evil in the Italian political and legal system to dismember the mafia. It was a fairy tale. The families would always exist to protect their own for they'd learned no outside help from law enforcement was available in Tuscany. And, as strongly as she believed in law and order it wouldn't change a thing. It was the illegal actions of those who chose the path that was the problem.

He didn't see her accepting this premise. She was all about law and order and from what Godwin confided to him she needed to look closer at her own family history. She believed the story her mama spun about her papa's murder.

No wonder she feared Lilia choosing law enforcement. Afraid, she'd learn the truth, and the same thing would happen to her as her father.

Godwin's investigation of her family was an eye-opener. Yet, he doubted Lilia would believe it. Her father was murdered when he did not protect the son of a leader of a clan. He was murdered in prison by a rival gang. They'd promptly ordered a revenge killing.

Her boss Di Donato wasn't the only one on the take. A slew of agents was on the Zarrella's payroll along with judges and influential people in Italy. Their robust economic windfalls from drug smuggling afforded them the best in security at all levels of government, politics, and society.

Probably some of the best warriors in the Zarrella's were killed in their bid to murder the boss of bosses, Angelo Simone. Did he think the defeat was enough for the leader to exile himself to the USA?

No, he'd come back stronger with new recruits for the cause. The drug smuggling business was lucrative and feeding the markets in the US and Europe. They wouldn't stop for their stronghold was a cash cow. Today's fight was won, but it didn't hold promise for ending a war. They'd be back. The question was could he and the Rocco families stop them?

Chapter 50

David had a business to run and thankfully Venturi stepped up to take care of the day-to-day activity of the Mandarino clan. Twenty-four hours a day their estate with grapevines and olive trees needed to be protected. They were supplying additional security for the trucking company taking over Sciarretta's contract to get their products delivered. For their new non-mafia trucking company didn't have the manpower or fear factor to scare hijackers away.

He felt comfortable giving this oversight to Venturi for he was highly organized and deliberate in his job. Like Donatella and Dorian before him, he'd provide a lucrative bonus for his obedience to the brotherhood. Quickly thinking about the villa Luca inherited from his father for his pledge to the family, he understood the reason for its location. He'd build a new safe house in Livorno where their warehouse was located to monitor their cargo boarded onto the container ships. Venturi could use it as needed for business and personal pleasure.

Luca was enjoying meeting family on his father's side he'd never met. All were fishermen with a long and proud history of fishing the Ligurian Sea. He wished his mama knew his father's history or perhaps she did. He'd taken down the watercolor painting from over the hearth and saw her name scribed at the bottom. She painted the landscape a talent unknown to him. His mama had more secrets than a Pandora's box. It was pastime for her to come clean, and he doubted it would happen or perhaps her age would play a role. He was now a grown man, and she didn't have to sugar coat her feelings.

He'd meet her away from the villa close to her home. She agreed. When he arrived, she was sitting at a rustic table in the courtyard at the ristorante. He watched her for a moment before walking over. She was still an attractive woman, and he'd love to see her smile. He greeted her with affection, and she asked, "How's retirement?"

"It's wonderful beyond my wildest dreams, and yours?"

"Life is as expected when you're put out to pasture."

"You have a home and friends, right?"

"Yes, but this wasn't my childhood dream."

Afraid where the conversation was headed but focused on learning about his mama's secrets he continued.

"A hobby might help you relax and make life exciting. Is there anything you'd like to pursue? Classes are available in the city for arts and crafts."

"I studied watercolors when I was growing up in Sicily and enjoyed creating seascapes of our coastline. Perhaps I need to pick up my brushes again."

"Sounds wonderful, hopefully you'll paint a keepsake for me to hang."

Silvana nodded and said, "Perhaps someday you'll invite me to your new home. You're living in Livorno now, correct?"

"Yes, but who told you? I haven't been gone a week."

"Dorian owned a villa on the sea and I figured you inherited it after his death."

He paused for a moment then said, "Oh, and have you been to his villa?"

"Yes, when I was a young woman and first arrived in Tuscany."

Luca wanted to back track the conversation and had no idea how to do it. The logical response would be to invite her to his new home. He sipped his drink and waited for her to continue speaking. The dreamy look on her face said she'd become nostalgic, and he visualized his future going down the drain. She was unhappy about something. Maybe she wanted a different life than the one she'd been living at the estate. He hoped the distress wasn't about problems in her marriage.

He changed the subject and said, "How's papa?"

"Much the same, he's still working at the brewery. He's training new workers in the business preparing for retirement in the future."

What he wanted to learn and was afraid to ask was did she still love his papa? Her happiness was important to him, but it couldn't fathom they're not being together. He said,

"Mama, what's wrong? The unhappiness shows on your face and is unsettling to me. I want to help."

Silvana shook her head as tears rolled down her face. "Mea culpa, I did it to myself. I made decisions when I was young and lived with the consequences of my choices."

"Are you talking about giving birth to me out of wedlock?"

"No, I'm referring to the cover-up and my marrying your papa."

"You don't want to be married to him now?"

"I have no choice for divorce is out of the question. He'd have no place to retire for the manor is my life estate. And I feel like I owe him a home for being a father to my children."

Her shoulders relaxed from carrying the weight of her secret. He said, "Mama, find something in each day that'll make you smile. You can come visit me when you need to get away or go to your home in Sicily for a spell."

She smiled. "Thank you for the invitation. Someday, I'd like to visit for the villa was a special place for us."

Chapter 51

David double-checked to decide if the Zarrella hit sites were clean and led no trail back to the Rocco family. The soldiers used a tractor loader to scoop up their bodies and weapons and dump them into trucks. Then crews drove them to a waste site off their properties. A deep hole dredged from the earth now held the remains from the clan war. His captains assured him they'd left no tracks and the evidence was covered and safe from scrutiny from the polizia stradale.

The rolling landscape was clear for the moment. The Zarrella's were applying balm to their wounds and recruiting zealot soldiers to continue their business. Until the leaders were killed, the fight would continue. He was glad their clan was a ghost to them.

He needed to update Simone about the hit on the day of his daughter's wedding. He'd call and request a meet at one of the locally owned family ristorantes. His response would tell him if the Rocco family or his esteemed position in the commission was more important.

They needed to prepare for the clan would try a feat on Angelo again to learn the leaders of the Rocco family. Simone's security needed tightening and since his identity could be compromised, he'd help for he was a member of the brotherhood.

For now, he'd leave it up to Angelo to step down as Padrino of the Rocco family. Internal conflict within the clan would hinder their preparation for the next visit from the Zarrella's death squad.

Simone agreed to their meeting at a blood brother's ristorante. Simone was already there when he arrived. He was shown into a darkened backroom where he was waiting. After the first greeting, Angelo said, "Let's order lunch before discussing business and enjoy our drinks while it's prepared. Their pasta dishes are some of the best in Tuscany."

David agreed, and along with Angelo placed his order with the smiling server. Simone said, "You said our meet was about life and death, whose?"

"You and your family are the targets."

Angelo's face became contorted and said, "By whom?"

"The Zarrella clan sent a death squad to your daughter's wedding and the Mandarino family interceded in your behalf as blood brothers."

David tapped his cell to play the video he'd downloaded from his computer and handed it to Angelo. Tears filled his eyes as he watched the bloody massacre of those attacking his country home on his daughter's special day. He wiped his now drooling mouth with his handkerchief and said, "Thank you, I thought my security would be enough to keep my family and friends safe."

"Angelo they won't stop until you tell them the names of the Rocco family. They've learned you're the boss of bosses and will torture you until you talk then dissolve your body in sulfuric acid leaving no trace of evidence. Do you have a hiding place until we defeat them? You can still give your soldiers orders from there."

Simone had lost his appetite and when their meal arrived, he shoved it aside knowing it was bad manners to not enjoy the meal. He said, "Yes, of course, I have a hideout for emergencies. But my daughter is now married, and her safety is her husband's responsibility. As members of the Rocco family, they'll join our coup for destroying the Zarrella clan. I'll be your point man to coordinate the attacks for I know each family's strength."

"We can work together. But, for now you need to leave your country estate. Call me when you're settled."

With his head bowed, and his optimo Panama hat partially shielding his face, Angelo left the meeting and hurried to his automobile. David exited through the kitchen with a view of the street to find if he was being tailed. He called and told him to remove the battery and ditch his cell out the car window. He'd understand what that meant. His delay to the meeting worked in his favor for like any other customer he walked in for lunch. Hopefully, no connection could be made back to him.

David returned to the estate to work on new plans to defeat the Zarrella clan. The financial resources were the family's best armor against prosecution for their crimes. Studying the states past attempts for bringing the mafia to justice for heinous crimes; he found only one that produced results. Unfortunately, the creator of the sting was murdered afterwards resulting in anti-mafia protests from the residents of the communities.

The Italian Anti-Mafia Taskforce Lilia was assigned to have the potential to produce comparable results. However, several of the members had already been murdered. With Di Donato and Marcos on the inside along with others from the intelligence community, more hits would likely follow. Their only hope was to strip them of their narcotics smuggling trade and to take over their financial empire. This would require an international initiative with carefully vetted members knowledgeable about shipping, and the tracking of their finances showing payments and receipts for the narcotics and protection rackets.

This would require a secret taskforce to block those on the Zarrella's payroll from involvement. Simone knew the political stamina of the Rocco family and could broker the deal through their members' contacts.

He'd suggest a joint taskforce with the US FBI for billions of dollars were made off the narcotics trade in the states. They would recognize the benefits of halting the flow of drugs to their country and claiming the assets of those responsible for the drug smuggling. Now, the hard part, was selling his idea to a fleeing mob boss. He'd wait until he called voicing his safety.

Chapter 52

Silvana took Luca's suggestions and joined a watercolor class in the city. He was right; it did make her smile again. She had an activity that brought her joy and filled her empty days.

She'd love to paint the picturesque coastline of Palermo Sicily again and feel the warm sunshine on her face. With Luca gone from the estate, and Antonia dead, there was nothing holding her back from traveling, and returning to her birthplace. Her husband, Armo wouldn't mind for he too had been thinking about retirement and visiting the city of his youth, Montalicino, a hilltop community well-known for its delicious bold wines.

Their marriage was never discussed for it was based on a contract. Her mind played tricks on her when wondering what might have been. She made plans to catch the Trenitalia train to Palermo. This time she would stay a month for less time didn't merit the sixteen-hour one-way trip. Armo would understand for she'd been antsy since retiring from the estate's kitchen. And there was only so much cleaning she could do in their home with her restless energy.

She packed her bags and stuffed a handful of banknotes inside from the hidden compartment holding the treasures of her youth and the euros Dorian gifted her. She'd tell Armo tonight about her trip over a glass of wine after she served him *Penne Alla Bettola* with spicy tomato-cream sauce one of his favorite Tuscan dishes. Afterwards, he'd smile and say, enjoy your stay.

The train ride provided a diversion from the flashbacks playing in her head. The scenery was breath-taking, as she relaxed against the seat, and floated to another place in time. As a child she was pampered, and had numerous friends all a part of her father's mafia family.

After her father's murder, her mother insisted she and her brother leave Sicily. They left with nothing much more than the clothes on their backs. Lothario was going with her to the Mandarino estate where he'd secured her a job through his contact in the city.

The next day when he left to join a northern clan was one of the worst days of her life. She was alone and helpless for after Lothario left, the guest suite wouldn't be available to her as an employee on the estate. Dorian, the estate's manager recognized her hopelessness and escorted her to staff housing.

With little to unpack, she was relieved the manor was furnished with the necessities. She thanked him for the main house was busy with the boss, Donatella issuing orders to the staff. She was glad to have her own space away from the loud banter.

Her new job was in the kitchen for she had no skills for other estate employment. Assigned as dishwasher, she was determined to learn the culinary arts, so she could advance to a cook. The heavy pots and oversized pans were difficult to scrub, and the head chef warned the staff to not interfere with her work. As time went by, she developed the muscles and stamina to stay in tune with the kitchen's workflow.

Dorian checked on her periodically to assess here progress. After working for nearly a year and being promoted to cook, he asked if she'd like to visit the seacoast again. Fearful he meant returning to Sicily, she hesitated. Seeing tears fill her eyes, he'd said, "I thought you'd like to visit my villa in Livorno on the Ligurian Sea."

She felt like leaping with joy for it had been a long time since the soft ocean breeze brushed against her face. The sounds of seagulls making a peacock-like wail, a mew, as they flew in and out of the waves feeding on the abundant sea life were fascinating to watch.

This is where their romantic adventure began. They often returned on her days off from the kitchen. When she became pregnant with Luca, she expected a marriage proposal from him. She was shocked and hurt at his betrayal and solution to her unexpected pregnancy.

Their relationship was never the same again although she returned to the villa at his request. When learning the reason for the invitation, she wanted to scream. She didn't know whether his idea was more for his protection or hers.

Apparently, he planned to hide his paternity but didn't want her accosted by the rumors of being an unwed mother. The stigma would burn a scarlet letter on her forehead in their world. She dreaded that prospect.

Dorian proposed she marries Armo Marino from Montalicino. He'd contracted with him for a lead job in the brewery and to become her husband and father to his child. She couldn't stop crying. Her youthful expectations of marriage were now a fallacy. He embraced her and said, "I'll always be your protector, but you must fulfill this contract for the both of us."

When she opened her eyes, the train was approaching Palermo, her stop. She hoped on this visit she could put Dorian in the past where he belonged. And, let go of the shame and humiliation from living a lie since she'd turned eighteen.

She'd packed light with just one carry-on for she had left clothes from her previous visit. She wanted to skip to the villa she once called home. After closing the door, she double-checked for vandalism in her absence and once assured everything was fine settled in with a nice glass of local wine from the bar.

Her rental agent, Marabella had developed a respectable listing of clients who visited and rented the villa during the season. The villa was kept maintained, and spotless on her arrival. She was glad to have someone there to watch over her inheritance for she rarely returned. There had been no mention of her play to make a fast commission with Ghio. She wondered who her latest lover was since the Sicilian boss was murdered by a rival gang.

She'd squirreled the income away saving for a rainy day. It had come in handy after her forced retirement and no longer receiving a paycheck. Yesterday, was the first time she'd touched the banknotes Dorian left her and hoped the last time. An investment into something that would supply a profit made sense; otherwise, it could collect dust in her hiding place.

Realizing it was getting late; she showered and dressed for an evening overlooking the sea at the local's favorite ristorante. Tomorrow she'd go to the market and buy fresh food. The short brisk walk was easily a daily outing.

On her last visit she'd searched faces hoping to recognize someone from her past. She wondered how they'd react to seeing her now and if the traitor stigma was still clued to the family name like the blood-sucking leech, Amabile Ghio, her father's boss intended.

The 1969 Ferrari 365 GTS was a treat to drive with its top down. The wind whipped through the sports car ruffling the scarf holding her hair in place. Shifting the gears, she took the curves with confidence and smiled at her newfound freedom.

She arrived at the seaside ristorante and pulled the soft top in place for the drive home. Entering the popular seaside ristorante, she smiled while scanning faces for friends from her past. The host took her to the table she'd reserved earlier. In minutes, a server arrived to take her drink order and appetizer choice. She ordered and relaxed while taking in the scenic beauty of the seascape in front of her. Just as she was preparing to order her secondi course, Alessio Volta appeared at her table. He said, "May I join you for your evening meal?"

Caught unaware of his presence, she said, "Yes, of course."

He spoke to the server and said, "Give us a few minutes while we decide on our entrée selection and ordered a glass of wine."

Volta said, "Silvana, I had no idea you were in Palermo. When did you arrive?"

"I arrived today for a short vacation."

"I see. I wish you'd called to tell me you're in the city for I'd make special plans for us during your stay."

"That would be unnecessary for I know my way around the city and treasure my time alone to paint the timeless seacoast."

"Of course, you should enjoy your vacation as you like. I just thought we could get to know one another better. You're a beautiful woman and I'd like to introduce you to my family. The sins of your father and brother's past will never be mentioned. You'd be under my protection as the new Padrino of the Sicilian commission."

She'd had enough of mob families, first her own then Dorian's. She sensed there was more he wasn't saying, and wanted distance from him and his family of made-men. Carefully, wording her response, she said, "Alessio, I'll be here only a fleeting time and don't want to interfere with your family's plans. Perhaps, on my next visit we can catch up and get to know one another better."

He frowned then nodded in agreement before saying, "I'd not want to intrude on your vacation, and perhaps you're right, next time."

They ate their meal in silence at loss for words to carry on a conversation. He quickly picked up the check and escorted her to her Ferrari before kissing her on the cheek and saying goodnight.

She had no idea what was going on but fear from the deepest recesses of her mind propelled her into action. She cranked her car and sped home to think about the proposal he made to initiative her into his Sicilian family. What as his wife or lover certainly not a friend from the past?

Chapter 53

If you'd told this kinky-coiled haired boy growing up in Atlanta with a successful mother who dared anyone to speak of his ethnicity, he'd be in Italy today running an empire and a mob family, he'd laughed. But this was his life.

Unknowingly she'd trained him for what would become his destiny with the best education and training to run her Italian family's empire. A secret kept from her by her father at the bidding of his mother, Donatella the godmother of the family, who believed in her fate and later Godwin her partner.

The family had always shielded his mother from a distance and allowed her to choose her legal fights as a top attorney in Atlanta. Donatella was proud of her as she took down human trafficking rings the family abhorred. It was filthy business and went against everything their clan stood for.

It wasn't until she'd exhausted all means to take down corrupt rivals that her friend Captain Thomason garnered her attention, and she agreed to an exit plan. Her father's family owned an estate in Tuscany that was safe to retreat to under an alias. She chose the name Gabrielle D'Agostino and using her new name became a relative to Sydney Jones.

He wanted to protect his mama at all costs. And, keeping himself safe from harm would be the best feat ever. For he had no doubt that Godwin would protect Gabby and had the tech company to continue updating security measures surrounding her.

The loss and ability to reunite with her son was what kept her going after she suffered extensive injury from a car-bombing. Making him an orphan with no choice but to move to their island home from Atlanta, in his former nanny's care where he made friends and continued his schooling.

He finally figured it out years later when she returned to the island after recovering in Tuscany. Their first Christmas was shared with a captain from the Georgia Federal Bureau of Investigations. She'd said they'd met once when she was visiting her cousin, Sydney. The rapport between them said differently.

Old friends would be a better description. His visit was his first sign he'd missed something important about Gabby. It wasn't until several years later he discovered the truth. Within a week after Godwin his mentor and friend on the island, made a shocking discovery. He learned their secret and confronted them both, and they owned up to the truth behind their secrecy. Hurt that he'd not known what happened to his mother, he understood enemies were constantly at their gates and agreed to never call them mother and father again.

He was terrified for her to learn he'd been murdered by a rival clan. She'd believe she'd brought it upon her only son and heir after years of protecting him from her own fall outs for making the world a better place. It wouldn't happen. For whatever it took to take charge of the Rocco family and bring peace to their Tuscany region, he'd do it.

He believed the tenets he pledged for his affiliation into the family, to do no harm and above all else live as honorable men. The strikes he'd initiated where the difference between life and death. He had no regrets for the actions he took to protect his blood brothers and the Mandarino estate to the bitter bloody end.

Now, he needed to get an ole school gentleman who'd never seen much action in the family to step aside. Angelo had lived the high life for years since Donatella's death reaping monies from the protection the clan offered to those in need. He didn't want to investigate how that came about, for all he wanted was for the Rocco family to concentrate on protecting their own.

Angelo and his family would've been murdered if not for his and Godwin's eavesdropping, surveillance, and attack on his enemies. He'd better deliver the names of political contacts in the family to make the new task force a reality.

He could see he was hanging on by threads, for he knew the families better than him. But, afterward, the older man should move over and initiate him as the godfather for his days of ruling the empire were over. He had no idea how to strategize against their enemies and didn't have the soldiers except for blood brothers to back him up. He'd been coasting on his good fortune as boss of bosses. The new world of entrepreneurs in the Italian families was something he wasn't prepared for.

And, like him he wanted to go back to when there was peace between clans, and everyone protected their products and services. But the narcotics trade changed everything. The drug smuggling clan in the north was proud of their anonymity and Sciarretta from their clan beamed a light on their enterprise with his rogue human trafficking deals. There was no turning back. One family in their clan who put profit before brotherhood sealed their fate. It was now death to the finish to rid themselves of this purge on their family.

Chapter 54

Luca was enjoying the salty life, fishing when he wanted and making friends at his uncle's ristorante. He'd come to realize a casual nod from Mezzeo meant the bloke was OK to befriend. He still wanted to meet and romance a woman. And, for that Mezzeo couldn't or wouldn't help.

He only wanted a woman to share a dinner with and you'd think his uncle could help. Numerous members of his father's family lived along the shore, and he didn't want to date a cousin again. But surely, they had friends.

On his own and thinking about his mama, he decided to invite her to his seaside villa knowing she'd probably never want to leave. But, what the heck, he'd not met the first female, not related, to date. Maybe she might help.

When she answered her exuberance from hearing from him was heartfelt. He said, "Mama why don't you come and visit me in Livorno for a few days? Pack your bags and I'll come and get you."

"I'd love to visit the coast. But I'll drive myself down."

Luca thought, since when did she drive or own an automobile? But it put it to rest, and said, "I look forward to your visit. Drive safely!"

Was this another family secret filled with mystery and intrigue? He decided fresh fish would be a nice welcome lunch for when she arrived. He launched the cabin-cruiser and motored to one of the coordinates in Dorian's fishing journal to cast out his lines. After catching a couple of sea bass, he returned to the villa to clean and prepare them for their lunch.

His mama arrived in a sleek vintage Ferrari, and he welcomed her into his new home. She brought homemade bread and his favorite jam for their snacks. He couldn't wait to learn about the sports car. He wasn't even aware she had a driver's license. His papa always drove when they went into town. He'd let his inquiry rest for they had time to discuss her new ride later.

Silvana couldn't believe it when Luca called. She'd missed him dearly for they'd talked every day and enjoyed a meal together at least once a week. His invitation to visit made her glad she'd decided to drive the sports car back to the estate. Maybe she'd visit more often with his not having to drive her back and forth.

Her husband, Armo was surprised when she returned home driving her mama's car. She explained the Ferrari was garaged for years, and she decided it was time to use it. He never learned about her family's history, and she wanted to keep it that way. He said, "Silvana, we need to talk about our future."

Surprised, she said, "Sure. What do you want to discuss?"

She went to the kitchen and poured two glasses of wine and returned to where he was sitting in the living room and handed him a drink.

He said, "I've put in my papers to retire by the end of the month. I plan to return to my family home in Montalicino. I've fulfilled my marriage contract to you. I've given you my name, and now Antonia is dead, and Luca has made a life for himself. While you were vacationing in Palermo, I had the papers drawn up to dissolve our marriage. So, we'll both be free to live life on our own terms."

Silvana was blindsided for she never suspected he craved his freedom. Since her early retirement, she'd been especially gloomy, feeling like she had to escape to breathe. Armo must have felt the same way for he planned his escape while she was away. She said, "Perhaps, it is time we split for you have honored the contract."

He handed her the papers and a pen then said, "Sign where marked and I'll get them processed immediately."

She did as ask, and handed him the signed divorce decree. Placing the documents back into the package, he smiled and said, "I wish you nothing but happiness in the future."

Silvana smiled and said, "I hope your retirement years are filled with love, peace, and joy."

He raised his glass to hers in a toast to their new lives. Then, said, "Goodnight," and turned and went to his bedroom.

She refilled her wine glass and went to the front porch to sit thanking her lucky stars she'd decided to drive the Ferrari home. If not, she'd been without transportation for his was the only car they owned.

On the drive home, she decided it was time to be open with Luca about her family history. There was something sinister in the way Alessio acted when she refused his offer to join his family. To protect her son, she needed to share the horrors of her father's business. For what if something happened to her? He'd be a target if someone came after the family with murderous intentions.

Luca would be surprised that she and Armo were getting divorced. She'd shared the lack of romance made her unhappy, but marriage was forever in their Italian community. The thought probably never crossed his mind.

She felt guilty for invading his happy life with news that no mama would want to share with her son. Yet, he was a grown man now and deserved to learn the truth.

For tonight, she'd enjoy being with her son. They'd have a chance to talk before she left to return home.

They enjoyed the fresh sea bass while watching boats come and go like moving dots on the ocean. Luca said, "Mama how would you like to dine at the Ristorante Del Sole this evening? I've made friends with Dorian's family and my uncle owns it."

Silvana's face blushed, and she said, "I'd love to sample the local cuisine and meet your new family."

Luca took her for a cruise along the oceanfront pointing out historical sites, and glamorous looking villas perched above the sea. By the time they returned, it was time to get dressed for dinner.

When Silvana walked out of her bedroom suite, he was shocked. She was even more beautiful dressed in a colorful floral dress that complimented her dark olive skin complexion. And somehow, she looked happier than their earlier meeting in Florence. Maybe she took his advice and found something to make her happy every day.

Luca drove them the short distance to the Ristorante Del Sole and opened the car door for his mama. Every man there would stare at her. In Italy, a woman was known to grow more beautiful as she aged and tonight his mama radiated confidence. He couldn't wait to introduce her to his uncle Celso.

The place was already getting packed but when the hostess saw them enter, she quickly escorted them to a table. His uncle was behind the bar with his mouth dropped wide open googling his mama. In a matter of minutes, he'd be at their table asking questions.

The server took their drink and appetizer orders and returned to the kitchen. Celso was speaking to one of his bartenders, and then came across the room to their table. He introduced his mama, and waited for their greeting.

Celso said, "I don't believe my eyes. Silvana it's a pleasure to see you again. I'd wondered when Luca would invite you to the coast."

Luca coughed then sputtered, "You two have met?"

"Yes, a lifetime ago," said Silvana. "Celso, I'm glad your dream of owning a ristorante came true for you."

"This would've never happened if Dorian hadn't partnered with me. Life has been good to me, and I hope the same is true for you."

"Every day has its own sweet fragrance like lilies in a garden."

"I hope we'll have a chance to catch up during your visit with Luca. The ristorante keeps me hopping, but I'll make time for you."

Celso left their table smiling shaking his head in disbelief. Luca said, "Mama you could've told me you've met Dorian's kin folks."

"I wasn't expecting to meet anyone tonight. The few family member I met years ago, are likely dead or fisherman on the Ligurian Sea. This was a treat to reconnect with an old acquaintance."

His mother was full of surprises. He wondered what the next insight would be. There was an undeniable chemistry between Celso and his mama. The sparks were popping, and he wondered if he should chaperone their meeting for his papa's sake.

Later that evening, his mama explained her family history and the breakup of her marriage. She'd confided the secret earlier about their marriage agreement, that part didn't surprise him. But, after all the years together to call it quits, was a shocker. He wondered if Armo wanted to continue a relationship with him. The thought saddened him for he'd been always his papa.

Luca said, "Since you're no longer working at the Mandarino estate, what do you think about moving here? You'd be near me, and the manor house will be empty when papa retires and leaves."

"Thanks, Luca. Your privacy is important to you so if I move here, I'll buy a small villa nearby. I have my family's home in Palermo I can sell to make the purchase. Former renters from the US have shown interest in owning it. Perhaps, they'll be ready to buy now."

"I'd feel better knowing you're not alone miles away from me. We'll look at some properties before you leave, and you can contact your real estate agent about securing a buyer."

He lifted his glass and said, "Great things are coming our way. You just wait and see."

Chapter 55

Angelo was working harder as godfather than he had in years. The new boss of the Mandarino family was putting him through the paces to protect the family from the Zarrella clan. He had no idea the size of their operation, but he was aware he'd let his own family slide into disarray. They'd been peace between the clans for years, and he'd slowly stopped recruiting new soldiers for it was money he didn't have to pay out for services.

After talking with clan members politically positioned, they offered their help to initiate interest in forming an international multi-task force. They swore allegiance for whatever it took to end the Zarrella clan's hold over their businesses and welfare.

The key would be the vetting of the members for the secret task force. For others had failed for the Zarrella's had politicians, police, and federal agents on their payroll. The leader of their political unit wanted names of trusted magistrates, and agents to give for inclusion. Angelo promised he'd have names by the end of the day after talking with David.

Simone called with news of the clan's support, and David supplied a list of Italian counterparts to the USA's FBI hoping they'd be equally judicious in their selection process. He'd added Lilia's name to the list for this would be her opportunity to make the arrests she'd been duped out of by her boss. Her involvement would also be a way he could track their success whether she offered the info willingly or from tracking her cell.

In months, the international task-force was officially inaugurated into a clandestine unit to fight organized crime. They had plans for each step leading to incarceration for crimes committed, against the state. A special prison unit, a large underground bunker to house the mafia prisoners would soon be under construction along with a court room for hearing the cases. Knowing the ferocity of the crime family, added measures including protection from incoming missiles was engineered into the design.

A member of the Rocco family received the bid on the construction for they'd been instrumental in the secret founding of the unit. The leader involved was a no-nonsense businessperson with years of experience in the contracting business. He deserved the building contract for his political acumen led to the agreement between the US and Italy.

Now, David waited anxious for the investigations to begin and members of the Zarrella clan to be arrested. There were billions of euros involved in their cocaine trade. They were financially more powerful than the Deutsche Bank with their cash reserves. The slush fund financed their protection to expand into new markets.

If the new unit could track the money, they'd end their take-over of law enforcement and the legal system. He expected Lilia's boss and co-worker Marco to be one of the first arrests. As they sifted through the agents, they'd find more on the take from the former drug task force.

Until the Zarrella's leaders were behind bars, he'd not chance a meeting with Lilia. He wanted to continue training her in martial arts for her new duties. But her safety came first for he was uncertain if the Zarrella's had discovered who sabotaged their attack on Simone. The bloody battle would be one they'd remember. He didn't want enemies at his gates with her present.

Lilia received a call from the head of an international multi-task force for organized crime. She listened intently as the magistrate asked her to meet him at his office and to tell no one where she was headed. Nearing lunchtime, she slipped out of the office and walked over to his office. She was at once taken to his chambers and briefed on her assignment with the task-force. Finally, she'd get her seat at the table to being down the criminal element that roamed their streets plying their trade.

Judge De Rossi said, "Lilia we're proud to have you join us and want you to profile the leaders of the clan as new information is made available. When arrests are made you will be in the trenches with the other agents. Are you up for this?"

"Yes, sir, I've been training in weaponry, combat strategies, and martial arts. I will be ready when we make arrests. However, don't you agree my involvement shouldn't be known until after my boss and all co-workers are arrested? I fear they'll suspect me and end my involvement prematurely."

"You're right. Continue investigating those in your unit and coordinate your findings with me personally."

"Yes, sir, I'll be in touch."

Lilia's thoughts quickly went to David for she suspected he could track down the information she was missing. Her boss was looking over her shoulders more lately and changing her assignments. Now, she was investigating the Sicilian family when the Zarrella's were at their front door.

Their office had no authority in Palermo, and she failed to understand her boss's interest. When she began her investigation the Sicilian secret society hadn't officially met since 1993. Then suddenly a cell from the Zarrella clan hit them killing the boss of bosses and his soldiers proclaiming themselves as the new Sicilian family. They were expanding their narcotics distribution into a new region.

She'd shared her finding with her boss, and he thanked her and left for the day. Without feedback, she was none the wiser about his involvement. The best guess would be he was using her profiling and investigation to up his take from the Zarrella's to verify their infiltration of regions.

The week had sped by and now her coworkers were leaving for their usual Friday celebration at a local bar. She waited until the last agent left before logging into the agency's website and downloading work assignments for her co-workers. She copied the files onto a flash drive to review later at home. Then cleared her browsing history from the computer and logged out. Spying her handbag nearby she slipped the information in, and zipped it closed and left for the weekend.

When she arrived at her apartment, she poured a glass of Acqua Minerale San Benedetto and inserted the flash drive into her laptop. She was cross-referencing her co-workers' assignments against known holding cells of the clan, their refineries, and the harbor in Livorno. Were they supplying protection for illegal activity and if so, how did they get paid?

She made notes on a spread sheet of the locations they visited. She found five agents assigned to key clan strongholds. After summarizing the data, she then emailed the file to Judge De Rossi for the investigative team of the task-force.

The goal was to turn one of the suspects into an informant in return for a lighter sentence. She thought her boss, Di Donato, would be ideal for he had higher rank and access to the bosses. He was a leader in their protection ring, how much further it went she didn't know. She'd leave that to the interrogators to discover.

She closed her laptop and pleased with her resourcefulness relaxed and readied for bed. The weekend would be ideal for down-time from her hectic schedule of working with two opposing task forces.

Lately, David had become her last thought before going to sleep. She wished he'd call her. But she suspected her last outburst still haunted him. When the Zarrella's were arrested she'd offer an apology and ask for what was now a third chance for friendship since they'd met.

Chapter 56

Luca and his mama were enjoying their seaside adventures. He was finally feeling hopeful about meeting a woman to romance. People gravitated toward his mama, and knowing her she'd play match-maker to introduce her son to a suitable Italian woman.

They viewed villas for sale along the coast with his mama becoming excited about a small cottage nestled into the rocky seacoast. She'd called her real estate agent in Palermo and instructed her to sale the family's villa. And she quickly responded with an offer from an American couple who had rented the villa earlier in the year.

After their earlier attempt to buy the property failed, they offered full asking price. His mama accepted the terms, and a quick cash closing date was set. The real estate lady was expressing the documents to the estate in Florence for her signature. On return the funds would be wired into her Florence bank account.

He went with his mama to the real estate office to make an offer on the seaside cottage. They'd wait for the seller to accept or make a counteroffer. Within hours the owner responded accepting the offer. They celebrated with a toast to her home ownership on the Ligurian Sea on an arm of the Mediterranean.

She'd delayed her return to Florence until his papa vacated their manor house. They'd already said their goodbyes, and she preferred to keep a distance. Tonight, would be her last night until she returned to claim ownership of her new cottage by the sea. He'd rented a truck to help her move for her sports car wouldn't carry much more than an overnight bag.

Silvana was ecstatic about the possibilities in her future. She'd just purchased the first home of her own close enough to Luca to stay in touch. Her life was over at the estate and her childhood home was just that, a memory from the past.

Tomorrow she'd return to the estate and sign the real estate contract to sell her family home and express the documents back to Marabella, her agent. The funds would be then wired into her bank account where she could then send the money to the agent in Livorno to complete the closing on her new home.

She'd carefully planned her exit for if Alessio should try to find her he'd not know to look in Livorno. Her tracks would be covered after saying goodbye to her former boss, David and asking him not to divulge her location if someone should inquire. If anyone would understand, it'd be him.

When she arrived home Armo had already packed and left for Montalicino. Looking around she noticed he'd not left a goodbye note with a forwarding address. Luca would be disappointed that he'd not wanted to stay in touch. She quickly checked her hiding place where she'd stashed the gift from Dorian and kept her family heirlooms. Her treasure trove was untouched.

There wasn't much packing to do for the manor was fully furnished when she arrived. She quickly tossed belongings she'd not want in her new cottage. She packed her personal keepsakes into the boxes the chef had provided from the kitchen. Going through her clothes closet, she culled items she'd never wear again including her chef wear.

When Luca arrived with a small moving truck, they'd not be much to load. She gathered her personal items along with the brief case full of euros, to carry in her car.

She walked the landscaped path to the back entrance into the kitchen for the appointment she had with David. He met her in the main hall. She thanked him for the opportunity to serve the family and thanked him personally for giving her closure about Dorian. He nodded his head, and said, "God's speed. I wish you the best life has to offer. You deserve it."

Tears came to her eyes, and he reached over and hugged her. "Goodbye, and stay safe," she said.

When she returned to the manor, Luca was backing the moving truck up to the door. Along with him, they quickly loaded the truck and in no time, she'd packed her overnight case and Dorian's satchel into her sports car, and they were leaving the estate. She didn't look in the rear-view mirror.

In less than an hour, they were pulling up to her seaside cottage and unloading her meager possessions. The cottage came with luxury furnishings as part of the sales agreement. On the bar was a bottle of Bruno Giacosa Barolo Falletto 2017 and a note from the earlier owner that said "Auguri nella tua nuova casa" best wishes in your new home.

She looked around the cottage for a hiding place to store the leather bag and family jewelry she'd inherited from her mama and never worn. The fireplace with its sea themed metal screen looked like a good hiding place.

She pulled aside the covering and noted there was a drawer under the hearth covered with a Mediterranean design. Curious, she opened it and inside was a storage space the bag and keepsakes would fit into. Inserting them, she closed the drawer and set the screen in place.

With a sigh, she hoped her hiding place was safe for the euros stashed were from the leftover proceeds from the sale of her family home in Palermo and the banknotes Dorian left her. She'd cleaned out her bank account in Florence and closed it after wiring the funds for the purchase of her cottage.

Luca had changed the locks after the closing, so she'd feel safe after moving in. Later, she'd open a bank account in Livorno to stash some of her monies. But not all, for she'd learned cash on hand came in handy in case of emergencies.

Luca helped store away the boxes for she could go through them when she had more time. The rental truck needed to be returned, and she handed Luca banknotes to pay the fee. He looked surprised then smiled and said, "No, mama this one is on me" and handed her back the euros.

She followed him to the rental truck center and afterwards they stopped in at the Ristorante Del Sole to celebrate. Celso joined them at their table and made a toast to her new life by the sea. After enjoying a succulent dinner, she dropped off Luca at his villa and traveled the short distance to her new cottage. She unlocked the door and with a smile said to the empty walls, "Finally, my very own home by the sea."

Relaxing looking out the oversized windows, and sipping a glass of chardonnay, she wondered how much of your life is based on fate or if all of us were free-falling until we landed in our place in the world.

Chapter 57

Lilia held her breath as members of her task force were arrested for their protection racket and kick-backs from organized crime. Within days her office was abolished, and she began collaborating with a new unit forged from the international multi-task force.

The new anti-mafia group, the Carabinieri (hunters) for their military like methods for finding and arresting leaders of the mafia families. Geared with bullet-proof vests, goggles for night vision, machine guns, and helicopters for tight spaces, they answered to the anti-mafia chief prosecutor, the head of the Anti-mafia Investigative Directorate.

Her boss, Di Donato was one of the first arrested and within three months was under house arrest due to his being allergic to beans. She wasn't surprised for his political influence ran deep and he feared his new prison mates would retaliate since he didn't protect them from landing in neighboring cells.

In return for his trumped-up freedom, he gave names and the locations of the hidden bunkers of the Zarrella clan leaders. His life was over regardless of his legal course of action. Whether he spent years behind bars after his trial, or was popped in his home, his life had taken a path with no U-turn.

Marco her co-worker didn't fare as well in the concrete prison dome. He would spend the most part of his life behind bars. And, if the recent photos were an indicator, he was not making friends easily.

The mafia trials were making headline news and residents were cautiously optimistic that their cities were being returned to them. The problem was a new breed of gangs was sprouting up throughout their region. The cities were ripe for takeover from opposing clans or rift rats looking for new strongholds and a fast payoff.

Her job was to continue profiling and investigating prime targets for capture. She itched for a chance to collaborate with the arresting officers, but her commander didn't believe she was ready for the grueling maneuvers necessary for the take-downs.

Spending her off-hours at the firing range she'd became an excellent shooter for moving and stationery targets. Other aspects of training for the missions were rappelling from a hovering helicopter, and it didn't appear that difficult. She'd already studied military grade videos for helicopter rope suspension techniques. Given the chance, training maneuvers with the team would be the tell-all.

Her hand-to-hand combat needed work and David was right martial arts were the equalizer for her petite size. Now, if she could convince him to train her again, she'd be prepared to take her spot on the elite search and seize team.

She was ready to do what it took to make things right between them including groveling for her earlier unkind remarks. She understood now, taking down the mafia wasn't a one or two-person sting. He was right and the commission was the source for penetrating their chiefdom to keep them from regenerating in their cities.

David was watching the news as another leader of a cell of the Zarrella clan was arrested. He shook his head for the family had more cells in Italy, and abroad. They'd multiplied like rabbits infiltrating every aspect of life from pizzerias to cement companies. The broadcaster noted they'd been nearly four hundred arrests of mafia associates stemming from the international multi-task forces joint venture. The prisoners were waiting for their court date in the concrete dome prison. He was certain the news would be promising to Italians longing for a peaceful country.

He thought about Lilia and her fierce determination to be a part of the exclusive team responsible for their capture. With a sizeable number of the Zarrella's behind bars, he felt safer in contacting her. But should he?

They were star-crossed with his inherited family connections the opposite of her ambitious anti-mafia stand. His romantic tendencies toward her needed to stop for both their sakes. Yet, when he thought about her propensity to gravitate toward dangerous situations, he wanted to protect her.

He wouldn't make the first move, but if she contacted him, he'd restart her martial arts training at the estate. She needed to know how to protect herself and take-down the enemy. It wouldn't hurt to offer training to others on the estate at the same time and it would give her partners to spare with besides he and Venturi.

The young adults on the grounds needed to know how to protect themselves. And, learning the arts would help with focus and self-discipline, a life-long skill. He'd build a dojo outside the parameters of the main house to keep entry into his sanctuary at a minimum. He'd assign Venturi the project for he grew up learning from the best and could head the design and construction of their studio.

Lilia tried once again to make the A-team and was turned down because she didn't have the training suitable for an elite force. The commander commended her on the job she was doing and told her to keep up the excellent work. Even with his accolades she left the office feeling dejected and unsatisfied with her work performance.

Driving straight home she thought about her options. Sure, she'd made higher rank than any other female in the organization, but their goals were much different. After completing her training, she expected equal opportunities for career advancement, including elite forces.

On entering her apartment, she went to the kitchen and uncorked the chardonnay and poured it into a wine glass. Relaxing on the sofa, she sipped her wine while contemplating calling David. After a couple more glasses, she decided what the heck, and finding his name on her contact list, pressed the call button and waited for him to answer.

"Ciao Bello," he said.

She giggled for the wine was already having a relaxing effect and said, "How are you?"

David thought she's a little tipsy and eased into the conversation. "Staying busy with the business, and you?"

"I just got passed over for a promotion, for the second time and could use your help to prepare for the next test."

David was shaking his head and glad she couldn't see his reactions. "What can I do?"

"I need to get combat ready and you were right, martial arts will help me win against men stronger than me. Also, if you've got a helicopter, I can practice rappelling out of would be a bonus."

Even after refilling her wine glass, she realized the impossible scenario she played out for him and started laughing.

David said, "If you'll call me back tomorrow, we'll talk about your martial arts training here at the estate."

"Oh, thank you, you have no idea how much this means to me."

She smiled then remembered she'd forgotten to apologize for her harsh words on their last call as she'd intended. When the call ended, David realized being a part of the anti-mafia force meant a lot to her. The downside was he could be training her for an attack on the Rocco family himself included. The sage advice from the Sicilian godfather Corleone applied "keep your friends close, but your enemies' closer" came to mind.

Chapter 58

Silvana was enjoying the freedom of living on the coast in Livorno. Comparing her homecoming in Palermo just three months ago, it was decisively superior. She and Celso had picked up the friendship enjoyed when Dorian introduced him years ago. They both shared a love for him in their own unique way. She, for he was her first love and the father of her son, for him someone who made his dreams come true.

Luca was in-and-out of her seaside cottage sharing the latest on his dating life since she'd introduced him to some young women she'd met in her arts and yoga classes. She'd begin painting again and a few of her works were now for sale in the local art gallery. The owner said they were among some of her bestsellers to tourist wanting to take a piece of their coast home.

Celso and she were close to becoming romantically involved and if not for Luca, they'd probably already crossed the line. She didn't want Luca to think she was a loose woman. He'd be forgiving if he was aware of the truth. Twenty-two years had passed since having a sexual relationship with his papa. A romance with Celso was her next step.

She'd still not figured out the reason for Armo's rejection that made her feel ugly and unwanted as a sexual partner. She suspected it was the marriage for contract behind his strict code of conduct. There were only sexually active a month in the entire years of marriage. And, when she became pregnant with Antonia their sex life ended. He wouldn't discuss it, and they formed a compatible union to raise Luca and Antonia for divorce wasn't in her catholic upbringing or a part of the contract she'd signed.

She remembered how shocked Dorian was when he found out she was carrying Armo's baby. What did he expect? He was the one that pushed her into another man's arms. Yet, he was tender and gave her time off with pay weeks before and after she was born. In hindsight with a different point of reference, she realized there was something she didn't know about Armo that was a secret only he and Dorian shared.

Celso's ristorante was booming, and his sous chef quit at the height of the season. While he was taking applications to fill the job, he asked if she'd mind filling in for, she'd worked in the estate's kitchen for years. Knowing she'd tossed her chef wear before leaving the estate, she didn't have a uniform to wear. Celso said, "Wear black pants, white shirt, and non-slip shoes, and I'll have a chef's jacket with our logo hanging in the storage room at the restaurant."

She agreed and drove to the nearest store to find chef shoes. She didn't want to slip and fall to injure herself when she was living her best life now. Finding the perfect fit, she went home to dress for the evening rush.

The excitement in the kitchen brought back memories to when the estate was popping with dinner parties during Donatella's rein. She realized her knife skills for prepping the fruit, produce, and protein was as sharp as ever. She smiled for Celso would be proud his diners would be served prompt with delicious food.

After her shift, Celso came to the kitchen and thanked her for stepping up and saving their arse during the nightly rush. He asked, "How would you like working through the tourist season?"

She smiled and said, "Feels good to slice and dice again. I'll take you up on that offer."

She left the restaurant and went home to relax thinking maybe she had two gifts, one in the kitchen and another swirling a paint brush.

The next day she arrived at her scheduled time and went through the back door to the kitchen to begin her daily prep list for the lunch bunch and evening dining customers. She could sense Celso's presence in the dining room. She overheard him talking to Sicilian men about their buying the Ristorante Del Sole. They were making an offer to buy the land and business giving him freedom to retire. She listened intently and realized the voice behind the pitch was Alessio

Volta, and she felt faint. Was he tracking her, or was he expanding his drug cartel into the city of Livorno?

Either way, she saw it as his creating a foothold into the place she now called home. She needed to talk to Celso at once, and keep him from making a decision that could forever impact her life, Lucas, and the city of Livorno. Celso was ready to retire but this wasn't the offer he needed to accept. But would he listen to her?

Chapter 59

Lilia drank a café latte regretting her impromptu call to David the evening before. She had to make things right, so he wouldn't believe her ambition was crazy, and she was prone to overindulging with alcohol when under stress.

She nibbled on some fresh bread covered with her favorite spread and thought about her options. If it was anyone else, she'd get in her Fiat and drive to their residence to sort things out face-to-face, but she didn't think she'd gain entrance through his heavily guarded gate without an appointment. When she sobered more and relaxed a bit on the weekend, she'd decide the conversation she needed to have with David. For now, she'd cuddle with a soft blanket and go back to sleep.

David and Venturi were going over the plans for the dojo and when he signed off, the construction would begin with contractors from the Rocco family. The project was small but meaningful to him. The building would be a place where those living on the estate could train their bodies for defense and their minds for clarity and self-discipline.

Living under the shadow of a potential hit from the Zarrella clan, the contractor pulled the men needed from other construction sites to speed-up the project. In no time, they were ready to open the doors for the first time. He decided it merited a grand-opening to make its presence known to all the workers on the estate. He asked Venturi to work with marketing to welcome estate workers and their families to the grand-opening on a Saturday when more would be available for the event.

On the day of the grand-opening he was surprised at the number in attendance. Mothers with small children hugging their legs, and school age kids gawking at the mixed-weight punching bags hanging from the ceiling, focus mitts, gloves, and ultramodern training equipment. A least ten male workers filed in late to register for the upcoming adult classes.

He recognized he and Venturi both would need to serve as sensei for the number enrolled exceeded his expectations. Workers were sensing uncertainty and wanted to learn self-defense with the uprising of gangs in the city making them reluctant to leave their armed gates.

They'd have to wait at least six months to start programs for school age children. The top student in the adult class would become their trainer to reinforce his/her skills and earn extra money. He thought about Lilia in this role but wanting her to be on the estate for short periods vetoed the idea.

Her curiosity would be fueled, and she might stumble upon information best kept away from her. He'd continue training her in his personal gym inside the main residence until students from the dojo proved to be suitable sparring partners. Then she could meet them for practice.

Lilia woke up from napping and took an over-the-counter Moment tablet from the pharmacy to ease her pounding headache. Having a dry mouth she brushed her teeth, and poured a glass of mineral water to moisten her throat and refresh her body. She'd not drink alcohol again anytime soon. She'd allowed the job stress to strip her of rational thinking last night. And her pent-up desire for David confused her thinking.

By Sunday evening, Lilia decided it was time to call David and make amends for her behavior earlier. She hit the call button and waited for him to answer.

After a quick greeting, he said, "Are you feeling better today?"

"Yes, much and I want to apologize for calling you while tipsy."

"No problem, I understand you want to make the strike team and when you didn't it sent you spiraling out of control."

"Ah, you noticed." She laughed trying to lighten the conversation hoping he'd forgive her for making excessive demands and her earlier unkind remarks when he wouldn't help her.

She said, "David I was out of line in our last conversation, and I hope you'll forgive me for my drunken call. That's not like me; I let the stress of failure mixed with alcohol snap me. I won't do that again."

Knowing it took courage for her to apologize, he accepted her apology and told her the news she wanted to hear. "Lilia, I'll train you in martial arts once a week until you master the techniques. We can begin next weekend on your day off. Plan to be here Saturday morning at 10 am for your workout."

"Thank you; I appreciate your help for getting my body combat ready. I also want to apologize for my unkind words when you wouldn't help me deliver my boss and co-worker to the authorities. I understand now it required the commission to oversee it properly. You were right."

"You're welcome and I'll see you next weekend. Take care and stay safe."

When the call ended Lilia smiled for now, she was on track for making the elite team.

David wondered what he was getting himself into by teaching her self-defense and combat maneuvers. The physical closeness in the workouts was a turn-on, and he had to concentrate to keep his mind from wandering. Her hot and sweaty body didn't help his focus quite the contrary.

He'd prepare himself in advance of her scheduled class the coming weekend. If he'd not inherited the family's secret, things would go much differently. Yet, he caught himself wanting to hold her in his arms and make love to her. The legacy was a drag on his romantic life. But, if he found an opening for them to have a future, he'd take it.

Chapter 60

The Ristorante Del Sole was packed all day and night over the weekend with tourist and locals enjoying the seaside view and excellent Italian dishes and drinks. Silvana caught sight of Celso occasionally serving drinks to tables when she had to run food for the kitchen.

She'd be ready to soak in her claw-footed bathtub after work tonight. As tired as she was, the fierce demands in the kitchen energized her throughout the evening. Afterward, she and Celso usually enjoyed a glass of wine before going home.

Tonight, she had something to discuss with Celso knowing it would involve sharing her family secrets. Hopefully, he wouldn't be over-tired from the day's work or have an adverse reaction squelching their romance.

The staff left after cleaning the kitchen and dining areas. She and Celso were alone, and he went to the bar and poured them each a splash of whiskey into a glass before returning to the table. The choice was a good one for their conversation.

After chatting about the break-neck speed of the staff that night, she said, "Celso I overheard you talking with Alessio Volta this morning. I think you should know we have history together for he took over the Sicilian family my father was a boss in when I was a child. I moved here to make sure he'd never find me, for we'd run into one another when I visited Palermo before moving here. I carefully planned my departure from Florence after selling my home in Sicily, so he couldn't find me. He and his clan scare me for I'm afraid they're expanding their drug business here."

Celso's tired face reacted to her disclosures with sadness in his eyes. He said, "Restaurants like mine are attractive to mafia families to shield their crime business and to laundry money. I could tell from his odor he was mafia just wasn't sure which one. Thanks for sharing your dreadful experiences. I'll never sell this business to a mafia family; I'd close it first if a legitimate buyer isn't found before I retire. You have nothing to worry about. You'll be safe here."

"Thank you for understanding. I feel like I need to call David make him aware they're trying to move into this area. For Livorno is where their warehouse is found for shipping their products on container ships throughout the world."

"That would be a promising idea for if they take over this region it could mean trouble for him. Call him and will keep this between us for all our safety."

"I'll call him tomorrow before coming to work. We're both tired so why don't we call it a night."

Celso reached over a placed a light kiss on her lips and said, "Good-night, sweet dreams."

Silvana drove home thinking about close she'd came to Alessio's seeing her at the restaurant. She'd be more careful in the future, and let one of the other kitchen staffers run food until the coast was clear.

The next morning, she got up early and enjoyed her morning routine before preparing to go to work. She had David's number in her contacts for he'd insisted she have it in case of emergencies. She called and he answered after the second ring. She said, "David, I saw Alessio Volta the new leader of the Sicilian mafia yesterday in Livorno. The Sicilian mafia tried to buy Celso Mezzeo's restaurant to cement their presence in the city. No one knows about this but us and Celso."

"Silvana thanks for calling me about their movement. I'll tighten our security around the warehouse near the harbor. In the meantime, you need to stay out of their sight for Alessio maybe tracking you."

"I'm being careful, and you don't need to worry about them buying Celso's restaurant, he won't sell to them."

"Good, call me if you need anything or find out other news about their activities."

"Yes, of course."

Her heart went out to David for handling the family history and the beehive he'd inherited. She wished him the best for keeping the family business afloat with enemies at every turn.

Silvana drove to work and parked her Ferrari in a space hidden from street view. She needed to buy another car to drive around the city until the coast was clear. She'd ask Luca to pick her one out, and she'd buy it before work tomorrow. Alessio would recognize the Ferrari for it was her family's car. She'd not considered that when she moved there for, she never expected to meet him again.

When she arrived at the restaurant Celso was already taking in shipments of fish, produce, and fruits. He nodded in her direction when seeing her walking toward the kitchen door. She waved back and opened the door excited about the foods they'd make and serve that day.

By lunchtime when they opened the restaurant doors, they were prepared to serve a host of diners. The day flew by with the kitchen workers taking only brief breaks from the frenzy. The chef constantly reminded them to keep hydrated for they were on warp speed for getting the orders out, and he didn't want anyone to faint from exhaustion.

That evening when everyone left the restaurant, she and Celso shared their evening drink and said good-night. She drove home and parked the Ferrari in the detached garage and closed the door.

Entering her home, she turned on the lights to walk around the furniture. Alessio was sitting on her sofa, drinking a cocktail poured from her bar. She backed into the kitchen pretending to make a drink, and reached into a drawer for a chef's knife and waited.

Alessio looked up, and smiled. "Greetings Silvana. I hope you're pleased about my arrival."

"What are you doing here, and how did you enter my home?"

"Well, Silvana you really do need to be more creative for hiding your house key outside. It was simple deduction to find it."

"Again, I ask you why you broke into my home."

"I wanted to learn why you ran off from Palermo with no forwarding address. I thought you understood you have a place in my family. After spotting your car yesterday at the restaurant, I followed you home, so we could meet today and set things right."

"Alessio, I think it best you leave before I call the Polizia about your entering my home without permission."

Alessio got up and walked toward her and said, "Silvana you're more beautiful now than when we were young. I was too busy becoming a made-man to fully appreciate your beauty or I'd snapped you up then."

Silvana noticed the lust in his eyes and readied for his attack. He sprang like a tiger toward her and when he did, she thrust the blade she was holding by her side into his body. She quickly gouged it further and turned the blade to cut deeper.

His blood was dripping from her elbow when he fell to the floor from his wounds. Her tunic was smeared from her counter defense, and she quickly dropped the knife into the sink and ran water over it while washing her hands to remove the stain.

She felt faint but had to hold it together and decide what to do. Should she call the polizia and report the intruder or call someone with sound advice to clean up the mess. She didn't want the scent of the mafia to curtail her newfound freedom.

With shaking hands, she splashed some whiskey into a glass and drank it quickly. Who should she call? Celso at once came to mind for he'd come to her aid, but he had no experience with the mafia. Although it was late at night, she called David, and he answered and asked, "What's wrong?"

"I've killed Alessio. He was waiting for me in my home after work. I slipped a chef's knife out of a kitchen drawer and hid it in my hand beside my body and when he attacked, I thrust it into his body. He's bled out on my kitchen floor and I'm uncertain about what to do. Should I call the polizia?"

"No, stay where you are, and I'll send over a couple of men from the warehouse to dispose of the body. They'll arrive by boat and tie-up at your dock. Let them in when they arrive, and they'll take care of the rest. Don't tell Celso or anyone else, including Luca, about what happened."

"Thank you, David. I'll wait for your men and keep this between us."

David was hoping the attack stemmed from Alessio's obsession with Silvana and had nothing to do with family business. There would be a hunt for him when he didn't return to their mafia headquarters. Silvana could still be in danger if his blood brothers were aware of his plans for the evening.

The good news was that the Zarrella clan's focus would be on the Sicilian family while they sorted through Volta's disappearance and nominated a new boss of bosses for the clan. The timing would be a perfect for the Zarrella's to take out their narcotics competition in Livorno.

He hoped the war between the clans would reduce both their forces, but realized the Sicilian mafia had always had the power to rejuvenate themselves. And, the Zarrella's had a steady stream of recruits stemming from their lucrative drug trade. Regardless, it would be a lengthy process giving him time to shore up counter-attacks from the Zarrella's on the home front.

David's security crew docked at Silvana's waterfront home and loaded Alessio's body onto their craft. She'd already cleaned up the pool of blood surrounding him when they arrived. Not knowing what to say, she said nothing. David wouldn't send them to her home if they were not trustworthy.

She scrubbed the floors after they left with his body rolled up in a tarp. The scent of the blood still permeated her home. She sprayed disinfectant all around. Tomorrow she'd meet her son outside for their trip to the car dealer where he'd found her a new car.

Opening the windows for the cool ocean breeze to cleanse her home, she went to bed and tossed and turned all night. Tomorrow she'd order a smutching wand with white sage online to remove any spirits from her home left over from Alessio. When it arrived, she'd go in every room to vacate the dwelling of any lasting remains of him.

When Luca arrived, she was ready to go buy a car, then motor to the restaurant in time for her shift. When the dealer showed her, the Renault Luca picked out, she shuttered. For it was an old woman car, no doubt the price tag said that too. She smiled and said, "I'll take it."

She paid for the car with a check from her bank and said good-bye to her son after thanking him for test-driving it for her. The Renault drove smoothly, so she understood why he chose it, but there were others on the lot she'd preferred.

Luca had no knowledge about her finances, and it may've been behind the reason for his selecting the cheap deal on the Renault. He was taken care of from his inheritance from his father Dorian. Something he never talked about, but it was obvious he couldn't live in the villa and not have an income. She'd let him have his secrets for hers kept piling up.

She parked in a space behind the restaurant and breathed out preparing herself for another busy day in the kitchen. The servers were arriving talking as they entered through the back door. Stopping off at the storage room, she pulled a chef's jacket from the rack and went to her station to begin prepping for the day. Looking around at the younger members of the staff, she wondered if they pictured her the way her son did, old.

Casting aside the thoughts, she was proud to be alive for things could've gone differently last night if she'd not been prepared. In minutes, she was in the flow prepping the food products for the day. She smiled and greeted the kitchen boss when he entered carrying his chef's bag with his personal cutlery.

When the overflow crowd was fed, and they began closing the kitchen, Celso stuck his head in and said, "I'll be waiting for you at the bar after you finish."

"I'll be there shortly. Just a few minutes, and I'll be ready to call it a night."

All the workers filed out except for Silvana. She met Celso at the bar where he'd poured a glass of wine for her and was waiting. He said, "We had another big day, and the kitchen ran like a fine-tuned machine. Thank you, for helping us out."

"I'm enjoying it and am glad to learn the customers were pleased with their visit."

Celso nodded his head in agreement and said, "You remember that Alessio fellow you spoke about yesterday? He's gone missing. One of the men with him the other day came by and asked if I'd seen him. Of course, the answer was no for he'd not returned. I thought you needed to know so you can check your surroundings."

"Thanks for sharing, but I don't think his blood brothers will look for me. At least I hope not. If they return, or you learn something new about Alessio or his clan tell me."

"Sure, I noticed you're driving a Renault today. Did you buy that to keep off their radar?"

"Yes, I was afraid they'd recognize the Ferrari as my family's car in Palermo."

"That was smart thinking on your part for garaging it and driving a nondescript car around the city."

They said goodnight for tomorrow would be an even busier day for it was the weekend. They briefly kissed before walking to their cars to drive away. The closer she got to her home the more she worried about unannounced visitors waiting to question her about Alessio. She prayed that wasn't the case tonight. A cold shiver ran through her body as she parked in the garage next to her vintage sports car.

Chapter 61

David was pleased the dojo was being used by workers and their families on the estate. The building had turned into a popular hangout for teens who wanted to learn how to protect themselves. Rightly so, with the Carabinieri still rounding up soldiers of the Zarrella's to rid the city of the drug trafficking group.

The trainers recommended that the teens not go into the city alone, but to travel in groups and look out for one another. For although it was said, they didn't kidnap people anymore, didn't mean they didn't.

When the leader became sickened by the media attention the mother of one of the girls, he kidnapped and brutalized produced, he pledged it would end. He had a moment of penitence. The narcotics business was much more lucrative and had less potential of being caught by the Carabinieri than from a public outcry from families of missing children.

When Sciarretta was arrested for human trafficking, it was believed he was a member of the Zarrella's even after the leader explicitly said it was untrue. This fired up the leaders to hunt down his associates and murder them. They wanted no attention on them to interrupt their drug trade. The anti-mafia chief prosecutor was already one-step behind them and the leader was forced to take cover in the mountains.

Lilia's martial arts were improving weekly and now was working out with the adults from the estate. This gave her chance to try different techniques based on the opponents' strengths. Bruised from the workouts, she kept coming and practicing.

Once a week with him to learn advanced techniques, and then she returned to work-out at the dojo. Her determination was contagious, and her fellow partners stepped up their training to not allow her to best them in a match. Unknown to her and the others, he had a cam installed to keep track of the activities in the building.

David was certain she'd not stop until she was selected for the elite team. There missions were the same to end the Zarrella's rein in the city. He decided to help her realize her career goals and called her.

"Lilia, drive over to the estate I have a surprise for you. Wear your fatigues, combat boots, and bring a flight helmet for you'll get a chance to practice rappelling today from my airport control tower."

She couldn't believe the words that came out of his mouth. "I'll be there within the hour. Thank you."

Quickly changing, she was on the way in record time. When she arrived, they rode in an estate cart to his private airport and parked in a space near the tower. He'd already prepared for the training. She could see nylon ropes hanging down from the top. Before taking the elevator up to descend from the tower, he said, "Let's prepare down here, and get you suited up properly and go through some basics."

He handed her all leather gloves, with double leather padding for the palms and fingers, eye googles, a deployment bag, a safety belt, and high-end harness and tether for descent control as a gift for her new adventure.

Already outfitted for the training, he said, "We'll do some role-playing. The ropes are anchored to the tower. Follow me and repeat my actions. It's important that you make a final check of your hook-up and rappel ring, before jumping. Pull on the rope to double check the anchor points connectors."

She did as he asked and waited for his next instructions. He took her through the steps from throwing the rope out of the helicopter before jumping, to the 180-degree position on the skid to rappel from, with the knees flexed to vigorously push away from the helicopter. Then he talked her through guiding herself to the ground roughly at 8' per second, with no jerky stops. She was to start braking slowly when half-way to the landing spot. With her brake hand out at a 45-degree angle to regulate her descent. When landing on her feet she was to pull the rappel rope through the rappel ring until the rope was free.

After repeating the exercise several times, he said, "I think you're ready to rappel off the tower."

They took the elevator up together, and she got in position. He reviewed her throwing out the rope and stance before saying, "Go" to make the jump. He stood guard in case she got in a 'possum' position turned upside down. With her rope he could turn her right side to continue here descent.

Her first jump was jerky from holding the hand brake too tight. By the end of the practice, she was much improved. He saw the tiredness in her face and said, "Let's call it a work-out and do this again tomorrow after work. You'll need about ten days of practice before we go up in the helicopter for the real training."

David pulled the ropes into the tower deck and tucked them away for her next practice session before driving them back to the estate. Lilia said, "Goodbye, and thank you for the gifts and training."

They continued the exercise and after ten days, he said, "You're ready to take your training to the next level."

Lilia was excited but anxious about the genuine experience of hovering over a spot and jumping out of the helicopter. At their next meeting, David said, "I've picked the perfect spot for training and later we'll try some tight ones in the mountain range."

David's pilot arrived, and they talked briefly before starting the engines of the Bell 429 helicopter with satellite guidance. They climbed aboard where David had stashed the ropes and equipment for rappelling.

With eye googles in her hand, the 9 mm pistol and ammo in a belt around her waist, and a dummy M-12 machine gun strapped to her back, she was prepared. She was carrying an extra thirty pounds of weight. This should help steady the rope for her descent.

David anchored the rope to the donut ring, and waited for her to snap-in and prepare to jump as the helicopter hovered. Lilia took a deep breath and threw out her rope, as David checked for tangles. From a seated position at the door, she swung her legs out to the skid, and took her stance to push away from the helicopter and descend to the ground.

The fierce wind was unexpected as she steadied herself on the skid. She pushed away from the helicopter with all her might and concentrated on her descent remembering to brake when half-way down. She slid to the ground like the rope was made of silk. Then freed herself from the rope as she was taught and was smiling when the helicopter landed nearby. They went back up, and repeated the jump three more times.

David said, "I think you're ready for a tighter squeeze," and they went to a new location. After successfully completing the training, he pulled out a pair of night googles, and said, "Your assignments will carry many night-time jumps. We have time for one or two before calling it a night."

The more she rappelled the better she became until David told the pilot to take them home. He was pleased with her efforts and suggested virtual reality training until rappelling became a natural experience.

Lilia legs felt like jelly when she disembarked the helicopter. She hoped her training would land her a spot on the Carabinieri's elite squad.

The next day she went into her boss's office and asked to try-out for the team. She'd already passed weapon proficiency, now she needed to prove herself in hand-to-hand combat and rappelling.

He looked up from the maps on his desk and said, "I'll schedule your combat readiness next Monday and rappelling later in the week if you pass the first test."

She thanked him, and smiling left his office. Later, she'd call David with the good news.

Chapter 62

David received a call from his warehouse's security to inform him that members of the Sicilian mafia were at the harbor asking questions about the disappearance of Alessio Volta. He told them not to worry for that was standard procedure when a boss goes missing and there was no way they could tie them to his demise.

The up-and-comers in the Sicilian mafia were ready to close the books on Alessio Volta. Whatever happened to him, they couldn't change. When the time was right, they'd have their answers, but in the meantime, they were sitting ducks to be taken over by the Zarrella mafia who wanted their heroin refineries and expansion into their territory.

Alessio led the barrage against the Zarrella's in Livorno trying to take over their cocaine operation and failed. His plans backfired with the Zarrella clan knocking at their door. They needed to nominate a new boss of bosses and initiate him into the clan before the fireworks from their opposition exploded. Their sources said they'd bring the fight to them and too many of their members were beyond their fighting years, and they'd failed to recruit new blood.

David was eavesdropping on their conversation and when the hit on the Zarrella was planned, he'd drop the hint anonymously to the Carabinieri's without a trace back to him. Why not take out both clans with one powerful punch.

All he wanted was peace and the ability to run the estate. Truth be told, he wanted Lilia, and he'd not have her until there was peace between clans or maybe never because of his family legacy.

Lilia received word her agency was to deploy to Livorno to take out the clans which included both the Zarrella's and the Sicilian mafias. She'd made the elite team who would be first on the ground to take them out.

She suited up for the rendezvous of fighting clans and boarded the helicopter flight to their destination. The fighting had already begun when she heard a voice, she recognized in her earpiece, David. "Listen to me and I'll bring you out alive."

She said, "Yes, give me your marks."

He told her where to hide and when to fire upon the enemy. His console was like a gaming board unlocking the answers. She listened and took out the main leaders of the clan which should capture her superior's attention and provide a promotion.

After a bloody battle the Zarrella's retreated with many dead or arrested by the Carabinieri. The remaining members of the Sicilian mafia were said to have limped back to their headquarters in Palermo.

When Lilac returned home, she called David to thank him for coming to her aid, wondering how he learned she was in a crisis. She owed him her life for she was pinned down when he contacted her.

She realized from working out with him she was far above her comrades, her boss included. She'd not stop until she was the head of their operations for, she'd been dead under her present commander. For by following his orders, she became separated from her unit and put in a deadly position. The Carabinieri's needed a new commander, her. That would be her next goal.

The boss called her into his office and thanked her for the outstanding take-down of the clans. He promoted her to lieutenant and said, "We're expecting some formidable results under your command. Good luck!"

Lilia could see the cog-wheel slowly turning toward her ambition of becoming the Carabinieri leader. She called David to tell him the exciting news and to thank him for training her.

After she blurted out the reason for her call, and waited. David said, "Why don't we celebrate. How about meeting me at Deano's Pizzeria after work?"

She agreed and smiled after ending the call. The rest of the day went by in a blur as she took on more responsibility in the agency. The promotion enabled her to view the tracking of the clan. Her boss was trying to pinpoint the leaders' latest hideout in the mountains. They needed heat-sensing technology to narrow the hunt for although he was in a bunker, he'd have to come out occasionally for nature breaks. She smiled knowing who could find him.

After applying fresh lipstick, she left the office to meet David at Deano's. He was waiting for her at an outside table when she arrived.

The ordered their pie and drinks, and relaxed enjoying themselves. When their pizza was served piping hot fresh from the oven, David slid a slice onto their plates, and handed her one. Then he looked around as if he expected someone to approach their table. She asked, "What's wrong?"

He pointed to the tiny three-legged plastic table in the center of the pizza, and said, "I wonder when Deano was taken over by the mob?"

Before he could say more, a gun shot was fired and the bullet grazed Lilia's arm. Not certain who was the target, her, or him, he pulled her to the ground, and unlatched his pistol to return fire. He couldn't see an assassin from where he was hiding. The outside diners had made a stampede indoors making it difficult to determine a shooter's location.

When not hearing another shot, he said, "Let's make a run for my car, and go home to check on your wound. I'll send workers from the estate to drive your car back later tonight."

Lilia did as he said, grabbing her handbag from the table as they fled. She said, "I need to call my boss for the shooter may try to take him out next."

She punched in his number from her contact list and waited for him to answer. When he didn't, she left an urgent message on his voicemail. She said, "Somethings wrong, or he'd picked up."

David entered the estate grounds with his secure code and parked in the garage. He opened the car door for Lilia and took her to the bathroom to clean her wound and apply ointment for healing. He said, "Lilia why don't you sleep here tonight, for a thug may be waiting for you at your apartment. You can stay in the bedroom next to mine, and we'll check your home tomorrow morning before you go to work."

He handed her one of his t-shirts and said, "Let me help you pull this on, and I'll rinse the blood from your blouse."

Her arm was throbbing, but she gritted her teeth as he helped her with a change of clothes. The scent of her own blood was nauseating, and she was glad when he took it to his sink and left it to soak. The first day in her new rank at the agency, and she was targeted for a hit, but by whom? And why hadn't her boss returned her call?

David called Venturi to pick-up Lilia's car and return to the estate. He said, "Take the bomb sensor from the garage to check under the Fiat before cranking it. Just in case, they returned to plant it after we left."

"I'll ask one of my work-out buddies to ride with me to drive back my car. I'll call when we return to make you aware the Fiat's here."

David thanked him and looked across at Lilia lying on the bed. Her face was frozen in fear, and he said, "What happened?"

She said, "My captain texted me and said the commander was gunned down on his way home from work. That was why he didn't answer my call. All our agents are requested to remain in a secure location until the polizia supply more information about the hit. Tomorrow we'll strike back against the army of thugs responsible for his murder."

David wanted to hug her for she looked so dejected but with her sore arm he wasn't sure how. He said, "Lay still and I'll make you a stiff drink to help you relax and soothe the pain from the wound."

Lilia sat up in the oversized bed and said, "Thank you, for everything. Now I realize I should've let you make our dinner reservations, as you suggested. For I believe that's how they learned I'd be there."

David was glad she shared the information for he'd not ruled out the hit was on him. Clearly the Zarrella's were aiming to take down the Carabinieri by taking shots at its leaders. The leader of the group had become bored in his hideout while others reaped the financial benefits of his drug business. He wondered what his next move would be.

He'd take the helicopter up tomorrow and search for his bunker with his high-tech sensing equipment. They'd not get another shot at Lilia if he found the hideout.

Lilia was getting sleepy, and he kissed the top of her head, and said, "Good-night."

He went into the adjoining room leaving the door open to check on her during the night. Her wound wasn't deep but worth observing in case of infection.

The next morning Lilia found her blouse where he'd left it drying and was dressed when he entered the bedroom. He invited her down to have a caffe latte before leaving for her apartment. She agreed and sipped it slowly while enjoying the garden view from the kitchen.

He followed her home and opened the door with his pistol drawn. With one arm in a sling, she carried her handbag in the other. He went from the living room to her bedroom and bathroom in her tiny apartment and found no signs of entry hoping that meant they hadn't learned where she lived. But that could change if she was still a target.

He said, "Lilia why don't you pack some clothes and your personal things, and stay with me for a few days until the crisis is over? They can't locate you easily, and my estate has a state-of-the-art security system."

"You don't mind?"

"Of course not, and we'll have a chance to talk. Bring your swimsuit and you can enjoy the pool. It has a spectacular view of the orchard."

He waited for her to pack a bag and change for work. He double-checked the lock on her door as they were leaving. "See you tonight, and don't eat early for the chef will prepare dinner for us."

Lilia mouthed the words thank you, as she drove away from her apartment.

David sped home to prepare for finding the leader of the Zarrella's and to grab his maps. He called Venturi and told him to meet him at the house and prepare for a work-out. He'd understand what that meant and would be dressed and armed accordingly.

Chapter 63

Venturi met him at the garage where he parked the Ferrari, and they took the estate cart to his private airport. He'd brought his clip board with the map and coordinates of possible locations to investigate. The heat-sensing equipment was onboard, an upgrade he requested when ordering the Bell 429. Today he'd pilot the helicopter to keep his airport crew from being involved.

When he found the bunker's location, he'd need a clearing to land, for he couldn't rappel down. They'd have to track through the woods to the hideout carrying their weapons. He'd packed his compound bow to make the first hit, to not alert others in his bunker if he had company.

He piloted the helicopter to the coordinates likely holding the leader. When nearing the spot, he turned on the heat-sensor and picked up activity below. Venturi said, "There a dirt road leading into his hideout. Can we land on the road, so we'll have a direct path to his bunker?"

"Let's make another pass to make sure there's no one on look-out. If not, we'll land in a clearing close to the road, and hike in."

Venturi smiled, "Just trying to simplify our entry."

"Yep, I'm with you on that. This helicopter runs quietly compared to others, but our target may have sensitive hearing." He laughed.

David eased the helicopter into a landing barely large enough to accommodate its size. He took the keys out in case their cover was blown to keep their ride from being hijacked.

They trekked through the underbrush carefully observing the path for signs of land mines or guerrilla style booby traps. When they neared the bunker, a man came out to take care of business. David snapped his arrow into place and released. The target fell to the ground. Unsure if it was a kill shot, he pulled his 9 mm and walked to where the body was laying while Venturi policed their surroundings.

He examined his shot and used his KA-BAR military knife to cut around the tissue of the arrow's entry to release the broad-tipped blade from his body. He didn't want to leave evidence with his signature. When the task was completed, he tucked the arrow into his backpack to dispose of later in a secure place.

There had been frequent traffic from the fresh tire tracks coming and going from the bunker probably bringing food and supplies and updating the leader about the hits he'd ordered.

He and Venturi crouched into the underground doorway and with his guerrilla warfare boots kicked in the wooden door. He entered while Venturi stood guard at the entry. The one room bunker was stocked with food and drink, especially alcohol. Magazines and books covered the table where he'd recently eaten. His plate, fork and knife were still moist from recent use.

He checked for a hidden passageway and found none. This one room bunker probably less than the size of his closet at home was his hideout for months from observing the clutter. He turned to Venturi and said, "Let's get to the Bell before anyone shows up to bring him updates and supplies."

The return to the helicopter was faster than their arrival for they'd already determined the path was safe. David inserted the key and the motor started at once. The Bell gravitated directly up from the ground, and when clear of the trees, David turned them towards home.

He didn't need to say anything to Venturi, for the Zarrella's were the Rocco family's enemies and were staging an attack on them for the sins of Sciarretta. Today, they'd done a good thing for the country by ridding it of a fierce, and dangerous Mafioso while making their clan safer from sworn enemies.

He was uncertain about how to inform Lilia the leader was dead. He'd listen to her strategies and make suggestions that'll lead her team to his bunker and dead body. Treading carefully, for her experience as a profiler could put him in a tough spot.

Chapter 64

Lilia's workplace was frantic with everyone sensing their mortality since the commander was murdered. Her captain stepped up to take over his position and promoted her to his former rank. She expected jealous remarks from her co-workers, but they congratulated her with sincerity. Perhaps, thankful they'd been passed over making it more difficult for the mafia to learn their name and rank for a direct hit.

She and her new commander decided upon a strike for their elite force. After talking with David last night, she'd determined the leader would need a service road of some sort to his bunker to command his unit and receive supplies and started pinpointing locations in the Zarrella's territory.

After they decided on a target, the commander called a meeting of the elite team and ordered them to secure the coordinates with her leading the strike. Pointing to the map as he spoke, they were to rappel onto the dirt road and trek directly to where it led.

The team suited up for their mission and loaded into the helicopter. She went through the hand commands she'd be using, and reminded them to do a safety check prior to their jump and to stick together on the ground.

She was the last one to rappel, for she was checking their lines for tangles and commanding the jumpers. When her feet hit the ground, she freed herself from the rope and pulled her pistol for quick action.

The unit was trekking up the dirt path observing their surroundings for a potential ambush. They followed the hilly road to an entrance into the side of a mountain. One of the agents waved her toward him. She looks where he points and lying on the ground outside the bunker was a man dressed in fatigues. From the damp stains lingering on the ground beside his body, he had relieved himself prior to the hit.

One-half of the team moved forward to secure the bunker, while she and others remained to examine the body. The hit was unusual, and she was unsure of the weapon used to murder him. It appeared to be a stab wound but could've been another weapon. She'd wait for forensics to issue their findings.

Lilia took a picture with her cell to compare to their database of leaders of the clan. When a hit came back, she realized it was the boss of bosses of the Zarrella clan. But who murdered him? Was it one of his own soldiers?

She ordered their medical team to pick-up the body for autopsy while her squad secured the crime scene. They would be there within the hour to take control of the body.

Her initial report of their findings would suggest a payback for the major hit on the Sicilian mafia to remove them from their drug distribution territory. Other possibilities included one or more of his soldiers took exception to the comrades murdered under his reign, and/or those jailed from the arrests by the Carabinieri.

The new leader of the clan would prove insightful for likely he was the one who ordered the hit on his former boss. Her investigative team would be on it. From the city streets, to restaurants, and tattoo parlors they'd have their eyes and ears scouting for information. A new boss was big news in a clan, and someone would be talking about it.

Lilia showered and changed back into street clothes before leaving for the day. She was looking forward to the conversation and dinner with David. They'd developed a routine that was relaxing and romantic to a degree. He was always a gentleman, and her best guess was he'd never come on to her while she was under his protection.

She was ready to find the next in line of the boss of bosses to superbly do her job as captain of the elite forces. And, to have a chance at romance with David. A double-edged sword she dared to pull.

Chapter 65

Silvana and Celso were enjoying their time together and Luca didn't seem to mind since he'd met Vitalia De Rose. They had Sunday brunch together after mass sometimes on her days off. She was slowly getting over the dreadful experience with Alessio and appreciated David checking on her and supplying updates.

She learned the Sicilian mafia appointed a new godfather Vito Trevisani, and she remembered him from childhood. Like her, his family was mafioso. The family owned a small trucking company they used to haul illegally butchered cattle to the city's wholesale meat market. He was a bully then and later pushed his way onto the city council to expand his business interests. His political ambitions were unchecked for he was supplying lucrative government contracts from his government position to his clan and their voting families.

Knowing him, he'd have no interest in popping Volta's killer for he had control of the Sicilian mafia something he always wanted. She was relieved to put the past behind her and begin another chapter in her life.

Lilia returned to David's estate after work and realized her stay wouldn't be much longer. Her team worked their leads until they discovered the new head of the Zarrella clan. Lotterio Allesi was selected as the mob boss, and she suspected he put the hit on his former boss Arduino Moretti.

The autopsy report revealed Moretti was stabbed and a chunk of tissue around his main organs was removed from his body. Another form of debauchery by the clan was suspected to send a message to traitors in their clan.

The Zarrella's were supplying stipends for their jailed comrades and their families to keep them flush, so they wouldn't talk to the chief prosecutor. But with the escalating changes in leadership, would they continue with their code of silence or take the immunity agreement they were offering?

The agency was tracking their movements to arrest the next-in-line, Allesi, but he was slippery in his dealings always one step ahead of them. She wondered if he'd retreat to a haven like the former boss and command his forces from there?

Lilia met David at his estate and wanted nothing more than to be in her apartment making it possible to renew their relationship where he wasn't her protector. In her mind, their romance needed to be set up on friendship, sexual attraction, and more than anything else love. She'd never know the answers if he was protecting her from assassins because of her chosen career.

The meal they shared was better than the top restaurants in the city. His private chef was extraordinary making her wonder why David didn't invite business friends and their wives to his home for dinner.

David lived an exemplary private life but there had to be a reason for the top chef in the city cooking for him. Then it dawned on her, having unlimited resources can buy you anything. Whether he dined as one, or parties with tables of ten, it was his decision. The potential was mind boggling; she'd only imagined living that kind of life.

When she became the commander of their elite team life would immediately become better. Perhaps, not her own chef but reservations for dinner anywhere she desired. She'd be able to say good-bye to her tiny apartment and start living a larger life. The goal was set, now to conduct her plans for redemption and life satisfaction.

Chapter 66

David noticed the restlessness in Lilia as they dined. He saw it as bad sign suggesting she wasn't interested in him. Perhaps, he'd misjudged her for he'd sworn a sexual attraction existed between them. While they enjoyed their night cap, he'd listen for clues hoping it was work related. And, afterward say good-night as a gentleman and protector.

She had work on her mind and quickly mentioned their hunt for Allesi, the new boss of bosses of the Zarrella clan. He wasn't surprised her agency offered deals to those from the clan now incarcerated.

They'd discover nothing unless one of the prisoners was feeling especially repentant like one of the bosses from the Sicilian mafia who cast the die for the code of silence for the Italian clan. The inmates and their families were being kept safe and flush during their prison sentence. Truth be known they had a racket inside and outside the concrete prison to supply drugs and hits on their enemies. They were not to be trusted.

He understood how suits in the law enforcement agencies believed they'd won against those responsible for the upheaval of their cities. But they were wrong. They'd just changed coping mechanisms for the prisoners still attacked when and how they desired. History had proven that the chief prosecutors and their replacements were being murdered by mafia hits while the godfathers were behind bars in their special designed concrete cells.

He was tracking the movement of Lotterio Allesi to end the targets on the Rocco clan. But no attack was planned, for his movement was devious. Did he think arresting or murdering the boss would put an end to the mafia wars?

No, the best he envisioned was from the heat of their being arrested, they'd relocate to the US with their cocaine trade. Then the agencies had an excellent chance to take them down away from their thick network of soldiers.

They'd be out of Italy, and the military police, Carabinieri's could monitor their shipping products inland while picking up more of their comrades. The joint efforts of the US and Italian task force could dismantle their drug cartel. The end was in sight, just not close.

Lilia sheepishly said good-night, and he voiced the same as she excused herself for the night. Knowing their relationship was headed nowhere, he decided to hand deliver Allesi her latest nemesis on a platter. The arrest had potential to skyrocket her climb up the military command ladder. And, then they'd have no reason to continue their friendship. He wanted no part of a woman who put her ambition above love.

Chapter 67

David now understood Jason's anxiety by allowing Tonia access to the estate. He'd done the same thing by courting Lilia who could expose his family for political and financial gain. Although, Godwin had infiltrated the criminal actions of her father while working with the polizia, he couldn't expose their methodology for obtaining the information. And, doubted he would for that wasn't the way he lived his life and won against enemies.

He needed to rein in his sexual attraction for a potential rogue Carabinieri who was after the accolades of bringing the mob down. Political power and money were her career path, and unfortunately, he'd assisted her to obtain those goals. She was trying to right her father's wrongs and make a statement about herself. And, even with Godwin exposing the truth, he did not recognize it. He was attracted to the enemy.

He'd serve up her next Zarrella mafia boss for it took down an enemy of the Rocco family and helped the residents of Tuscany. Then he'd leave for he wanted no part in her celebration. He could let her go and get on with his life.

The holiday season was Gabby's favorite time of the year. He'd book a flight and get his pilot to drop him off at the airport and retrieve him on his return. Unlike past years, the airport wasn't overcrowded for private aircraft, and it'd save time coming and going.

He couldn't wait to see Gabby and Godwin and his friend Jason and his family. And, of course, Daniela who took care of him until his next of kin arrived to become his guardian. Jason said he was dating, and he wondered how serious it was. But with his mother's oversight, he'd bet she'd passed scrutiny, or she'd not be in his life. His friend's mama, Nashoba, was no one's fool.

Godwin met him at the airport, and he hugged him for it was good to be home. They had plenty to talk about, and he could trust him with the details. But first the fanfare for Gabby's special occasion.

Their friends on the island would be in and out. The men would be fishing on Godwin's charter boats, for fresh fish and outside adventure. And his charter boat captains, and their families would be invited to the festivities leading up to Christmas morning.

Gabby's friend Thomason who relocated to Barbados at her insistence, and who later met and married a native would be over for the Christmas celebration. He'd bet that

Thomason kept his nose in agency affairs, even though he was retired. He'd kept his home in Atlanta for Gabby insisted he retire to the island at her expense for saving her life.

There was much love shared on the island with Godwin and Gabby between friends and family. He couldn't wait to go to their man cave and catch up on the latest tech and information about the family.

The Olympic sized pool on their veranda overlooking the Caribbean was welcoming. This was where he lived most of his life with Daniela until his aunt from Italy arrived, and they moved into the next-door villa his mother had bought before her murder. Now Daniela had a daughter in school where her mother taught. Gabby, he was sure was her god-mother and spoiled her probably to her best friend's delight.

His life in Barbados had been much better than living in Atlanta where the color of his skin made a negative impact on making friends, except those known by his mother. The fierce attorney who was feared by international criminals and human traffickers.

David was enjoying the star-lit night above the Caribbean. He loved the scenery from his Tuscany villa of the orchards, but this was home to him walking out and viewing the Caribbean Ocean from the villa.

There was nothing like the ebb and flow of the ocean, and the waves crashing against their man-made sea wall. He'd planned to build Venturi a safe house on the Ligurian Sea but perhaps he was too impulsive. Since learning about Lilia's plans for advancement, perhaps he as boss needed the alcove. And, he'd made sure it had every exit away from opposing clans and Lilia's Carabinieri.

He couldn't believe what he'd allowed himself into by desiring Lilia. It was like moths being attracted to flames. Likely she didn't know the Mandarino allegiance to the Rocco mafia family for they protected their shipments abroad.

Her knowledge about his personal life was limited. He was a tech genius from an early age that was no secret. With some difficulty he'd maintain a distant friendship to seek out her agency hits. He'd been played. But understood how to play back for information about their next take-downs in the mafia.

He now understood Dorian's cringing instructions about a hit on his own son, blood brothers first. Lucca was never a member of the family he swore allegiance to and for good reason, he was weak-minded. Dorian was aware, and likely blamed it on the man he installed as his father, Armo Marino, and his mamas over protection.

Dorian was trying to save a man who was gay and had the business skills the family needed and was living in a homophobic community. After his friend was beaten beyond recognition, he realized his life was in danger too. Dorian's proposal was a god-send away from the tyranny of those opposed to his lifestyle.

No wonder he was surprised when Silvana became pregnant with Antonia. He was trying to give Armo and the love of his life freedom from oppression. Dorian already sensed a bounty of his head for his link to the Rocco mafia family. He was trying to protect Silvana and his unborn son.

David smiled during Gabby's festivities to make her happy and unsuspecting of his sadness. Godwin he couldn't and didn't want to fool, and needed his council. He said,

"Why don't we go to our man cave tomorrow before Gabby awakes, and talk."

"Sure, I'll be up early, and we can leave."

They took Godwin's jeep to his office, and made more island coffee for their morning brew. He spilled his guts, telling Godwin how he'd been played and waited for him to say I told you so. He didn't. Godwin said, "I understand being attracted to someone who doesn't fit in with your lifestyle whether forced or chosen. I've been there and the picture isn't pretty nor one I'd redo."

"You've awakened early enough to cut your losses; you can be thankful for that. The best thing you can do is show Lilia, she doesn't control you for your attraction is elsewhere. That should take her innuendos about romance off the table, and we'll keep your island romances outside of her reach.

I've got it covered from here. By the way, Gabby has someone she wants to introduce you to. But go-slow her mama is friends with Nashoba, and you know what that means."

"I got it a big sparkly ring on her finger and a fancy family gathering to announce my intentions."

"Island protocol. You don't mess with the maidens without the mama's blessings."

"So, when is Gabby going to spring this on me?"

"Tonight, matter of fact."

Shrugging his shoulders, he said, "Well, thanks for your head-ups."

After talking about their security precautions concerning Lilia and some time to up their own security perimeters they left. For David, it felt like home again. He and Godwin working magic with their new apps.

Chapter 68

David went to his bedroom to shower and change before Gabby's house party. He wanted to make a good first impression to the young woman and her mother who he was to be introduced to that evening.

The sound of people giggling and talking floated upstairs, so he smiled in the mirror and closed the door to go meet them. A beautiful native girl was standing next to Gabby. She looked familiar, but he didn't remember ever meeting her. He'd learn soon as he strolled up beside Gabby to be introduced. Gabby nodded toward the older lady and said, "Abelina this is David, who I'd mentioned earlier."

She smiled and said, "Nice to finally meet you," and softly touched her daughter's arm before saying, "And this is my daughter Zana."

"Pleased to meet you both. May I refresh your drinks?"

He took Gabby's glass and Zana her mother's, and they went to the bar on the terrace to get fresh ones. She said, "Awkward, I hate it when mama introduces me to a man. You're aware she was sizing you up as a potential suitor, aren't you?"

"Not a problem, that's the way of Bajan families looking out for their own."

She giggled. "Then you realize the lofty expectations."

They handed the drinks to the ladies and excused themselves to continue their conversation.

"Oh, yes, they were drummed in my head years ago. My question is why haven't we met before now?"

"I travel a lot with my cosmetic business, and you haven't lived here in a while."

"True, but I'm glad we finally met."

Seeing his friend Jason with his girlfriend, Rose, they walked over to where they were standing. When he opened his mouth to introduce Zana, she started talking to Rose like they were old friends. He was surprised that everyone seemed to be acquainted with her, but him.

They talked about their weekend plans and decided to double date that Saturday night. By then, he'd ask Jason why he'd not met Zana before now.

His cell phone lit up with messages from Lilia. They'd arrested the Zarrella leader, Lotterio Allesi, and she wanted him to meet for drinks. He texted her back, "Congratulations! Sorry to miss your celebration, but out of the city for a while."

She sent back a sad-faced emoji in reply.

The friends met at a swanky new Bajan restaurant to be among the first customers at their grand opening. The ladies said it was the talk of the town and quickly snapped photos to post to their Instagram accounts. Seeing her handle, @Zanacosmetics, he'd flip through her selfies later.

They made plans for a picnic at Brownes Beach located on the outskirts of Bridgetown. The calm waves were ideal for swimming and the crystal white sand was great for laying on blankets and tanning. He'd ask Godwin about driving his jeep to pack their supplies in and pick up Zana from her home.

He was certain it wouldn't be a problem for he rotated driving his motorcycle and jeep. Besides, it was Sunday a day he usually spent pampering Gabby. They'd probably not leave their bedroom. He smiled thinking about their commitment to one another.

He was enjoying the time spent with Zana and after her mama invited him to Sunday evening dinner, he assumed he'd passed the test as a suitable match for Zana. They'd spent the day frolicking in the Caribbean and catching sun rays. By the late afternoon, they were ready to pack-up the jeep and go home. He promised to see Jason the next day at their orchard and catch-up. After dropping Zana off at her door, he went home to clean out the jeep, shower, and dress for the evening.

Knowing a gift was expected for Zana's mama, and flowers for her, he called in his floral order to be delivered prior to his arrival. He'd let Gabby pick out a bottle of wine from their collection to gift the hostess. She'd know her taste better than him. When he'd vacuumed the sand out of the jeep, he went into the kitchen where Gabby and Godwin were cooking their evening meal.

Gabby turned when she heard the door close, and said, "They'll be plenty leftover if you're still hungry after dining at Abelina's." She pointed to a gift basket on the bar, and said, "I thought Zana's mama would appreciate a bottle of wine to go with dinner."

"You're reading my thoughts. I've already ordered flowers for Zana to be delivered about now."

He took the stairs two at a time to quickly shower and dress for the evening. Gabby would want to give some last-minute suggestions, so he hurried to make time for her check list prior to leaving. He pictured Godwin's face now hiding a smile or an outright belly laugh about her counseling him.

She still treated him like a kid, but he didn't care for it was wonderful having her in his life. And, as humorous as her matchmaking strategies were to Godwin, he felt the same way. No doubt, both would be awake when he returned to get the latest news about his evening.

Chapter 69

Lilia was getting agitated for more of the Zarrella soldiers were turning state's evidence prior to their court dates. She didn't have the manpower or the technologies to verify their statements faster, but David had the resources.

He'd been out of the city for almost a month according to the limited information she received from him. This was the longest time since she'd met him, and she wondered where he was. He was probably chasing down a new green energy solution in the US.

Should she text him and ask when he was returning? Time wasn't on her side, for springing the prisoners by verifying their statements to the chief prosecutor. She gave in and texted him about his return date. He didn't respond immediately, unlike her previous attempts to make contact. Had he seen through her veiled attraction to him to further her career goals?

She didn't think so, for a strong sexual attraction existed between them. She saw it when he came to her suite at the resort in Florida. And had been using it to her advantage since being named to the task-force.

David felt the vibration of his phone but declined to check it at Abelina's dinner table. Zana's mama would be furious and make sure their courtship ended, and he'd finally met a decent girl. The logistics for dating was a problem with him living in Tuscany. But perhaps her skincare products were sold in Florence. He hoped so for then staying at his villa regularly made sense.

He zeroed back in on the conversation at the table where her extended family gathered. By the time dessert was served by Zana and her mama, he'd learned a lot about the family. They were a proud Bajan family with an interesting history on the island, and an enterprising spirit that propelled Zana into business for herself.

After he thanked Abelina for the delicious Sunday dinner, he said good-bye. Zana walked with him to the front porch, and he said "good-night, I'll call you tomorrow." She smiled and said, "thanks for meeting my family."

He cranked the jeep and went the short distance to his home. Gabby and Godwin would still be awake probably waiting for him in the living room. He'd relay his thoughts and go to bed for it had been a long day. He was sure Gabby would get the low down from Abelina soon.

Tomorrow he and Godwin would go to the office where he could check on the estate's business using his state-of-the-art computing system. Venturi had stepped up and was making his days flow smoother. He'd offered him Silvana's manor to live in since she'd left for it was closer to his office at the main house.

They'd hired more soldiers to keep their products moving to Livorno for shipping abroad and through Italy to their vendors. When he returned, he'd meet with an architect to design an escape house on the Ligurian Sea. The site was necessary for them to safely monitor their shipments from the Port of Livorno.

He told Godwin good-bye and climbed on his motorcycle to meet Jason at their orchard to learn the latest about their new hybrids. A unit was being constructed for aging the wine after the grapes were harvested and processed for storage. The architect provided a genius plan for constructing the cellar above ground on their tropical island. He couldn't wait to view it in person, for the photos Jason sent wasn't the same.

Jason showed him the freshly planted vines he'd brought with him from the estate's orchard when he arrived. The others were taking root and maturing as expected. In a few years, they'd have their first harvest and a reason to celebrate. They chatted about Rose and Zana, and plans for taking them out again that evening. Unfortunately, Jason had no answers to why he'd not met her before now. He was leaving in a couple of days and hoped Zana, and he developed a long-distance relationship.

They had a leisurely dinner at a restaurant in town. When the musicians started playing, he asked Zana to dance. They swayed to the music, and he felt her heart beating against his chest. Jason and Rose went to the dance floor for the next song, and he and Zana talked at their table. He asked, "How would you like to visit me in Tuscany next month?"

"Yes, I'd love to see your villa. I've never traveled to Italy so this will be a first for me."

"I love forward to your visit, and will send you an airline ticket and meet you at the airport on your arrival. We'll have lunch in town at one of our swanky restaurants before going home."

"Sounds fun and an interesting kick-off to my mini vacation."

They enjoyed the evening together and left with Jason and Rose. He to drop Zana at her house and Jason to take Rose home. He decided to kiss her on the cheek to say good-night. Her skin was smooth as silk. She looked him in the eyes and leaned in, and he kissed her on her mouth. Zana responded and he kissed her again before saying good-night.

He was leaving the next day after Godwin dropped him off at the airport. Saying good-bye to Gabby was always difficult and this time more than ever for he suspected her match-making was geared toward enticing him home. And right now, she was doing a surprisingly excellent job of it.

Chapter 70

David had barely walked into the door when Venturi met him and said they needed to talk. He said, "Sure, let me drop off my bags and I'll meet you in my office."

In minutes, he'd opened the secure door and was waiting for Venturi to arrive. When he did, he welcomed him and offered a beverage. Getting right to the point, Venturi said, "Angelo called and said he was ready to come out of hiding and wants to know if the coast is clear. He sounded panicked. I told him you'd get back with him later today."

"I'll return his call for he must have serious cabin fever to run the risk of kidnapping by the Zarrella clan. I'll try to coax him into staying put, until I can verify their activities. Have any of our soldiers seen them around our business interests?"

"No, but they've learned more of the leaders have been arrested by the Carabinieri and are being cautious to stay off their radar."

"OK, I'll investigate it and try to determine what level of bosses are being arrested. Without leadership directing them to capture Angelo, he'd not a prime hit. They're more likely concerned with moving their products to keep their cash flowing to make good the men who have been incarcerated and reinvest the capitol into more drugs."

"Oh, by the way, Lilia tried to visit while you were gone. I had her stopped at the gate, and told you were not in residence."

"Excellent work. She no longer has access into the estate unless I'm here and have granted permission which will be seldom if ever again. Our relationship is strictly business and can be conducted in the city."

"I understand. It's your decision to ban her from the estate."

"Thanks for the update and the excellent running of the day-to-day communications while I was away. I plan to build an escape house in Livorno near the port where we can keep our eyes on shipments if there's a problem. You are welcome to use it for business and pleasure to take a break from the estate."

"Sounds great, I've always liked the coast of Livorno and the beautiful beaches. And having a safe house is a wise decision given the potential of clan wars."

David was aware Angelo was ready to resume leadership of the Rocco family from his country estate. For he'd broken a cardinal rule of their clan by talking to Venturi for he wasn't apprised of their plans nor a member of the family.

Venturi was prepared to battle his enemies as a member of the Mandarino clan when the hit was ordered for his daughter's wedding, but he never shared the family affiliation with him. He'd hoped helping a fellow grower would be his understanding. Angelo didn't keep his discussion private between him and/or other bosses in the Rocco family. He'd make sure he understood for his future calls.

Lilia was his next call to find out what she wanted and to try to learn about the latest Zarrella arrests. He punched in her contact number and waited for her to answer. When she did, as usual she blurted out her needs, pinpointing the location of the clan who were given-up by their comrades. He asked, "Lilia, are these low-level soldiers who are turning on their captains or does it go higher?"

"Yes, most are foot soldiers in the clan with a few bosses scattered in from the busts at the harbor. This will be a huge take-down, and we don't have the resources to capture and interrogate them before their trial dates."

"Have you tried to postpone their hearings?"

"Yes, but we're already backlogged from the last bust."

"Send me your list of the members of the clan, and I'll search for their locations, and let you know what I find."

He heard her breathe a sigh of relief from his offer of help. She said, "Thank you, I'm taking heat from not acting fast enough."

He immediately ended the call, and pulled up her email with the list of members of the Zarrella clan with photo identification. The bosses were his top priority making it safer after their arrest for Angelo to leave his safe house.

The timing was perfect for trying a new app he and Godwin had developed on the island. He inserted the app onto his computer and went downstairs to grab a sandwich while it uploaded.

While looking around at his empty home he remembered Zana and would send her airline ticket before going back to work. He wanted to deliver all the information to Lilia before her arrival. So, she wouldn't be calling for updates.

When he returned to his office, he sent Zana her airline ticket, and opened the new app with state-of-the-art surveillance built-in and located the bosses on Lilia's list. Then he uploaded the foot soldiers' photo, and the app began sorting through locations. Using the spread sheet, she'd provided he auto-filled a column with their locations and hit the send button to return it to her. He commented, time is of the essence to capture them at these locations. Spear-head their take-downs now.

He hoped she moved fast enough to put Angelo one step closer to returning home. Since meeting Zana his interest was reduced in becoming the godfather of the clan for the imminent danger surrounding the respected title. He'd still monitor for possible hits on the clan, but Angelo's role was secure for reducing his chances of exposure as boss of bosses.

Thinking about Zana, he met with his housekeeper while his sandwich was being prepared, and instructed her to freshen the bedroom next to his and place a floral arrangement from their garden on the nightstand.

Tonight, he would call and as usual say hello to her mama to maintain goodwill with the family. Gabby would be pleased with his manners for Abelina would tell her. He imagined the smile on her face now.

Lilia texted him that they arrested the bosses on the list, but didn't get all the foot soldiers. She asked, "Would he mind redoing their locations tomorrow?"

He replied, "Yes, send me your updated list and I'll pinpoint them if they've not gone into hiding."

In minutes, he had the listing and there were twenty left. And he feared tomorrow she'd have another list from those arrested today. The potential of her seeking his ability was an interruption especially having qualified staff available. He shook himself and remembered her files were another resource to track the Rocco family enemies.

Chapter 71

The next morning after having a healthy drink made with fresh fruit, he went to his gym to work-out to start his day. Venturi sometimes worked out with him, but lately had been using the equipment in the dojo to exercise with the workers. Making friends came easily for him, and he was dating a sister of one of his new friends. His plan to find a girlfriend was working, and his happiness was refreshing.

Running up the stairs to his office, was an extra cardiac boost for sitting behind his desk until time to pick-up Zana from the airport. He logged into his app for finding Lilia's arrests for today. And, sipped fresh Bajan coffee from home while it sorted through the data. When the app dinged signifying the results were completed, he sent the info to Lilia with a reminder to act now.

Depending on the results of her raid, he'd call Angelo to tell him if it was safe to return home. Their discussion yesterday didn't go well for he missed his family and the day-to-day operations of his citrus business. Only after being reminded of the gruesome tactics of the Zarrella clan, did he calm down and agree to stay in hiding until notified differently.

Checking the time, he left his office to go to the airport to meet Zana after making a purchase at one of the luxury jewelry stores. He'd made a lunch reservation at one of the city's highly-rated restaurants for after her arrival. He planned to give her a scenic tour of their city before traveling back to the estate.

When he recognized her, Zana looked beautiful with a colorful tropical scarf wrapped around her head. She was a natural for marketing her skincare products made from the combination of herbs her mother's family used for years on the island.

When she saw him, she smiled, and he walked over to where she was standing and kissed her cheek. He said, "Let me get your travel bags, and we'll go to my car."

His Ferrari was parked close by, and he opened the passenger's door for her and waited until she was seated. He placed her bags in the storage unit and turned to greet her. "You look beautiful today. How was your flight?"

"It was smooth all the way. Thank you for the invitation and ticket."

"Are you hungry? Our reservations are ready by now."

"Yes, I'm starving, and I've been looking forward to sampling some authentic Italian dishes, not like the Chef Boyardee that's on the shelves in our grocery stores."

David slid the car into a parking space, and walked around to open the door for her. When they entered all eyes turned to them for, she was strikingly beautiful. The host showed them to their table where a server waited to take their drink and appetizer orders.

Zana said her wine preference, and he ordered an appetizer for sampling a taste of Italy. Her smile was contagious as she leafed through the menu and said, "Their selections read like a book. How do you decide what to order when there's so many to choose from?"

"Just take your pick from ones that appear tasty to you from the descriptions. You can't go wrong by any dish you choose for they're all excellent."

When she'd decided on the Linguine Piccole with Grilled Swordfish and Parsley Anchovy Sauce, he wasn't surprised for Bajan's had numerous recipes for cooking fresh catches from the ocean. This was a dish she could add to their collection for cooking at home.

The server took their order, and they sipped their wine, and she filled him in on the latest from the island. He was pleased to learn her mama liked him and had no problem with her visiting his home although she was a grown woman and could make her own decisions.

He briefly scanned the restaurant to figure out if he recognized anyone he knew. His eyes rested on Lilia dining with the Chief Prosecutor from the task-force. He thought she'd be out leading the raid on the clan members she'd identified for arrests. But instead, she was making moves to advance her career.

Saying a silent prayer, she'd not come over to their table to be introduced, he smiled at Zana. When their food arrived, her eyes lit up at the ample serving. "Oh, my, I had no idea the serving would be giant sized."

"Just eat what you want, no one will mind for their known for their hearty lunch menu."

"Thanks for the tip, I was afraid the chef would come out angry and express distain for my not cleaning my plate."

He laughed and said, "You've watched to many Italian movies, they're not quite as volatile as they're represented in film."

After finishing their meals, David paid the check and pulled out Zana's chair, and they left the restaurant to go site-seeing. They parked and walked around the historical sites, and he told her a brief history of the city. Pleased to walk off their lunch, they returned to his car and headed home.

The drive was picturesque as they toured the wine country leading to the estate. When they arrived, he grabbed her bags and escorted her into his home. Leading her upstairs to the bedroom to stash her luggage, he said, "Take your time to freshen up for you've had a long flight, and a hearty lunch. My suite is next to yours, just knock on my door when you're ready to explore the villa. And later if you'd like we can go for a swim."

"Thanks, I think I'll rest a little if you don't mind, and check my business emails."

"Take your time and when you're ready, we'll take the tour."

He went to his suite and turned on the TV to see if Lilia's task-force was making news by taking down more of the mafia clan. Her commander was heading the strike force and had rounded up the stragglers from the bust yesterday. Lilia didn't message him as usual after a raid. Was it in response to seeing him with Zana at the restaurant? He called Angelo with the news he could return home but recommended he keep a low profile. He'd update him as more information became available about the Zarrella clan.

Chapter 72

Luca was enjoying his life on the coast of Livorno with his mama close by and a girlfriend, Vitalia who enjoyed fishing and sunning on his cabin-cruiser. He'd been thinking a lot about his papa lately and realized if he'd tried to get in touch with him or his mama at the estate, it would be impossible. Remembering his mama had said he was retiring to his homeland, Montalcino he started searching for him there. He couldn't find anyone with the Marino name living in the city.

Knowing his mama's reluctance to talk about him and bring up painful memories of their past, he decided to call David and ask for his help for locating him. He called and quickly recognized David was a happier man than when he'd left for the coast. After making polite conversation about he and his mama, he asked if he'd help locate him. He agreed and said, he'd text him his address.

David was at his computer console when he called and dropped his name in for a search. He found him living in Florence and sent Luca the address. He hoped it wasn't a mistake for clearly the man didn't want to be found by not leaving a forwarding address.

Luca decided to make an overnight trip to Florence to scout out where his papa moved before contacting him. Now, to keep his plans from his mama would be the difficult part. She was busier than in the past by working at Celso's restaurant and painting more seascapes to sell at the galleries, and her dating life.

He made reservations and packed a bag for an overnight stay and drove away from his villa. He felt like a schoolchild sneaking out at night by not telling his plans to his mama. But this was between he and the man he called papa all his life. How could he cut-off all communication since raising him as his son?

Luca checked into the hotel and left his overnight bag. Then he drove to the street address David supplied him. The housing was upscale for a retired supervisor at a brewery making him wonder if his retirement was funded from his pay-off from Dorian. If so, he waited a long time to cash it in. Seeing a restaurant nearby, he decided to eat lunch and people watch to see what he could learn. With a table by the window, he watched as people strode by with their bags from shopping.

As he was taking a bite of his pie, he saw Armo walking hand in hand with a man. He'd spit the pie on his plate, if not for catching it in a napkin when he choked. Now he had the answers to his mama's perplexing love life with him. He wasn't attracted to women, and she'd suffered neglect all those years for nothing. He was biding his time, until he could be free to be himself and have the bankroll to do it.

He was sad to learn his papa was right in distancing himself for he'd be too ashamed to explain his new lifestyle to his son or didn't feel he owed him an explanation. Either way, his freedom was important to him. He'd let him be and return to the villa tonight lessening the chances of his mama's scrutiny.

Quickly checking out of the hotel, they gave him an extra night's stay anytime he wanted to return to the city. He took it but doubted he'd return anytime soon. This was one time when he agreed with his mama that sometimes things are best left unsaid.

A mother always knows, and Silvana sensed Luca discovered a new and painful secret. He was distancing himself from her, steering clear except for occasional Sunday brunches. Something was eating at him, and she wondered what. For one thing, he had too much time on his hands. He needed planned activities, like work, to make his days count and have pride in his life.

She'd suggest he work at a nursery for there was no doubt he had a green thumb. Even part-time work would get him out of his villa until something better came along. When he came over Sunday morning, they'd talk, and she'd try to learn what was wrong.

Chapter 73

David was on top of the world with Zana living at his estate. They dined on the garden terrace and sunned and swam often. They'd taken day trips to neighboring Tuscan cities for her to get the feel of Italy. She was running her cosmetics business online while he took care of the estate business. He was happy for the first time in a long time.

Tonight, he planned to call Abelina and ask for her blessings to propose to Zana and apologize for not making a personal visit. When they returned to the island, they'd have an engagement party at Gabby and Godwin's home for both families.

He called Godwin to tell him the news first. He was happy for them and looked forward to their homecoming. Then, he called Gabby who shrieked with joy when hearing the news, and was ready to host their engagement party and said they had a surprise for them. He asked they keep quiet about his proposal until Zana said yes. They understood and would keep mum until he called with confirmation they were engaged.

He couldn't wait to get Abelina's blessings, and he called her to ask, and she said, "Yes, we'd be glad to have you become a member of our family."

Now, the suspense was would Zana say yes to his proposal. He was excited and wondered if she would love the diamond ring he'd chosen. If not, they'd return it tomorrow while in the city giving her a chance to make a choice.

The chef planned an elaborate dinner for the special occasion. After dessert was served, he took Zana's hand and led her to his bedroom suite. When she relaxed on his bed, he presented her with a diamond engagement ring, he said, "Zana will you marry me?" I'll love you forever and a day."

Tears came to Zana's eyes, and she said, "Yes, David we are one."

They kissed, and he said, "If you don't like my diamond selection you can choose your own."

She laughed and said, "Yeah, if they can dig deeper into that mine where you found this diamond."

He knew he could've done better with his mafia connections but didn't want the Rocco family to know he was marrying to protect his family at all costs.

Their wedding would be in Barbados far away from the Rocco family connections making it possible to not invite any of his blood-brothers. If the boss of bosses should learn of it, he wasn't invited to his daughter's wedding for much of the same reasons. Besides, he'd shielded him and his family from death when the Zarrella's were itching to dissolve him in an acid bath.

David said to Zana, "I'm returning home with you and when we arrive in Barbados, Gabby is ready to throw us an engagement party. All our family and friends will be invited."

"Oh, my mama will love planning the wedding parties with Gabby for we will be the talk of the island locals."

"Why don't we stay there while you're planning the wedding, and pick out our island home somewhere between your mama's and Gabby's. That'll give them something else to do besides giving us advice for a happy wedded life."

That night they became one he and the only women he wanted as his wife and life partner. He'd finally came home again, with the love of his life.

Afterwards, they face-timed both families with their happy news. He could only imagine the happiness of both families and their excitement for planning the wedding and their homecoming.

David prepared for commuting between Barbados and his home in Italy. Family was important to him, and they'd spend most of their time on the island. Perfect for then they'd be miles away from the mafia connections he'd inherited along with the estate.

He bought a Bombardier Global 8000 his pilot was licensed to fly to make the flights. In the meantime, he would up his rating to fly the craft as needed in case of emergencies.

In the tour on the estate, he'd shown Zana the tunnel leading to their private airport and explained the nuisances of Italian businesses leaving out the word's mafia. The preparation for potential takeovers from opposing clans was a real and constant threat to their business.

She understood it at once from the guerrilla sabotage of her cosmetic brand. Most of her problem was online where he'd shut them down since she arrived in Italy.

She was the face of her brand, and want to be Zana's were dwelt a fierce blow. That was the least he could do for his soon to be bride. And, from here out he had her back, no more damages to her brand.

He went to sleep the happiest he'd been in his life with his soon to be bride nestled beside him.

Chapter 74

Lilia was not happy. She was banned from David's estate where she had enjoyed working out in his dojo and the lessons, he provided her once a week. The women she saw at the restaurant was probably the reason behind her exclusion from him except for business.

She'd snapped a photo of them there and realized his date was from his island. Probably his love interest from the get-go. She wouldn't be put down by his present love life. She needed him to help her rise to the rank of commander in the Carabinieri. The goal was set to become the next leader for taking down the mafia and nothing would stop her.

Working in the trenches, she'd gotten her hands dirty. Now that her career path was at stake, she had motive to chance it all. David was her sure winner for making a name against the mafia machinery, and she'd not let his love life interfere.

Without any remorse, she'd strike against Zana to get her out of the picture, so David would continue working with her. The sooner the better before they married, and had a child.

David and Zana returned home to Barbados to begin making plans for the wedding. They'd agreed to have the ceremony at Saint Patrick's Roman Catholic Cathedral where they'd both attended mass when on the island.

Zana went to her mama's home to stay until they were married. There she would plan the wedding, send out invitations, and order her wedding gown from a local tailor. Her friends were already planning a wedding shower, since learning about their engagement.

When Zana and her family arrived for the engagement party at Gabby's he realized she had many relatives. His friend Jason, and his girlfriend Rose were eager to congratulate them and were one of his first friends to arrive. He wondered his delay in proposing to her for they had dated longer than he and Zana. He wouldn't ask for it was his personal business.

Their families toasted their engagement with masterful prose wishing them a happy married life together. They thanked their family and friends for sharing in their happiness. And he whispered to Zana how beautiful she looked tonight.

Everyone left the party except for Zana, who he would drive home later. They said, goodnight to Gabby and Godwin, then walked outside on the terrace to be alone under the full moon over the Caribbean.

She felt soft and cuddly in his arms, and couldn't wait until they could be together again as one. Hesitantly, he said, "I suppose it's time to call it a night or Abelina will worry."

"You know my mama's trying to keep me on the straight and narrow until we say our vows."

"You are loved, and she's doing what she thinks is best for you. And we have a busy day tomorrow viewing houses to select our new home."

Zana smiled and said, "Yes, our island love nest awaits us. I hope we find one that's furnished to our liking."

Understanding what she meant, he said, "Yes, and with a quick closing date."

They laughed, and he dropped her off at home where Abelina had the front porch light on and was waiting.

He shook his head, and said, "Soon this'll be behind us."

Tomorrow he'd wake up early to go with Godwin to the office. He'd ride his motorcycle over for Godwin to drive home after he left with his jeep to pick-up Zana for house-hunting.

He'd called the realtor to verify the time for them to meet her. And was excited to be one step closer to living his married life on the island.

Godwin was up drinking his morning coffee when he went into the kitchen. He handed him a cup and said, "Drink up, and we can hit the road."

"I'm right behind you for I suspect you've created an innovative technology since I was last here. And can't wait to show me your new toy."

Godwin smiled. "Soon you'll see for yourself. I think you'll appreciate the extra security measure for your new home."

"Now you've got my curiosity peeked for I want the best for my new wife."

They left home after Godwin reset the security to protect Gabby while away. When they arrived, he pulled up his new security package and ran it for David to observe its operation.

David said, "I'm impressed. Have you put this on the market yet?"

"Yes, to my elite clientele and of course you."

David laughed and said, "We probably need to upgrade the orchard and distillery for its close to operational."

"Excellent idea, for Jason would have a heart attack if someone damaged the property."

Remembering the sabotage in Italy, he said, "You're right for he's put his heart and soul into building the business from the ground up."

After brewing more coffee, Godwin said, "Have you figured out how to keep your family secrets about the Italian estate from Zana?"

"I'm working on it and plan to run the operations from here as much as possible. I've ordered a private jet for long-distance travel back and forth as needed. My Italian family connections aren't invited to our wedding, nor have I told them about our engagement."

"Just keep a low profile with the Rocco family and step away from taking more responsibility for its oversight. Do your surveillance quietly to keep the ranking members inline or popped by an opposing clan."

"I agree. My life will change drastically after the wedding which reminds me, will you be my best man?"

"I'd be proud to stand with you. And I'll check with Jason about our planning your bachelor party."

"Good for I've planned to ask him to attend the wedding as my groomsman. I'll do that later today before going to Zana's for dinner tonight."

Checking his watch, he said, "I've got to go and pick-up Zana to meet the realtor. Thanks for the use of your jeep until mine is delivered."

"No problem. Good luck in finding your new home."

David smiled when he winked knowing that he and Zana would love to have a place to themselves for privacy.

Chapter 75

David and Zana arrived at the Realtor's office and went in to go over the properties she'd planned to show them. They ruled out a couple from the photos that didn't suit their architectural style. Then they followed her to the first home for sale and lacking a beautiful waterfront they passed. The second home was more like a bachelor pad in its layout and fully furnished rooms. Thinking their day was wasted, he said, "Does the next home have the amenities we requested? If not perhaps, we should reschedule when you have more to show us."

"The next home is a newly listed waterfront home, with a master bedroom, and separate bedroom upstairs and two more downstairs. The house comes fully furnished and since the family has moved back to the states, a quick closing is available."

He glanced at Zana, and she smiled. "Sure, let's go check this one out."

Driving up to the palatial home, he felt better about viewing the inside. The Realtor opened the front door and allowed them to enter first. From the entry the floor plan opened to a large great room overlooking the Caribbean. She was right, the home was lavishly furnished in tropical décor. They walked through the house picturing living there.

He wanted to know Zana's thoughts. He asked, "Should we keep looking, or does this one suit you?"

"Yes. This one fits our island lifestyle and is close to family."

They made an offer on the home, and would wait to hear from the Realtor to learn if the sellers accepted. They left excited to be one step closer to owning their own home.

On the way to Gabby's to share their news, his cell rang, and he answered. The realtor said, "Congratulations, you're the new owner and the sellers will close on the date you suggested."

After hanging up, he kissed Zana and said, "We're new homeowners. The seller agreed to all our terms."

They entered through the garage where he'd parked, and Gabby was waiting at the door. In minutes Godwin arrived home on his motorcycle for Gabby must have called him. She had chips and dip, and fruits spread on the bar for everyone to snack on. After pouring wine, she said, "How did your house-hunting go?"

"We made an offer, and the owner accepted our terms with a quick closing date."

"This occasion deserves a toast." Raising her glass, she said, "May this be the first of many positive steps you take in your lives together."

With Godwin by her side she added, "We'd like to purchase the home for you as our wedding gift for two special people we love dearly."

Both David and Zana were star-struck from the unexpected generosity. Afterward, they thanked and hugged them and left for Abelina's to tell her their good news and enjoy the authentic Bajan dinner she'd prepared.

Chapter 76

Lilia was pacing her apartment for David wasn't returning her calls, and she needed to make more busts on the Zarrella clan. Her team was putting effort into finding them but so far, no results. She planned to meet with the chief prosecutor again to find out if any of the prisoners turned for a lighter sentence.

Her commander was on her back to take them out completely. And it appeared they'd scattered to the ends of the earth. They were sitting at the harbor waiting for cargo to be shipped in or out. The crew from there was gone. She'd bet to another seaside port.

She'd send her team to the nearest ports to look for drug related activity. In the meantime, maybe David would call from wherever he was hiding.

David went to the tech office and logged into his satellite security for determining the safety of the Rocco family and the Mandarino clan. Afterward, he called Venturi to check-in with estate business. When he answered, he was breathless from working out at the dojo. He said, "All is fine here, boss. How's everything with you?"

"Looks on target from here. How are the Mandarino soldiers working out for protecting our cargo?"

"There hasn't been a problem. The trucks come in and leave without hassle with their riding shotgun."

"I hope it stays that way. When I return, we'll have your annual performance and salary review. Call me immediately if you see any problems."

"Of course, and I suspect you know Lilia is trying to contact you and tried to weasel your location from me."

"Not to worry, I thought she got the hint by now; but I'll phone her when we hang up to put an end to her pestering you."

"Thank you, sir. She can be scary with her innuendos, and I don't know how to manage her blatant disregard for privacy."

Checking his phone line for security for he didn't want her tracking his location, he called. She answered and said, "Where are you? I've been looking everywhere for you because I need to locate and capture the rest of the Zarrella clan."

"Lilia, we need to straighten out your expectation from me. I don't work for you or the Carabinieri and my life is private. Don't contact my staff again about locating me. You have the resources you need to do your job. Don't contact me again. Do you understand?"

"Yes, but I thought you wanted the same thing I do, to rid Tuscany of the mafia."

"Lilia, you need to get your employment goals straight for their yours, not mine. Now, good-bye, and best of luck."

She was in shock when he ended the call. Where did she go wrong and lose his tech-savvy aid? She'd bet it had something to do with the woman named Zana he was with at the restaurant. She'd looked her up online from her photo ID and found she owns Zana Cosmetics. He was likely with her now.

If he wasn't involved with her, she'd bet their relationship wouldn't been sidetracked. The right idea would come to mind for taking care of the gorgeous business tycoon. She'd wait to strike and be available to comfort him in his grief.

On the eve of his wedding, the rehearsal followed by the rehearsal dinner went as planned. Just one more day, until he and Zana would be married in the eyes of God and man, and they could spend the night together in their new home.

Godwin wanted to personally install his new security package while he upgraded the Island Grove Distillery. They completed their tasks in record time and were set for his wedding day. He called Zana to tell her goodnight, for she'd been busy with last minute wedding details.

They arrived at Saint Patrick's, and everyone prepared for the traditional wedding march and Zana to walk down the aisle. He had butterflies in his stomach excited to see her in the gown she designed. When she entered all eyes were on her, he felt like he couldn't breathe for her beauty was captivating.

The priest led them through the ceremony and pledge to one another. They signed their wedding certificate in the presence of family and friends, typical of island weddings, and then invited everyone to the reception.

They cut their wedding cake and teased one another while touching the slices to their mouths. The music started, and they danced the first dance as a married couple, then invited family and friends to the dance floor.

The night was special for now he could show affection to Zana without hesitation and with Abelina's permission. Seeing Gabby and Godwin dance to the island sounds, he knew they were a forever couple even if they didn't have a marriage license for security reasons. When they could take their leave, well-wishers sent them away with gaiety and laughter.

In minutes, they were at their island home where he lifted Zana and carried her across the threshold. Taking a minute to reset the alarm after entering, he and Zana went to their master bedroom. They took their time pleasing one another throughout the night until both were fulfilled.

Tomorrow they planned to stay-in and enjoy the comforts of one another in their new home. Godwin offered to do security checks on their businesses for a few days giving them uninterrupted time together.

Godwin arrived at his office early as usual and started security checks. Someone was trying to find Zana's current location online. He booted them off the internet from her social media site.

Tracing the stalker, he found it came from an Italian government server, and the computer assigned to Captain Lilia Siciliano. His adrenaline was pumping for this woman was obsessed with finding her now. He'd give David another day of privacy before sharing his findings. In the meantime, he'd flag her IP address for tracking her searches. Siciliano was up to something, and his gut said it was a dirty deed.

Chapter 77

David and Zana were enjoying their new home and planning a cookout to invite family and friends for a housewarming party. David, Jason, and Godwin planned to catch fish earlier in the day to grill for their dinner.

Zana returned to her office in Bridgetown where her manufacturing company was located. She had a new line of skincare products coming out for the holidays. He was working from Godwin's office like old times.

On his first day back, Godwin explained that Zana had a stalker and showed him the results of his scans. "Unbelievable," he said. "I was just trying to help her achieve her career goals with intense training. Looking back, I should've kept the work flirts to a minimum or just not gotten involved period."

"When you explained her family history, I recognized the potential for a problem and was hoping she'd chosen a different path than her papa, the crooked cop."

"I'll add her photo to our airport security surveillance so if she enters the country, we'll be alerted even if she uses an alias."

"I need to return to Florence for a face-to-face with Simone next month and to give Venturi his annual review and raise. First thing, I'll check-in with the department heads to get their opinion about Venturi's work performance. The business needs to continue growing regardless of the clan wars. And he frees up my time by managing the operation on-site allowing me to check the business from here.

Zana wants to stay here and prepare to launch her holiday products. Keep an eye on her while I'm away. For you never when our enemies might pop-in."

"No problem. She's welcome to stay with us while you're gone and I'm sure Abelina would love to spend time with her."

"I'll tell her she has options to not be alone while I'm gone. And, let her make the decision. We both are aware she's safe in our new home."

"You're a natural at pleasing the lady. I'll be watching so don't worry about her safety. Go and take care of business."

The days flew by as they worked and enjoyed family and friendships on the island. Zana drove him to the airport to catch his flight to Florence, and he dreaded saying goodbye. They kissed one last time, and he went to board his flight.

After take-off, he opened the proposal Angelo sent him for buying a trucking company to run as the Rocco family.

Most all of them had trucking needs, and feared taking on a new blood-brother after the betrayal by Sciarretta. He suspected Simone added a fee for his services which was not shown. His accountant would need to sign-off on the numbers before he reviewed it further to decide.

He wondered what the other bosses would think about the deal he proposed. For himself, he didn't have the time or inclination to oversee the management of it. Living on the island made him happier. The trucking company he contracted with was working out with his soldiers tracking their shipments. He'd keep an open mind for he pledged the tenets of the Rocco family to put blood brothers first and knew the punishment for breaking them.

Venturi met him at the airport and briefed him about current business on the return home. He said, "Congratulations on your wedding." Aware his boss liked to keep his personal affairs private, he asked, "Do you plan to wear your wedding band to your business meetings?

"Yes, except for one that I'd rather not share my personal life."

Venturi didn't have information about the meeting and believed his boss would tell him if his involvement was required. He parked the car and walked around to open David's door and grab his bag.

When they walked into the villa, he said, "The chef will have dinner ready at your usual dining hour."

"Thank you, it appears you've got everything under control here."

He took the elevator to his floor, and after entering his suite took out his cell to call Zana to tell her he'd arrived and to check on her day. They talked until time for him to go down for dinner.

The next morning, he awakened early and worked out in his gym before preparing for meetings with his department heads. He'd call Zana before she left for work to wish her a wonderful day. He'd arranged a floral delivery to her office with a card that read, "Missing you, I love you, David."

When he thought she was up and drinking her morning brew, he called. He visualized her dreamy sleepy-eyes and wished he was there. When he said, "Hello beautiful," she giggled and said, "My love I missed you last night."

They talked for several minutes, and she said, "I'm staying over at Mama's tonight and will make sure I set the security system before leaving."

"Enjoy yourself, and tell Abelina I said, "hello.""

"Will do. Take care of business and return home soon. I love you!"

He'd never smooched on the cell, but he blew her kisses and said, "I love you!"

He was ready for his scheduled meetings beginning with Pauli at the orchard office. Then with all department heads, in the wine business. By lunch, he was ready for a break to dine on the chef's delicious dishes. They had a meeting scheduled afterward.

In the afternoon, he met with marketing and the business accountant. Marketing wanted to reestablish the wine tours, but he placed a hold on it until he was certain the mafia war was over, and the numbers were up for tourism. He gave his accountant Simone's proposal and asked him to investigate it for a joint venture with other growers.

Tomorrow he would meet with the department heads in the olive side of the business. From now on, he would have a monthly face-to-face with his managers. In the interim if there was a problem, they'd be asked to contact Venturi or him depending on the severity of the problem.

He'd asked the captains of the Mandarino clan to join him for dinner. They'd have a feel for what was happening with the Zarrella clan and any problems with shipments and delivery of their products.

He also wanted them to check into the trucking company Simone proposed buying. Then their soldiers could snoop around to learn if they were affiliated with any mafia group. He'd run them through his programs prior to the meeting to see if anything new popped up.

The captains arrived for dinner and drinks, and it was a pleasurable meeting. Learning the remnants of the Zarrella clan were in hiding, with many leaving the country to expand abroad was good news. He was feeling more secure about Zana returning with him for meetings. By then, the new jet will be delivered for quicker flights.

One more day of meetings, and he'd return home to Zana. The dreaded meeting with the Rocco family was next and feedback from the members about Simone's business proposal. He called Zana to say goodnight and send his love. She was cheerfully optimist for his homecoming and would meet his flight.

Chapter 78

Godwin saw Zana with his surveillance program and after David called to tell him she was staying at Abelina's he felt better about her not being alone in their new home. The security system he installed was top of the line but wouldn't help if she opened the door for a would-be assailant. He recognized her as the innocent she was, like Gabby when he first met her. But she quickly became knowledgeable about a world she was never exposed to and learned to protect herself. He hopes Zana was up to the challenge for her married family was often targeted.

He was at his office early to counterattack anything against them. Zana went to her office as usual, and he poured himself another cup of coffee and leaned back into his desk chair. His airport security feature started bleeping, and he opened the app for closer inspection. Lilia Siciliano landed traveling under an alias. His gut was right, she was targeting

Zana to do bodily harm and sneak away in the dead of night according to her departure ticket.

Always armed, he rubbed his thumb against his 9 mm pistol and then withdrew it, loaded a fresh magazine, and returned the weapon back into the hidden pouch. He didn't know what tactics she'd used to meet Zana. But she was on their island for a deadly purpose.

From his live video feed, he saw her climbing into a minibus provided by a local resort. He tapped into her cell phone to listen for outgoing calls. The minibus stopped and let her off at a local internet café.

She was clever for not using her cell to contact Zana leaving no traces of her call. She'd use the internet and message Zana to meet. He latched into the internet café's webserver and waited for her message. When she sent one, he blocked the communication from Zana's social site, and responded to her request for a meeting.

Her detective skills for making the hit were obvious. She'd selected a remote site with rough, turbulent surf that only the staunch die-hard surfers entered. He knew the area well; bodies were dumped there and never recovered for the Caribbean ran deep and deadly near the shores.

Pinging her phone, he realized she'd called a cab to drop her off close by. He sat in his jeep and waited for her to walk to the shore. He slid out of his seat, and with native steps quietly walked up behind her.

"Taking a little late-night stroll?" He asked.

She turned with pistol pulled, and he shot first. He checked for a pulse and found none. In minutes, he'd rolled her body, handbag, and gun into the deep cove for the tide to take her remains out to sea. By tomorrow morning they'd be no sign of their meeting. This inland mecca held Caribbean secrets best left untold.

He cranked his jeep and returned to the office to make another safety check on his family before returning home to Gabby. He'd like his son to come home, and find there were no problems. Eventually, someone would report her missing and attribute her murder to a mafia hit from her work with the Carabinieri.

His best wishes were for his son to have the opportunity to enjoy his bride and the takeaway be a spiritual connection forever. For that was what brought him and Gabby together again. Otherwise, they'd missed the sweet joy they now enjoyed, and he'd never known his son.

David removed his wedding band and gently placed the gold ring on his nightstand. He didn't want to but feared repercussions from the Rocco family if they learned he'd married and not issued them an invitation. He'd drive to the restaurant belonging to a blood-brother and wait for others to enter before him.

The Mandarino family provided protection for his business against rival clans and gangs. He'd slip in the kitchen door before the meeting so no one would see him enter. The members were all seated in the darkened back room when he arrived. Taking the empty chair around the usual set-up, he waited for the boss of bosses to call the meeting to order.

Simone reviewed the family's status of not having a trucking and delivery company as a member. Then proposed the Rocco family buy the trucking company he'd selected. David observed his blood-brothers closely to decide their reaction to Angelo's idea.

Simone opened the floor for discussion and members voiced their concerns one at a time in an orderly manner. Questions were asked about what boss would manage the operation, and would the existing drivers work for their new company.

The members were in consensus that they needed more time to decide if the Rocco family's delivery needs would be best served by his proposal. They would meet again in a month to take a roll call vote to enter into an agreement with the seller. The meeting was dismissed as was customary for the family.

David hurried out to his car to not be sidetracked by a blood-brother wanting to learn his thoughts. He was missing the touch of his wedding band on his finger and sped home to place the ring back in place.

He planned to dine with Venturi tonight and discuss his annual performance review. While meeting with managers throughout the estate, he heard nothing but glowing reports.

When he arrived for dinner, he mixed them a cocktail and asked him to have a seat. "Venturi, you've done an excellent job in your new position as overseer of the estate. Beginning next week your pay will increase by fifteen percent and when I return next month for a week, you can take vacation time."

Elpidio smiled and said, "Thank you for the opportunity and I appreciate the raise. I want to propose to my girlfriend, and would like to buy her a diamond ring."

"Congratulations! If you want to be married at the estate, that'll be fine with me."

"Thanks, and as lovely as the vineyard is, she wants to be married in church."

"Do what the lady wants, and you'll have a happier life or that's what I've always been told."

They enjoyed their dinner and drinks and said goodnight. The next morning, he was catching a flight home to Barbados and kiss his beautiful wife. He quickly called to tell her she was missed, and he couldn't wait to get home. He missed her special womanly scent and the soft touch of her hands.

The next morning the pilot would meet him at the helicopter for a quick lift to the airport. He'd already packed his overnight bag with the gift-wrapped present for Zana. The solid gold heart necklace was bought on the way to the meeting with Simone. Tonight, he'd sleep and dream about his homecoming and Zana.

He was beginning to believe in the possibilities of living in two worlds. One being his mafia family business and the other living the life of his dreams with his wife. If he drew breath, Zana would be safe from the Barbary tactics of the mafia clans. May he always live to die another day to protect his family.

The End.

Acknowledgements

The fictional portrayal of the Italian mafia would have been impossible without the scholarly research and the personal experience of writers before me who recorded the history of organized crime throughout its history in hopes of a united peaceful Italy.

From the Author, Carolyn Bowen

Thank you for reading *The Death of Me*, Legacy Series, book 1. Stay connected for details about special offers and giveaways to gift your friends and family.

Word of mouth is crucial for any author to succeed. If you've enjoyed the novel, please consider leaving a review, even if it is only a line or two; it would make all the difference and I would appreciate it very much.

Follow me on my website for the latest news about my new releases and fun social promotions. As always, I appreciate you!

Carolyn Bowen, Author—cmbowenauthor.com

Made in the USA
Las Vegas, NV
26 August 2022